ABERRATION

NICHOLAS J. RIPLEY

This is a work of fiction. Names, characters, places, and incidents either are the product of the author's imagination or are used fictitiously. Any resemblance to actual persons, living or dead, events, or locales is entirely coincidental.

Copyright © 2025 by Nicholas J Ripley

All rights reserved. No part of this book may be reproduced or used in any manner without the written permission of the copyright owner,
except for the use of quotations in a book review.
For information, write to: projectsuncloud@gmail.com

First paperback edition January 2026.

Cover design by Nicholas J Ripley
Editing & Proofreading: Rachel Oestreich, from The Wallflower Editing, LLC.
Typesetting: Ines Book Formatter
Author photograph © Kirstin Dietza, from Dietza photography

ISBN 979-8-9887588-5-3 (paperback)
ISBN 979-8-9887588-4-6 (eBook)

Published by Project Suncloud LLC
www.nicholasjripley.com

Special thank you to Shannen Velasco, Diana Tennyson, Chai Simone, and the Screenwriters Club for helping this book come to life. Appreciate everyone's support.

Content Warning:

The following book contains alcoholism, blood, body horror, cannibalism, dismemberment, drowning, drug use, existential dread, extreme violence, foul language, graphic depictions of gore, gun violence, mentions of sex work, mentions of abuse, mentions of suicide, mutilation, profanity, sexual content, suicidal ideation, themes of abuse, themes of mental health, trauma, and some loose religious imagery.

PREFACE

The year of 2016 is one that will live in infamy for the House of Ripley. In my early twenties, I was living in LA and it was probably the most chaotic period of my life. 2016 was the year I had the most painful breakup I've ever had, was sleeping in my car most of the time, almost drowned, and got into a car accident that totaled my Kia Rio. It was a supernaturally unlucky year .

This happens to also be the year I wrote the first couple pages of *Aberration*. It was always supposed to be a vehicle to tell a story about my childhood boogeyman: The Man with the Hat. At the time, I shelved it because I didn't know where to go past the inciting incident. Skip forward to early 2024, I stumbled on those couple pages buried away in my documents and inspiration struck.

This book was a healing process. *Aberration* is a personal exorcism. A brutal examination of the worst year of my life. Rachel is very much so my worst traits amplified to eleven, her friends are faint reflections of my friends back then, and Jennings is based on an actual neighbor I had that would leave me threatening, misspelled messages. Even the trippy imagery is heavily based on nightmares I've had. When I finished this book, it was one of my most emotional writing experiences.

Now, all this being said, this is not a literal interpretation of events. *Aberration* is a surreal work of fiction. This story is my Arthouse, A24, David

Lynch movie. Is it weird? Yes, intentionally so. Is everyone in it kind of a terrible person? Yes, intentionally so. I will likely never explain just what is going on in this book, but know that every detail was carefully placed. Things that may seem random are not random in the slightest. There is a puzzle that can be solved, but our POV character is not smart enough to put it together. One of the most amusing things for me as the author has been my readers coming up with wildly different theories as to what is happening. I'd love to hear your theory, though, dear reader. Is it all a dream? Is it something supernatural?

Just what is The Red? . . .

With that, I give you *Aberration*.

PROLOGUE

It was raining. I'll never forget it. Rain in LA in the winter is icy and cold, seeping through your clothes, even the thickest of your coats. No matter what you do, you never feel dry. It comes in waves—much like the waves of the ocean that's only a couple of hours away with traffic—at times with biblical fury, and at others like an old man hovering over your neck spitting on you. The old streets allow the water to puddle in miniature lakes you could probably drown a small child in. The freeways become wet hellscapes, and the plants get a little less brown.

I hate the rain.

I especially hated it that day.

The morning after a night of heavy, heavy drinking. The morning after some models I was hanging out with ditched me at a club, leaving my fate to whatever scum may have been lurking in the murky streets of the so-called City of Angels at two or three a.m. The morning after, when I was throwing up my guts into a toilet. After I called *him*.

I swore I would never talk to him again. I swore I would never write him another text. My friends had assured me multiple times that he wasn't worthy of me. Not after what he did. But I was scared, and I felt like he was my safety blanket. A faulty wiring in my brain yearned for him. Despite everything that had happened. Despite everything . . . Looking back now, I know that logic was fucked. How could *he* be safety? How could he be anything other than the—

I called him more times than I'm proud of, lost in Central LA without any way of getting home. Got home by chance that night. A kind stranger at a Denny's called me an Uber. It was only in the morning that he called back. That rainy, winter morning, after one of the scariest nights of my life. That was when my ex finally called.

I was still inebriated. I still could barely speak a coherent sentence. But he decided that he was going to . . .

I don't want to talk about it. It was only a phone conversation, but I don't want to talk about it. I still have nightmares. The rain beat hard, and as horrible as it was, it did its purpose. It hid my wails and screams as what felt like a part of me died during that phone call. With only words, he murdered me . . . and he got away scot-free.

I pretend he never existed. It doesn't make him go away, though.

He never goes away.

CHAPTER 1

"Can't stop," I said to myself from behind the lens of my camera. Photography had always been my passion. Had always been something I love. My earliest memories were of me as a little girl, holding my dad's camera in my hands. All my life I had taken pictures. Now . . . it all led to this. This very moment, I lay everything on the line. My most private and controversial photo yet.

I adjusted the settings carefully as my target came into view. I held my breath, not allowing myself to properly breathe until the shot was perfect. Sweat began to form on my brow as I bit my lip slightly, staring intensely at the subject that was to have their soul defiled by my tool of personal debauchery. I had one shot at this. Only one. Feelings of nervousness pervaded my entire body, yet my hand remained ever steady like a surgeon's. This wasn't my first outing behind my blunt instrument of truth. The camera, my best friend and lover, neatly fit into the crevices of my fingers as I stared at my subject with the intensity of a prize fighter.

"Won't stop," I whispered to myself. Almost had the shot . . . almost had it . . . I had to adjust the lens just right. Only one shot at this. Now or never. "Can't . . ." My finger hovered over the button.

Click.

I breathed out a sigh of relief and unfolded from the uncomfortable position I had laid in on the ground. The crick in my neck felt stiff as the photo printed out of my Polaroid camera. "Owowow," I muttered, putting one of my hands to my neck. I needed a chiropractor. I stared at the little bastard that had given my neck such grief. A tiny green bug on the leaf of a bush outside of my favorite coffee shop. "Your soul is mine, little aphid. Mwahaha." I said it with an inflected voice that only I found funny. I was hilarious. A stand-up comedian for myself, and probably only myself.

I looked around, noticing the passersby giving me strange looks as I did my best to appear normal. Nothing to see here. Just a black-haired lady putting herself in an awkward position with a camera in front of a random bush. I thought I might've heard somebody laughing, but it was drowned out by the street nearby. Sticks and stones. I know, I'm a weirdo. I don't think I was ever anything in my life other than a weirdo. Well, that and a professional photographer.

With a small hint of discomfort, I grabbed the photo and looked at it as it finished developing. It was perfect. A perfect portrait of the small green critter on a leaf. "Rachel Hannigan strikes again!" I said gleefully to myself, then I placed the photo carefully in my pouch. My sacred, sacred pouch. I looked around and moved my long hair out of my eyes, still hoping no one noticed my little weirdness.

This town was weird, though. Forgive the common trope, but LA had always been pretty goddamn weird. Now it was just . . . decrepit. A former shadow of itself. The city seemed to be in a permanent state of decline. There was talk of people supporting the outcasts and nurturing art. Ironically, the City of Angels always had a way of *stifling* art. Even from my viewpoint, me being professional photographer extraordinaire. Don't worry if you've never heard the name Rachel Hannigan, though. Us behind the camera aren't as well-known as those in front to begin with. Plus, it's my real name. My professional name is Eveline Apple. Clever, right? Cause you know, Eve . . . forbidden fruit . . . Yeah, you get it. I was very proud of myself when I came up with it. Long story short, I'm known for one type of photography and only one. God forbid I expanded my portfolio. Like, for example, this picture of this little aphid I just took? It wouldn't fly. People I work for, people that are fans of my photos, they just wouldn't get it. As for being an outcast, well . . . I don't feel any more welcome in LA now than I've ever felt my entire life. I'm not complaining, just saying how I feel.

I guess I go through . . . long bouts of depression sometimes? I don't know, never got a diagnosis or anything. Just have a lot of moments like . . . This is it? This is all I have going on in life?

I'm sure I'm a prime case for mental health advocates.

It was still morning and I had just barely rolled myself out of bed after yet another shitty night of sleep. I still felt exhausted as I continued to walk up the sidewalk, California sun already beating down, making the crisp morning air warm despite it only being April. There were people jogging by wearing shit-smeared plastic smiles that cost more than my rent. Me and my gray hoodie were lazy and just barely up in time to be functional enough for a photoshoot at eleven a.m. Needed a chai tea to start the day. Tea before I dealt with any models. Tea before I whored my talents for the talentless. I breathed in as I gathered up a little courage to go into the little coffee shop with a Buddha in front of it, praying no half-baked Instagram model would recognize me and want me to photograph them.

Cue eye roll here. (It's happened before.)

I walked in, felt the warmth of the coffee shop, and breathed a sigh of relief as I realized there weren't any Instagram hopefuls here. A young actor or writer or something working at his computer, an old lady, two people talking about showbiz, typical LA sights. A cute spry girl behind the coffee counter flashed me a huge smile with crooked teeth. Doe-eyed, probably her whole life ahead of her. At least her soul-sucking job wasn't her passion yet.

"What can I get you, miss?" she asked in a squeaky customer service voice. Couldn't blame her, I've had to use that voice too. Even to this day I occasionally used that voice. Customer service voice, a natural occurring phenomenon used by those of the service industry, specifically for assholes and dipshits.

"Chai latte, please." I smiled back at her, remembering when I was in my late teens. The writer/actor looked up from his computer and we shared a brief gaze. Skinny, short hair, earrings, skulls on his shirt, probably late teens or early twenties. I could tell he was into me by those eyes of his. I lifted my eyebrows in disinterest before I turned back toward the girl. Dream on, kiddo, I'm probably at least ten years older than you. Definitely flattered, though, admittedly. Not like men my age typically look at me like that. And I looked like a hobo today. No makeup, didn't shower this morning, dark circles under my eyes. My face without makeup looked like Skeletor's long-lost cousin. It was my ass, wasn't it? Always looked pretty good in these jeans. Definitely my ass. That was always *his* favori—

This coffee shop, The Happy Buddha, was just bohemian enough, yet fancy enough, to be something that I loved dearly. It was a quaint little coffee shop, though it had hopped on the health-freak bandwagon that all of LA seemed to be on recently, but I was okay with that. It was pricey . . . but organic was better than whatever Starbucks was. Healthier, and to me, tasted better. I mean, I wasn't about to hop on the bandwagon of being a vegan. I didn't have the funding to live comfortably *and* do that with how much LA charged for essentially being alive. But . . . vegan food actually wasn't *that* bad. Healthy food was a person with depression's best friend, so I've heard. The healthier the body, the more endurable the depressive episodes. Course, I didn't believe in therapists, so I assumed they were only depressive episodes. They say exercise and healthy food is good, though, so hey, there's that. My organic chai latte was evening out all the crap pizza I'd been eating lately, according to my admittedly biased math.

After getting my latte I sat near a window and got out my pouch. This camera I had with me wasn't anything special—it wasn't my professional camera. It was my side hoe, my romantic affair from the soulless, black beauty digital camera I used for work, this simple and plain old-school film camera. It wasn't professional enough for a dark room, but it did its job well enough. This film camera was the precious farm boy I fell in love with before my father married me off to my cold and cruel lord husband, the digital camera. May my digital camera husband never find out, lest I shame my royal family. I smiled to myself as I held the film camera in my hand. I definitely watched too many historical dramas.

I looked at my schedule for today. Well-known model, Swedish. Matty was going to meet with her first, prep her, and then I'd arrive on scene. Do my thing for an entire day. Bing bang boom, easy money. It was really unromantic, the business side of the arts. At times you felt like a cheap hooker, selling your services for a price, doing what other people wanted you to do. It was never about *your* enjoyment, only what *they* got off on. It was about the invisible *they*. *They* were always hungry. *They* were never satisfied. And the gatekeeping powers that be? *They* were the ones who actually profited from your hard work. The arts were much more soulless on the commercial end . . . and I was a complete sellout.

Apparently, I hadn't lost all my appeal, despite my commercialism and capitalist value. The boy across the way eyed me hungrily. It was a shy look here or there, but he was eye fucking me. I looked back and watched him as he squirmed behind his little computer. He had to be, what, twenty-two? I could eat him alive. He was skinny, but the way he looked at me . . . I don't know. Made me a little . . . I licked my lips a little and flashed him a smile. He looked around awkwardly, then back at me. I sipped my chai and leaned in, staring at him, smiling at him. He immediately looked down at his laptop like he was trying to ignore me, but he couldn't for long. Older woman deliberately sending him signals? Let's see how brave he was. I flashed him an even bigger smile and then looked away, back at my camera. Out of the corner of my eye I could see him get up awkwardly, grabbing his laptop and what was likely a school bag. He fidgeted this way and that as he stumbled my way. Deliberately, I looked out the window, away from him.

"Uh . . . e-excuse me?" he asked, almost sounding a tad too young. I turned back and looked at him, feigning surprise.

"Hm?"

"I-is anybody sitting here?"

I folded my lips and shrugged. "I don't know. Is anybody?"

"I—I mean . . . can I sit here?"

I sipped my chai latte and grinned. "Technically you could sit anywhere you like, and I wouldn't be able to stop you. But yeah, you can sit there."

He had a youthful grin and nodded before sitting down. "Cool." He sat across and looked like he had won the lottery, or a bet. Whichever made guys his age happier.

"You got a name?" I asked.

"Uh, Jason. You?"

I smiled. "Rachel."

"Nice . . . nice . . . Um, that's a—that's a cool camera you got. What kind of camera is that?"

I thanked him and told him. I could tell from his blank expression that he had no idea what I had just said.

"Uh, that's really really cool. You a, uh, photographer or something?"

I merely smiled. "Or something. What about you, you writing the next big screenplay?"

"Nah, just uh, working on some homework."

A college student, nice. I could be the Mrs. Robinson in his life and corrupt him at my whims. "Ooo, big-time scholar. What kinda homework? Pre-law? Film?"

He smiled and awkwardly nodded. "Chemistry."

Chemistry? How far into college was he? That had to be in the first couple years, right? I smiled, playing it cool. "Nice. What's your major?"

He blinked. "Uh . . . major?"

What the hell was that tone? Is that his major or . . . Oh no. "Yeah . . . your . . ." He *did* have some pimples on his face, but twenty-year-olds could also have . . . "Your *college* major . . ."

He smiled and chuckled. "Oh. I'm, uh, I'm in high school."

Everything in that moment dropped, including my will to live. Oh. He was even oblivious to my face dropping. That was evident from his puppy dog enthusiasm. "Ah." I breathed out roughly. I fucking hate my life sometimes. On that note, I stood up and began gathering my stuff. "Well, Jay-lin—"

"Jason."

"Yeah, um, it was nice chatting with you. Good . . ." The kid stared at me with a cherub level of innocence. I almost wound up on the FBI's Most Wanted. I knew how to pick 'em. Insert facepalm here. ". . . good luck with your homework." Jesus, I must be getting desperate. I almost ran away from him as fast as I could with my tail between my legs. This was just pathetic.

I have not had any luck in this department since . . . Yeah. But trying to reel in someone that young by mistake? What the hell was my life coming to? As I wallowed in my misery, something like a high-pitched squeal rang through the air. At first, as I touched my lips to my latte, it sounded like my ears were ringing, but in milliseconds it got louder and louder until a deafening sound of crunching metal made me jump and spill the hot drink on myself.

In a rush, much of the café I was in rose to their feet. It felt dizzying as my heart raced from the sudden jolt. It was a shock to my system, like I had plunged into icy waters and was rudely woken up. I dropped my cup but my hand remained clenched in a fist, shaking. Slowly, I turned toward the source of the noise.

The noise was from the other side of the window, but what was happening there wasn't what caught my eye. A large, metallic piece of what looked like a car part was staring straight at me, stuck in the window. A jagged bit that looked like some sort of pipe from an engine or something. It was surreal, like looking at a piece of modern art. It was at roughly eye level with me, staring right where my skull was. It reflected in the light like some twisted beacon, a spear that would've gone right into my head had the thick glass window not acted as a buffer. A spear that I'm sure would've torn through my flesh cleaner than a knife through hot butter. I let out a shudder, eyeing that thing. The window was severely cracked, with veins webbed all from the central point where the window protected me from meeting my demise, making it hard to see anything through it. But something was happening on the other side; most of the café were already on their way to see.

I backed away, still staring at the iron spike, my VANS tennis shoes slipping slightly on the spilled chai latte under my feet. I looked around to see if anyone saw what I saw, but most of the café, if not all, were standing outside. I breathed out big before deciding to see what the hell was going on out there. As I made my way out front of the café, the first thing I noticed was the screaming. It was high-pitched and young sounding. The smell of gasoline pervaded the air, hitting my nostrils worse than a gas station. I moved my tiny body between people, squeezing myself toward the front of the small crowd to try to get a better look.

It was an accident. A horrible, horrible accident right on the street in front of the coffee shop. Smoke rose from the hoods of the cars. That screaming was louder than ever. I stood bug-eyed, gazing at the wreckage in all its glorious and stupefying carnage. There was so much to take in all at the same time, and my stomach wanted to hurl what little of the chai latte I had back up, but I managed to maintain composure enough to not. There was a tickle at the back of my throat, though, and a dizziness as if someone pressed on my stomach.

The crash wasn't like any sort of crash I had seen before. It looked . . . *unnatural*. It was two cars, completely demolished like broken Lego sets all over the street. It looked like they had gone ninety miles per hour straight into each other in a head-on collision. Car parts were everywhere, like a brutal accident on a highway . . . but this was a surface street. A quiet little surface street that was not normally all that busy. There was no reason for it to be this—this *revolting*. The thought of survivors didn't even cross my mind, it was such a wreck. Flies had already begun making their presence known nearby as I crept closer to the accident.

I think a part of me went numb upon viewing the carnage. One of those . . . things where you are so overstimulated by so much going on at the same time that your mind can't decide what horrible thing it should be freaked out by. In the bright sun, almost none of it looked real. There was a sort of uncanny valley effect where you knew what you were looking at was the real deal, but nothing registered as anything other than the kind of fake gore you would see at Halloween Horror Nights at Universal or something.

Where do I even begin to describe this? I suppose as plainly as possible. There is no other way I can figure out how and . . . I don't think there is a respectful way to describe what I saw.

My eyes followed the droplets of red liquid until they discovered a man lying on the ground, bisected. He was slightly overweight, Hispanic, his top half lying on his stomach, missing an arm. Blood trickled down from his head, which was facing sideways, revealing a prominent mustache. His internal organs streamed out from the light blue Kia Rio, the lower half of his body still inside. It was like he'd been ejected through his windshield and scraped along the pavement. A young child wearing a dress writhed on the ground to the side of the car as if she had fallen out of the back seat, glass embedded in her face, and the skin of her right arm and leg had been completely torn off. Her limbs were twisted wrong, and she lay on the ground like some misshapen, stepped-on spider, screaming in Spanish for her mother at such a high pitch that it hurt my ears. In the passenger seat of the Rio, a woman looked trapped. At least, from what remained of her head and context clues, I thought it was a woman. Hard to tell with the front of her skull and head completely crushed against the dashboard, brain matter in front of her agape melon-like head like bits of porridge spilled from a knocked-over bowl. Finally, I looked over at the other car, a purple BMW. There was a man I couldn't see too well, lying on the ground. Glass and car parts littered the street and the sidewalk around him. He looked like he had been ejected by his car as well, but his body was mostly intact.

"*Somebody get an ambulance!*" I heard somebody scream from what felt like a mile away. The smell as I inched closer to the man from the BMW was awful. It didn't smell just like gasoline anymore. It smelled like . . . like defecation and burning flesh. Like burned barbecue. Something crackled and hissed like burning fat on a skillet as I moved forward as if in a dream. People began to gather around the accident, all bewildered. I know it was a mere few steps away and that time moved much faster than this, but my move toward the man's body felt slow. It felt longer than hours despite being seconds. I didn't quite feel like I was even in my body as I took the few steps to the driver of the purple BMW. The smell almost seemed to go away, the sounds got more muffled. I looked down at the driver, feeling every breath as my lungs slowly expanded and retracted.

It was . . . disgusting and revolting. Yet, for some reason that I can't explain for the life of me . . . it intrigued my wormy little brain. It was like . . . a magnet. I looked down and stared at the corpse at my feet, and it was like there was nothing else in the world. Best way I could describe it was like being underwater but not drowning. Holding my breath but not suffocating. The man was older, probably midforties. At least, what remained of his skin made him look that way. Bald . . . Some sort of Hollywood big shot by the looks of it. The broken Rolex, bloodstained and torn white button-up shirt, the hip shoes he wore without socks gave an air of Hollywood status more than any condo ever could. His BMW looked possibly even more destroyed than the Rio, yet his ejected body was more intact than any of that family from the other car. What struck me as odd . . . I guess I should say what *entranced* me . . . what made me drift into some sort of state wasn't how bent and contorted his body lay, nor was it how shiny his chrome dome head was in the California sun.

No . . . it was his face. Or rather . . . the lack of. It looked like it had been completely sanded off. Not just the skin, but most of the muscle, tissue, and somehow the eyes too. It was just bloody bone. A crimson skull staring back at me. I remember asking myself, how the hell did the eyes get scraped out? The holes where his eyes used to be were like a dark red abyss. One that my eyes seemed to sink into. I couldn't look away. In a weird way too, I suppose, it felt like they were looking right back at me. The skull stared and I couldn't move my eyes from it, as horrible as it was. I felt my body move by itself as I got closer and closer to the lifeless corpse of the man. It was awful, but as I stared into the vacant red holes, a strange *impulse* came over me. One that . . . I can't think of having any reason for.

I have no way of explaining it. It was a strong impulse though. Probably one of the strongest impulses I've ever felt. Stronger than an impulse to scratch an itch. Stronger than an impulse for sex. Overwhelming . . . like a starving, homeless orphan's stomach yearning for food. Or better yet, like lungs screaming for air when drowning. My mind went blank as I got closer and closer to the corpse, drawn by some strange, horrible beauty. Without thinking, I obeyed the impulse. I knelt close and took a picture with my camera.

Almost immediately, a young woman pushed me down, knocking my camera out of my hands. A flurry of angry Spanish words I didn't understand came out of her mouth as I barely realized what I had just done.

"*Yo, what the fuck, lady? The hell's a matter with you?*" her boyfriend, who stood nearby, yelled at me, seemingly from worlds away as I was forced back into the present. Into reality. Why did I do that? Why did I take that picture? I didn't have an answer. Confusion set in as the boyfriend held back his girlfriend. She continued yelling obscenities in a language I was only vaguely familiar with. She tried desperately to swing at me but I immediately backed away, my eyes watering. Angry tears rolled out of her eyes as she continued her tirade. I looked around, startled that people were starting to look at *me*. I quickly picked up my camera and made a barely audible apology before fast walking away, hearing sirens arriving at the accident not too far behind me.

CHAPTER 2

What the hell was that about?

I had never done anything so—so *disgusting* in my life. That was . . . horrible. I felt awful for doing it. Completely unforgivable. I briefly looked at my camera and the photo that had come out. It hadn't developed yet and . . .

Goddamn it, my favorite camera was broken. I focused briefly on the damage, but kept fast walking. I looked behind me to see if I was still being watched. I wasn't, but . . . I couldn't shake the feeling of shame from being seen committing such a disrespectful act. I still feel . . .

I got into my car, a tiny black Prius, and sat myself in it, hyperventilating.

Eyes.

Vacant, dark red holes that saw through everything I am and ever was. An abyss that stared into my soul. Even now, I still feel like I was looking into them. Even now, I still feel watched. My breath slowed as I looked into the mirror, into my own eyes. My little hazel orbs stared back at me, slightly red and watery. His eyes were gone. Where did his eyes go? Where the fuck did his eyes—

"Fuck," I whispered to myself, starting the car. I shouldn't think about it. I couldn't afford to. I shifted into drive, eyeing the crowd of people gathered around the smoke in my rearview mirror.

The drive is a blank for me. I remember the sun shifting through the trees as my thoughts dwelled on the faceless man. The meatless bone caked with blood, surrounded by flesh, how everything but the corpse seemed to fade from existence as I looked at it. I briefly looked over at the camera and photo in the seat next to me. For a moment, I saw red on the picture, but I quickly turned it over onto its face. The rest of the car ride I spent frequently looking at the back of the photo, still drawn to it like a moth to light. It was only once I arrived at my studio that I even realized I was late to the photoshoot I was scheduled to have today. When I finally parked, I quickly changed my chai-stained shirt and hoodie into a black tank top. Then, I stuffed my broken camera and the photo into the camera pouch and rushed into the facility, pouch in tow.

When I got to the studio for the photoshoot I could see the Swedish model I was to shoot rolling her eyes. "There you are, Eve!" my best friend and assistant, Matty, called out as I rushed past him and into the restroom. The bodies, the accident, the picture . . . that didn't just happen. That *couldn't* have just happened, I thought. I breathed hard and put my pouch on the bathroom counter. The vacant red eyes pervaded my mind and made me nauseous. My head spun and I felt out of breath. I closed my eyes hard and couldn't get the bony face out of my head. I gasped and pulled the photo I took out of the pouch.

It was horrid. More horrid than I remembered. How the hell did I have a fascination with *that*? The flesh, the blood, the twisted carcass. I was disgusted with myself. *What the hell was I thinking, taking that picture?* In anger and self-disgust, I tore the photo in half and tossed it. Immediately after, I rushed to the toilet and upchucked whatever was left of the chai in my gut. My entire body shook and convulsed. I breathed hard and leaned against the seat. God, what did I do? Am I so desensitized? I never thought myself capable of doing something so wretched. Something so *against* my own code of ethics.

Regaining some composure, I flushed the toilet and stood up. It took me a moment before I looked into my own eyes in the mirror. I had bags from my poor sleeping habits. My pale, almost sickly skin glowed in the light of the small deco bathroom. My black hair was frayed. I took deep breaths in. I looked more bone than human. Like some gollum-esque creature with slimy skin stretched just barely over my skinny frame. What was wrong with me? Who even was I anymore? I didn't used to—

Suddenly I heard a knock at the door.

"Eve, you okay, hon?" Matty's effeminate voice called out through the door. Images of the accident flooded through my mind. The child, the mother, the bisected man, and the faceless corpse. The horrible skeletal face that had already burned deep into my subconscious. I wiped my teary eyes and breathed in, quickly getting some gum from my purse and chewing on it.

"One moment," I told my best friend. It was just a dumb accident. I had seen accidents before. No biggie. I had to get my shit together for this photoshoot. *This* was my *job*. I had to keep my job in order to support my little duplex in Burbank. Showing up late to the shoot was unprofessional enough. I couldn't let this affect me. Not right now.

"Subject is getting pissy, *come on, Eevee*," Matty added. With that, I sighed. Okay. Okay, I could do this, I promised myself.

It felt like a momentous occasion, getting out of my bathroom and presenting myself to my BFF. He stood there, a freshly dyed bleached streak in his dark hair. Now, there are gay men, and then there's Matty, who has my vote for possibly the *most* flamboyant gay man to *ever* roam West Hollywood (which, mind you, is the gayest part of Los Angeles). He was a tall, built, Filipino man that had multiple piercings in his ears and an unhealthy obsession with Sailor Moon (he's spent many Pride Parades dressed as Sailor Mars in particular). He's . . . someone without an off switch typically. Right now, his muscular, tanned body leaned against the wall next to the doorway, putting all his weight into his hip. Today he was wearing the pink "Badass Diva" shirt I gave him a few Christmases ago. The expression on his face when he saw me come out said it all.

"Shut up," I muttered, walking past him.

"Psh, I ain't sayin' *nothing*, girl," he said before following me.

The model, Michelle Heirman, was a beautiful immigrant from Sweden. Big, big model. Famous. Ultrathin, tall, blonde, tan skin, shiny blue eyes. She looked me over and wrote me off immediately.

"Oh, are we gonna have the photoshoot today after all?" she said, slightly mocking, through her thick accent.

Matty and I exchanged a quick glance before I began looking over my equipment. "Just let Matty and I finish setting up equipment, then we'll get started," I said coldly, still thinking about the horrible skeletal face. She replied with a simple *mmm*. I worked in silence, setting up lighting, but I felt her eyes watching me like a hawk.

"Do you know if it's a boy or girl yet?" she asked, feigning concern.

I stopped in my tracks and shot her a look. "I'm not pregnant . . ."

She looked me over one more time. "Sorry, I just assumed." I exchanged a look with Matty (who gave me the *oh, girl, she didn't* look) and sighed.

"Let's get this done," I stated, readying my cold digital camera

As the photoshoot began, two professionals at work with a . . . less than favorable subject, I began to feel alright with the world again. As the pleasure of my work overtook me, the red skull drifted away. "Can't stop, won't stop," I whispered to myself as I took the photos of Michelle. She posed seductively, staring at my camera like it was a lover. For a moment, I forgot how much of a bitch she was. For a moment, I was able to forget the horrors of the accident. It became a synchronized dance between the camera and I. Photography brought me back to my happy place. "Can't stop, won't stop," I whispered as I took yet another photo.

"I'm sorry, can you not whisper like that?" my subject asked suddenly. In an instant, I was pulled out of Rachel-land and into the soul-crushing grip of reality, snapped out of my creative daze and staring at a prima donna who apparently didn't like the way I worked. I swallowed and smiled.

"Pardon?" I asked in a voice not unlike that of the female barista I saw earlier that day.

"You're whispering. It's distracting. I do better work when I'm not distracted. Can you stop?" she asked, her accent making her words sound even bitchier. I smiled a fake smile.

"Oh, it's just a—it's a calming thing. Li'l mantra, helps soothe me."

"Well, can you say it in your head? You're distracting me."

"Sure thing, girl," I said, keeping the words I'd rather say to myself. "You do you, I'll get the shots." I felt Matty giving me a disapproving gaze. In silence, and completely disconnected from my creative energy, I finished the shoot with Michelle.

"I need to powder my nose," Michelle said afterward, making her way to the bathroom like she was too good for this world. As soon as she closed the door, Matty turned like a wheel toward me. I analyzed the shots, trying to ignore him.

"You let her walk all over you. Few years ago, you would've ripped her hair out," he remarked.

I shook my head, still not looking at him, choosing to keep my gaze on the shots instead. "That was then, this is now. Gotta be professional, Matt. She's one of my biggest clients yet. If I'm not, I could lose potential future clients her caliber."

"Just saying . . ."

I didn't care. I just wanted to go home. Today had been a shitty day. I knew we had things later tonight. Things that couldn't be avoided, especially before *tomorrow* . . . But fuck, I wanted to not go. I wanted to lay in a fetal position underneath my big cozy blankets, watch old-school *Charmed*, and drift off to sleep. I wanted to forget about the accident and the photoshoot. Sooner rather than later.

Matty continued. "Why were you late, anyway? You should've heard her. Never realized angry Swedish could sound so Third Reich before she spewed it."

"It's not important."

"All fourteen-plus years I've known you, you've never been late to anything. Even post—"

I gave Matty a look. A long, hard look. He was about to bring up what my few friends knew to never bring up. He was about to say it, and realized mid-sentence he fucked up. I watched his face drop before he breathed out and nodded.

"Just saying it's weird. That's all."

I sighed, looking up and seeing Michelle exit the bathroom. "Really don't wanna talk about this right now," I said solemnly.

"You never do," Matty whispered as the blonde bimbo walked up to us. Michelle and I talked business, which she did while texting, I might add, then she began gathering her things. For a brief moment, I saw that she texted something in English. Something with a bunch of laughing emojis.

She look like crazy cat lady, she will die alone

Ow. Bitch. A flash of . . . certain people ran through my head and I felt a small dagger in my heart. I sank at that very moment, and continued the business talk. Professional as ever, am I. Bitch was lucky my studio was a place I considered a sanctuary. She might have lost an eye or two otherwise. Soon, she left and it was just Matty and I cleaning up equipment, and I remained quiet.

I would die alone?

A memory of rain poured into my head. A moment where I was the most alone I'd ever been. Memories of a familiar man with a shaved head that I had once called mine. His arms around me, warm embrace. Small echoes of words he told me over the phone . . .

A flash of the man without a face went through my head. As far as I could tell, he had been the only passenger in his car. I highly doubt he knew the people he hit. Did he die alone? Like a cat trying to get under a closed door, I could feel depression attempting to sink its claws in me. A weight creeping into my being and skull, dragging me further and further down. Not today,

I told myself. Not now. No, I wanted to be happy. But my thoughts didn't stop at my request, as if they ever did. I was in my thirties and unmarried. Not from lack of trying. I almost was . . . But I missed my shot, and now I was destined to be an old crone nobody loved. I was married to my passion, and even that was an unfruitful marriage. I had three friends at best, one of which being my own mother. No real social life to speak of. Dana was engaged to her man, Matty and his boyfriend were beginning to go steady, Mom could croak any minute. Soon . . . I would be alone. Wouldn't I?

No.

No, I couldn't think like that. Couldn't afford to. I was a successful young(?) woman working in the field of my dreams. Was that not fulfilling enough? I wasn't lonely. Why should I be? I am an excellent photographer . . . was . . . am.

As I tried to scrape my self-esteem back together, lift myself from the endless sea of tar, temporarily cure myself of my disease, Matty approached me. "Matty, can you do me a favor? Never book me with that Swedish *skank* again," I tasked, leaning against the table in the studio.

Matty smirked. "When she told you to stop whispering to yourself, I *knew* that was the end of that. Don't fuck with Eevee's process."

"Yeah, she was a real piece of work."

"Real bitch is what you mean, Rach. She ain't here, you gotta use the *professional* lingo," he said with that prissy little grin he had. That got a chuckle out of me.

"Force of habit at the studio," I remarked, finding mild humor as my depression lifted ever so slightly. "I needed today to end way sooner than it did."

"What? And miss out on the IKEA experience?" Matty leaned into an exaggerated pose, putting his hand on his hip and giving himself a duck face. "Oh ja, I shit rainbows and sparkles, ja? My hair was blessed by unicorns, I'm just so perfect, ja."

At this, I felt my depression successfully fended off. For the moment, anyway. I giggled almost uncontrollably.

"Miss Photographer Girl?" Matty continued. "Could you change my litter box? Could you do handstands while you photograph me? *I cannot work with distractions!*" he said with comedic bite, exaggerating his movements. My giggles turned into full-on laughter. Depression defeated . . . For now.

"Dead-on."

Matty hugged me and rubbed my back. "You feeling better, girl?" he asked sweetly. I was still laughing.

"Y-yeah. Fuck, you should get an Oscar, that was a stellar performance. You got her down to a T."

"I did always say my agent didn't know what he had," he chimed, full-on smile. "Come on, girl. We gotta meet up with Dana and Trevon. You'll feel better after a few drinks."

"Depends how much he talks . . ." Matty snickered, finding humor in my statement. I sighed. "Still don't know why they have to drag us all the way to fuckin' Hawaii to have their wedding."

"Damn girl, literally an all-expenses, paid-for trip and you *still* have a reason to complain?"

"I'm skeletal and I burn easy. I have reasons."

The drive over to Matty's favorite bar near WeHo was fun. For a moment, I forgot all about what had transpired earlier in the day. Matty blasted music that brought us back to our teen years, sang at the top of his lungs, and sped through LA, being the typical LA driver everyone hates by cutting off other vehicles and tailgating. It was fun, reminded me of the teenhood I had glossed over in my head and fantasized about, even though looking back, I hated it at the time. The past never is as good as the present, but the grass is always greener. I did occasionally miss those days, the days where I literally had nothing to worry about. 'Cept for school and the mean girls, I guess. I look back, and there are moments where I think I was happy, more innocent, more carefree. But if I really think about them, my depression was just as bad back then as it is now. Nothing's changed. The monsters in my closet are the same ones that have always haunted me. I guess now, they just take different shapes.

Shapes like Greg.

What was I talking about? Right. Sorry, got sidetracked. We got to the bar and found Dana. Shit, I haven't talked about her, have I? Dana is . . . a character, or at least she was. I first met her back when we were both going to the same college. She *used to be* wild and crazy, but always a damn good subject for my work. She was my first real model. In a way, we built our careers off each other. Her seductive look, beautiful ebony skin, perfect body. I still remember when she used to be all about partying. I think one time we were both so drunk we even made out! She was always, always the craziest one out of the three of us . . . that is, until she met Trevon.

Trevon. That . . . *douchebag*. Complete jerkwad. Didn't know what she saw in him. He seemed awful. If I was with him, I'd want to strangle him. Literally the most pretentious, garbage human I knew personally, other than that Michelle bitch from earlier. And I worked with models, some of the most pretentious people on the face of the Earth. But Trevon . . . he turned my wild and crazy tigress friend into a purring feline, not unlike the kitty I grew up with. Domesticated. After the two of them got engaged, there was a serious disconnect between her and I. I may have been asked to be the maid of honor . . . but I'd be lying if I said I was completely on board with it. And I felt completely out of the loop with everything wedding-related lately. She had changed since meeting him. It was like crazy college-girl Dana was replaced with middle-aged, mature "may I speak to your manager" woman Dana overnight. I couldn't make the same stupid jokes that she used to enjoy anymore. Talks of work became boring somewhere along the way. It just . . . felt odd. As that one song says: "I guess this is growing up."

Dana greeted us as we got to the bar, dressed in a faded purple dress, a necklace with a pearl, and gold bracelets on her right arm. Her natural hair was dyed blonde and in a short perm. God . . . after all this time she still looked like a goddess. I almost smiled until I saw Trevon in a black dress shirt next to her, his *fancy* barber-cut and goateed face looking in slight disdain at Matty and I as we crept to the bar. He always looked *fancy* with stupid expensive clothes and jewelry, and I think a part of me hated that. Like he was always trying to visually claim superiority over everyone else in the room. Pretentious tool. If there was ever a nepo-baby I knew in my profession . . .

"Rachel! Baby girl!" Dana greeted, in a way semi-familiar to how she used to say it in our college days. I hugged her, smelling the coconut lotion she loved to wear.

"Hey, hey, hey," I said as I smiled back, embracing her tightly. Matty hugged her shortly after I did.

"'Sup, Rach," Trevon said with his stereotypical head jerk that was like a reverse nod and his way of waving.

"Hi." I was not in the mood. Not for Trevon. Not right now. Matt and Trevon exchanged greetings as Dana kept her attention on me.

"You drinking, boo?"

"*Fuck yes.* Please," I said with a sigh.

"Uh, bartender?" Matty said. The bartender's attention turned to him. "Get this girl the meanest, fruitiest, pinkest drink you can possibly make. She's had a bitch of a day. Keep 'em comin', sweetie," he stated very effeminately, putting both of his hands on my shoulders.

"Sure thing, Matt," bartender said with a wink, turning to his bottles. Trevon gave the bartender a look before looking back at Matt. Knowing Matty, my money was the two had slept together before.

Dana rubbed my back. "That bad of a day, huh?"

"You've no idea. Matt, I can't afford . . ." I began. Matty winked at me.

"It'll go on *my* tab. My treat for you having to deal with Nazi bitch today." He grinned. I sighed.

"Nazi bitch? German model?" Dana asked.

"Swedish. Michelle Heirman," Matty said with a matter of fact turn.

"Oh yeah, I know her. Took photos of her last week," Trevon added. He then sipped his drink and gave a disapproving chuckle. "How was she a *Nazi bitch*?"

I stared at Trevon. I thought: Yeah, you *would* like Michelle, huh? Why don't you go fucking marry *her* instead of my best friend? Asshole. Luckily, the bartender finished my drink and pushed it in front of me.

"Ooooh, well, I've heard she's hard to work with," Dana said. She began rubbing my arm. "Poor Rachel . . ."

"I don't know, I thought she was cool," Trevon added yet again. Dana gave Trevon a look. "I dunno, maybe she had an off day or somethin'."

Off day? More like off life. Girl was lucky I didn't tear out her jugular.

I glared at Trevon before turning my attention back to Dana. "I-it's fine . . . prima donna wasn't what made my day shitty today." I sighed and looked around the bar. Somehow, despite never meeting any of these people, I felt like I'd worked for at least half of them in the course of my life.

The group must be used to my shitty days by now because shortly after, the topic was forgotten. Dana rubbed my back and half-heartedly told me that if I needed her she was there for me. And that was it. I hate to say it, but by now, me having a shitty day had become commonplace. I don't blame them for not asking. There's an unspoken rule about friends and breakups. After a month or two, you're expected to move on. Or at the very least, shut up about your ex. Shut up about your feelings. There was a time I used to blab about things. Maybe a few relationships ago . . . But I knew now about the rules. I also knew my friends cared . . . but there were limits to how much they would listen. So why bother? Matty and Dana chattered for a bit before Trevon decided to rear his presence into our space.

"So *this* is the itinerary for tomorrow," Trevon stated proudly, showing off his phone. He showed us and as soon as he did, a small part of me started to regret this trip. Immediately he began to go over flight details and details about the hotel we were staying at for two weeks. This trip was basically a wedding and a honeymoon all in one at a Hawaiian hotel named Tropical Springs. I was the maid of honor, but Dana had already planned with Trevon in conjunction where each would hold a bachelor and bachelorette party. I had literally no part of the planning. I mentioned I was *excited* for this wedding, right? Totally *excited*. Sarcasm.

I couldn't explain any of what Trevon was telling us cus frankly I wasn't paying attention. No, the booze in my hand was a much more interesting conversationalist. It kept telling me funny jokes about how big Trevon's head was and how stupid he looked and how beautiful Dana was. Trevon just kept talking and talking without saying much of anything. Was that mark always on Trevon's—

"Rachel, you good? You looking at me like a space cadet."

I blinked. What? I cleared my throat. "What?" I chuckled. It was now that I noticed Dana, Matty, and Trevon all focusing on me. Deep discomfort set in. I blinked and cleared my throat. "Damn, Matty. Your guy mixes a hell of a cocktail. Think I'm a little tipsy."

Trevon gave me a look of disdain and Matty nodded his head. "I'll make sure she's up tomorrow and on the plane," he said, putting his hand on my arm.

Trevon glared at me. "Right."

As if on cue, Dana tapped me on the back and clutched me from the other side. "Hey, I need to pee. Do you?"

I caught her gaze on my other end. She had a look on her face that I had come to know. I nodded. "Y-yeah. I could pee. I'm pro-peeing."

Dana's not-so-subtle pull away where we both went to the bathroom is a move I think most girls are familiar with. Safety in numbers, and all that. It also was useful when you needed to talk about something out of the range of your guys. That was apparently what this particular instance was about. Dana pulled me into the bathroom, quickly checked to see all the stalls were empty, then sighed. She leaned against the sink counter and folded her arms as she looked at me.

"Okay, what's going on?"

"What do you mean?"

"What I mean is this cryptkeeper routine you're doing. You've been off tonight."

I shrugged and chuckled lightly. "I told you I had a bad day."

"'Kay, but what was it? Time to *actually* spill some beans, Rach. I don't want whatever is bugging you messing up your trip."

I sighed and shook my head. "It's nothing. Just . . ." Images of the accident from earlier spilled through my head. The bisected man, the faceless woman, the child, and of course the man from the other car. A thought of his red skeletal face passed through my mind. How did I even begin to dump all that onto her? After a moment, I decided against it. "I . . . I'm okay."

"No, you're not. Ever since—" I gave a look, which stopped Dana mid-sentence. She scoffed. "Ever since *he who shall not be named*, I've been watching you wither away. You've been losing weight like crazy, you've been drinking more, you've been . . ."

I swallowed and looked down. She wasn't wrong about those points. I just had nothing to say. No fight in me to combat any of it.

"I'm just worried, okay?" Dana said with a sigh. "I—I want you to be *happy* this trip. It's gonna be one of the happiest moments of my life. I wanna share that with my best friend. Okay?"

I nodded, ashamed. "Yeah."

"I'm serious when I say I'm here for you. You *know* you don't have to be strong around me. And you always *know* there's also groups you can reach out to worst case—"

"I'm not going to a group. You know how I feel about that," I said, sounding more nasty than I meant to. My eyes watered a little. "I told you once, I'll tell you again, Dana. I'm fine."

Dana breathed out uneasily. "Okay." There was a tad bit of awkward silence as we stood across from each other. "Uh . . . One more thing, I guess. Before we all go on this trip together . . . can you *try* to get along with Trevon? For me?"

I flinched before jerking my head into a nod and grinning with the side of my mouth. "Don't know what you're worried about. Trevonathy and I are the best of buds." Dana gave me a look that made me squirm. "Yeah . . . I'll do my best. That should go both ways, though. He may be your fiancé, but your bestie was here first. He has to share."

Dana smiled. "Before the wedding, I'll make sure we get some time together. 'Kay? I promise."

I smiled back. Bold-faced lies, but she didn't know she was lying. Tre had a way of sweeping her away. I'd heard that one before. "'Kay. Sounds good." When we headed out of the bathroom, Trevon and Matty were waiting outside for us. We must've been in there long enough to worry.

"What's up?" Dana asked.

Trevon shrugged. "Was thinking of getting a seat outside. Too loud in here to talk," he said, plain faced. "Y'all good?"

Dana began, "Yeah—"

"There was this one bitch in there that would *not* shut the fuck up," I interrupted. "Poured her *whole* life story to us while doing lines. Was hard to break away. She may or may not have killed someone, it was kinda wild."

Matty snorted, probably sensing I was fucking with Trevon. Trevon gave him a look. "Right . . ." With that the group began heading outdoors, Trevon folding his lip like he had something to say. "Actually, uh, y'all go on ahead. I wanna talk with the maid of honor 'bout plans."

Dana gave us a look of concern. Matty blinked with uncertainty. "Uh . . . sure!" Matty said. "Not a problem. Girly, you want another drink?" he asked me.

I nodded my head. "Fuck yes. Definitely." Trevon lifted an eyebrow, glaring at me. I cleared my throat. "Water. Gotta . . . hydrate. Health, ya know?" I added to quickly save some face. Dana *had* made a comment about my drinking back there. If I had to guess, Trevon had talked to her about it at some point. She was dick-whipped like that. As Matty and Dana walked away, I was face-to-face with my nemesis. No, "nemesis" was giving him too much credit. My biggest annoyance. The fly at the picnic. The pain in my ass. There we go. Face-to-face with my biggest current pain in the ass, at least for the next two weeks. Trevon stepped forward. I shrugged in a challenge.

"You wanted to talk, Tre?"

He folded his lip and breathed in, nodding. "Yeah . . ." He looked like he was searching for a way to word his thoughts. "Look, bruh, I—I don't mean to sound disrespectful—"

"*Probably* gonna come off that way, though," I said, cutting him off.

An evil glint was in his eye. "Look . . . just wanna be on the same page with you 'bout somethin'. These next two weeks? They're about Dana and I. *We're* getting married and having our honeymoon. This is gonna be all about *us*."

I twisted my face into a grimace. "Am I supposed to interpret what that's supposed to mean?"

"It means she ain't gonna have time for you," he said bluntly. "The way she hovers 'round you, checking in on you, all that? That's not gonna happen these next two weeks. She's gonna be *busy*."

I scoffed. "'Kay, and?"

"And? Frankly? I don't want you bringing her down." I glared at him; he continued. "You're a part of this wedding, but make no mistake, Rachel, it ain't about you. I don't want you pulling no dramatic shit and getting her involved like you do. 'Kay? These two weeks gonna be copacetic."

I felt like punching him. "Dramatic shit? I—*I* pull *dramatic* shit? Really, Tre?"

Trevon scoffed and shook his head before grinning wryly. "Look, I'm sorry your man abused you and all, but that shit ain't *my* problem. And it ain't her's neither. During this wedding, I want it to be as stress-free for Dana as possible."

I couldn't come up with anything mean to say. He had mentioned the unmentionable. The skeleton I didn't want to acknowledge. I could have strangled this fuck boy and probably would have if I thought I could get away with it. Absolute fucking pig. My eyes watered a bit.

Trevon breathed out. "Look, I ain't trying to pick a fight or nothing just, you know . . . Be considerate. 'Kay?" With that, he walked away to the outside patio. All I could do was stare blankly ahead, feeling humiliated.

CHAPTER 3

The hiss of the shower hit the ceramic in a rhythmic fashion. It served as white noise as he sang. I heard them both from down the hall. He couldn't carry a tune to save his life. It was some crappy Top 40 hit; he never sang *good* music.

I didn't care.

I crept up the hallway, slowly taking off my clothes as I silently stepped into the green-walled bathroom. I was going to surprise him. My body tensed with anticipation and my heart pounded with sincerity. My bare feet felt the transition from our rough wooden floor to the wet tile floor beneath. The cool air hit my chest as I exposed it. Now that I was closer, his off-key singing was accompanied by the music playing from his nearby phone. The top of his shaved head peeked over our shower curtain. A grin grew on my face as I wrapped my fingers around the curtain. In a sudden jerking motion, I pulled it back and yelled, "Whoa!"

You were easy to get over—

I awoke with a jolt in cold sweat, death-gripping my pillow in a bear hug as I felt a tightening in my chest. My body shook uncontrollably as I struggled to breathe. I grimaced as I felt a sharp pain somewhere inside all over again. A sharp pain I'd felt ever since *that day*. Lines from the phone call swirled around in my head, replaying the incident all over again. That rainy day. My head over the toil—

I don't want to talk about it.

If the pillow were a small child, I'd have crushed its windpipe. My face crumpled as the salty tears slipped out and burned my eyes like acid. I screeched like a dying animal without any consent of my own, trembling as if buried in ice. I pulled my covers over me, but my body couldn't get warm. Not with the cold sweat under my clothes.

Why am I like this? Will I ever be normal again? Will I ever be happy again?

His words from the phone conversation repeated even though I didn't want them to, tearing me apart again and again. A vicious act of violence, not even his worst, but through words. At least I'm a little better now. I used to cry like this any moment I was alone. Now it was reserved for the times I slept alone. I refused to cry in front of anyone else since the phone call, though. Never again.

"Why, God, why?" I mumbled through my sobs for nearly an hour. It was the wee hours of the morning still. After a bit, my whines and whimpers began to simmer down as that thing that happens when you cry too much began to happen. It was like a part of me began to numb again. Numb enough to continue existing despite the pain. "Can't stop, won't stop."

After gaining a shred of will to do anything I peeked out my blinds to see it was still dark. Okay, well, guess I was up way earlier than I had any right to be. Sleep didn't seem achievable at this point. I decided to upload the photos from yesterday's photoshoot to my computer. As I hooked up my digital camera to my computer, I eyed my pouch where my Polaroid camera lay. After pressing the download button on my computer, I pulled my beloved Polaroid out of its bag, which had become its crypt.

Fuck.

Pieces of the lens dropped in broken shards as I lifted it. I was going to need to buy a new one. From its sorry, banged-up state, there was just no saving it. I cursed and lit a cigarette, breathing in the sweet smoke and feeling more alert as I did. If my friends knew I had gone back to smoking, they'd be pissed, especially Matty. My little secret, though. I studied the Polaroid camera, remembering the accident from yesterday. Still crazy that it happened. For a brief moment, I thought about the corpse of the man with his face sanded off. The blood-covered, exposed skull. Those vacant red holes he had for eyes. I don't know what attracted me so much about them but I almost felt like they were staring back at me . . . Watching.

It gives me the creeps to think about it.

I took a puff of my cigarette before looking back at Michelle's photos, which were still uploading. As the hundreds of shots passed over my computer screen, showcasing her different looks, it almost looked like she was a stop-motion figure doing a little dance for me. There was something entertaining about the thought that she was a little puppet on display for me to watch, like a perverse reversal of power. I grinned as I took another puff and breathed out. God, the euphoria of the cigarette fought off any feeling of dread, if only for a fleeting moment. It was like with each puff a weighted blanket was lifted off my head. The images passed as the phony asshole in front of me smiled like a little plaything. I watched in awe like a five-year-old watching *Jurassic Park* for the first time.

"World's a stage, bitch."

Then, in a blink, I saw something. Something in one of the photos. It was brief, but I could've sworn . . . I pulled up the file where the photos were downloading and searched for what I thought I saw. I clicked on a photo and began searching through them again. It looked like—like some sort of figure in the background. It was weird. I could've sworn I saw . . .

There. I briefly saw the same figure again before accidentally skipping past it to the next photo.

Shit! Missed it!

It was like a . . . like a man with a flat-brimmed hat. He was dressed in black. I went back to the photo where I thought I saw the figure behind Michelle.

Nothing.

There were some shadows back there, but nothing physical. Nothing but the background I had chosen to shoot Michelle in front of. I leaned back, analyzing the photo. Checking that it wasn't the photos before that one, and finding nothing that looked anything like the figure I thought I saw. I twisted my mouth. What the fuck was that? Was it the lighting? Was I seeing things? To be safe, I clicked through the photos again.

Nothing. No man with a hat.

I blinked and puffed my cigarette. "You're losing it, Rachel," I told myself. I rubbed my eyes before looking at my clock. Five in the goddamn morning. Matty would be coming by to pick me up for our flight at nine. I needed sleep. Luckily I had packed my bags a week in advance, knowing that otherwise I'd wait till the last minute. I huffed before lifting myself off my chair. "And with that, the nefarious Rachel Hannigan returns to her mysterious den of slumber yet again." I put out my cigarette in the little bowl I used as an ashtray before dropping onto my bed like a falling tree, face-first. "Awaiting the next seventy-five years until she devours yet another hapless man." I sighed, closing my eyes. "Leaving nothing but bones." I pulled my pillow to my face and buried myself into it. "If only." With that, I drifted into the warm embrace of sleep.

Doors. Countless wooden doors. White ones, red ones, black ones, maroon, beige, gray. Doors opened before me as I sank deeper and deeper down into the void ahead. Countless doors I opened, equalizing pressure in my ears like changing altitudes. Keeping my feet vertical, despite somehow traversing straight down. The doors didn't stop. I kept heading down, a primal dread in my gut. The doors didn't stop.

I awoke to a thunderous rattle at my front door. "Rachel! Come on! I'mma leave you behind!" The sunlight was blinding as I tried opening my eyes. I thoroughly believe that the world was only getting brighter due to global warming.

And we were going to Hawaii, where it was bound to probably be even brighter than this. Joy. I barely lifted my head up. More banging on the door.

"Jesus! I'm getting up, Matty! What the fuck?"

"Then get up, bitch, let's gooo."

I got up and let Matty and his partner, Frankie, in. Frankie was a blond twink in contrast to Matty's twunk. Pretty sure they met on Grindr or at the Abbey in WeHo, but Matty likes to tell a more romantic tale. If you believe Matty's version, it was two soulmates that found each other while shopping for clothes in West Hollywood. They both wanted to buy the same expensive designer shirt and wagered a bet for it: If the next person that came into the shop was brunette, Frankie could have the shirt. If the next person was blond, Matty could have the shirt as well as a date. Apparently it was a slow day in WeHo and the two spent a good half hour talking, waiting for someone to come in. The guy that came in next was bald. Matty and Frankie hooked up that night.

I once asked Frankie about this story; he looked at me like I was a space alien. If you knew Matty like I do, you would know he'd exaggerate the truth in service of telling a better story. Especially when it came to his conquests. In those cases, I think it was the chubby, shy gay boy I knew back in high school telling me those stories rather than the slimmer extrovert that was Matty now. I think somewhere deep inside, he was still looking for approval from the popular girls.

Matty gave me a look while Frankie quietly greeted me with a shy nod.

My bestie twisted his mouth before picking up my luggage. "One suitcase? Really?"

"And two carry-ons."

Matty shot me an evil look. "There better be more than Kiss and Black Sabbath T-shirts in here."

"There's like a fancy wedding dress in there. Plus, *as if* I'd forget Van Halen."

Matty huffed, which made me chuckle as I grabbed my carry-ons. Frankie politely took one of my bags before I could, as if gently trying to lead me out of my own house. I quietly thanked him and sighed as the three of us began to make our way out of the duplex toward Matty's silver Subaru. Matty opened his trunk and stuffed my case in like a body bag into a cabinet at the morgue.

"For real, though, Rach, we are gonna go on a shopping spree after we get to the hotel. You need more clothes."

"You're just jealous my ass looks better in jeans than yours."

Frankie laughed a hearty laugh and Matty screeched a loud, shrieking, "*Hey!*" that made his voice break. "You can't weaponize your ass! We had an agreement!"

The drive to LAX was sleepy. Frankie drove, Matty was in the front seat, and I was in the back. When we first got into the car, Matty began blasting 2000s girly pop. I asked him if it'd kill him to get some Ozzy into his life. He turned it into an Ozzy and Harriet joke. Other than that, most of the conversation was between him and Frankie. The two feverishly talked about people I didn't know, gossiping about their WeHo friends. It was a group that I'd met in passing, but Matty was spending more and more time with. I guess they were originally Frankie's friends but were adopting Matty through couple symbiosis. The sun peeked through trees as Frankie drove us along the freeways of LA. My eyes rested on Matty's and Frankie's hands as they held on to each other while driving, and I stared for a moment before looking away. I was half asleep when Matty finally addressed me again.

"Rach! We gotta go to the Pearl Harbor memorial! There's also that one place they filmed *Jurassic Park*—"

"Kualoa Ranch," Frankie added.

"*Oh my God* we gotta go there. Maybe I'll photoshop a T-Rex eating us, huh, Rach?"

I sighed and chuckled. "If alcohol is involved, I'm in."

"Honolulu is beautiful pretty much year-round," Frankie said. "You guys will have a lot of fun."

Hopefully. As soon as we landed on Waikiki, we were going to meet the other bridesmaid, Penelope, and the groomsmen. From what I understood, Tre's friends were probably going to be piggish clones of him. And Penelope? I wasn't sure what to expect, but I knew she was a successful OnlyFans model. Hopefully she was cool. That business was definitely not *my* scene, though. I've photographed nude models before, sure, but filming people fucking? Having to edit photos of certain body parts and fluids? No, thank you. That seemed like a circle of hell I never wanted to step foot in.

After an hour and thirty minutes of driving, we finally reached LAX. Matty and I rushed out of the Subaru to the correct terminal, where we met up with Trevon and Dana. Thank God I was wearing sunglasses, because I could feel Trevon's judgmental gaze on me. I decided to pay him no heed and hugged Dana tight upon greeting her. The greeting was brief before we boarded the plane that would take us on an over five-hour flight to our destination. A small bit of genuine excitement began to stir in my gut. I'd never been to Hawaii, and even my overly cynical nature couldn't overpower the hope of the new adventure that awaited. Upon actually sitting down, however, and waiting for the flight to take off, that hope turned to unease. Statistically a person has a one in 1,708 chance of dying in a plane crash, the leading cause of plane crashes being pilot error. Still, there was the chance this was that one exceptional moment. I closed my eyes hard then looked over to my side, where Trevon was watching me from across the aisle, giving an evil eye while Dana chatted with him. I glared back until Matty sat in the seat beside me, blocking my view. He looked around excitedly.

"The people going to Hawaii are ugly *as fuck*!" he whispered with a mischievous grin. "Like that one to our right, in front of Dana and Tre? He looks like that troll from Harry Potter. Look at him, look, look."

I looked over to where Matty indicated and lifted an eyebrow. Just an ordinary older white guy who was balding and wearing a Hawaiian shirt. Not particularly attractive, but calling him a troll definitely felt undeserved.

"Ain't gonna be a *troll in my dungeon*, if you know what I mean," he said, snickering.

I turned to Matty and glared. "You're a *mean*, mean bitch, you know that?"

Matty scoffed and pretended to be offended. "Oh my God, Rach. How could you say something so *absolutely true*?" He jerked his head while repeatedly blinking his eyes, pressing on his chest. "I am *hurt*. It's like you know me or something. Ew."

I sighed, looking out the window, seeing Matty fidget out of my peripheral vision. He was being annoyingly energetic. I turned back. "What's got *you* hyped up?"

Matty smiled a huge smile. "I've been waiting for this for months! This trip is *finally* happening! Frankie has been telling me all about Waikiki and Tropical Springs. It looks like it's out of *Barbie*, Rach!"

I smiled. A genuine smile too. If nothing else, Matty was going to bring a smile to my face this trip. Could always rely on him. "Does it? I haven't looked it up much."

"Oh, yeah. Like, it's not the pink hotel, but *oh my god*. The exterior design of Tropical Springs is like this almost Mediterranean-looking style, but the inside has this interesting little cottage vibe. Oh, and the men? You don't even wanna know. Fucking gorgeous."

"Frankie and you have hall passes, I take it?"

At this, Matty got a little uncomfortable, his grin winding down. "I mean . . . He said it was okay to hook up while out there, but I don't know. I'm not sure I really feel like it, you know? What Frankie and I have . . . I don't know. It's different."

I smiled, rubbing his hand. "Aw, our little Matty is growing up."

"Shut up. As if." Matty adjusted in his seat. "In any case, I'm so excited I don't think I'll get any sleep."

It was less than thirty minutes after takeoff that Matty fell asleep and began snoring obnoxiously. I listened to the Kiss song "Detroit Rock City" in my headphones on repeat as I tried to ignore the loud snores beside me. I couldn't sleep. No matter how I tried, I couldn't for the life of me. I found myself blankly staring at the ocean, listening to Paul Stanley's voice tell me to get up and move my feet. My mind wandered as I stared blankly out the window. The clouds rolled by peacefully as I continued to stare.

About an hour into watching out the window, my right ear started to hurt. It started as a small irritation but it got worse, making the sound of Kiss painful. I adjusted my headphones, but that didn't seem to help. A high-pitched ringing began in my ears. I took off my headphones, trying to quell it, but the sound got louder. Did I need to equalize my ears? I looked around; it looked like everyone around me was asleep. The biggest tell that my hearing was compromised, though, was looking at Matty and not hearing his snores above the ringing in my ears. The pain kept getting worse and worse. It was like someone jabbed a spike into my right ear. I put my finger inside my ear canal and winced as I felt my flesh enter like a Q-tip.

I felt . . . liquid inside. Warm liquid. I swallowed hard, trembling from how white-hot the agony of my ear felt. I looked down at my fingers and saw dark red caking the tip.

"And you must be Rachel!" a squeaky, annoying voice said as pink acrylic nails landed on my arm.

What?

I blinked and saw a woman I had previously only seen pictures of standing before me. Light brown hair, tanned skin, big nose and eyes. Before I could even properly process what was happening, I was pulled into a hug. Her scent was the slightest hint of tea tree oil mixed with a sweet perfume. "I've been so excited to meet you, girlie!" her nasally voice jeered.

"Uh, me too . . ." I said, completely unsure of how I got there . . . or how there wound up being a lei around my neck.

The girl pulled away to reveal a heavily made-up face. At first glimpse she looked white, but the longer I looked, the harder it was to pin down her ethnicity. Her light brown, almost blonde hair was tied up in a ponytail and her prominent hooked nose didn't necessarily take from her beauty. If anything, it added to it. I was captivated. She was absolutely stunning. She was definitely shorter than me but her brown eyes were intense, wise beyond their years, and she had a huge smile on her face and wore a pink shirt and jean shorts, loudly chewing gum in a way that'd usually annoy me . . . but it didn't with her.

Where was I? I was just on the plane . . . I *swear* I was just on the plane.

The girl laughed the way a fairy in an animated movie might. "I am *such* a fan of your brand. Honestly, your work as Eveline Apple? Some of the best I've seen, like ever."

"Uh, thanks . . ."

Let's see . . . I was at what looked to be a front desk. Matty, Trevon, and Dana were standing nearby, along with a Polynesian guy and a white guy I didn't know. The Polynesian guy seemed to have a particular interest in me, staring at me as I stood there, holding on to my carry-on bags and suitcase. I breathed out, looking around. The halls were lavish, off-white with art deco furniture for guests to sit on. The front desk was large and wooden, with several hosts standing behind the desks. To my right, the sun was peeking in and a late afternoon view of the beach was nearby. There were people outside enjoying the sun, playing volleyball. We were already at Tropical Springs? That meant that those guys were Trevon's groomsmen. And that meant this woman was . . .

"Can't say I've ever seen your work, Penelope, but that follower count doesn't lie," I said, and chuckled.

Right . . . we got off the plane, were greeted by people that put leis around our necks, took a cab, and wound up here. How did I forget all that?

Penelope laughed the weirdest fucking laugh I'd ever heard. It was like a cat getting electrocuted. "Please, call me Penny. And I know! Just made top twenty in OF last week!"

Dana walked up. "Forreal? You didn't tell me that!"

"Girl, we have yet to talk! I have tea!"

"Oooh, sounds like girl time with some drinks before dinner," Dana said with a smile. She turned to Matty and I. "How's that sound? Get settled into our rooms and meet up in Tre and I's suite and explore a bit? Tre and his boys have some catching up to do. So, girlie time before dinner?"

Matty and I exchanged looks. "Uh, yeah, that sounds fine. I guess," I said.

Matty smiled. "Sounds great,"

I looked over, noticing Trevon's Polynesian friend still staring at me. His mouth widened into a grin. He was kinda cute. He had hair slightly on the longer side, a decent build where you could tell he worked out, and some sort of tattoo on his left forearm. Looked tribal. Maybe he was a Native Hawaiian? Hard to tell based on looks alone.

It didn't matter.

He was one of Trevon's friends. Probably meant he was a douchebag too. With that in mind, I coldly looked away without acknowledging him. Soon after, Matty and I split off to find our rooms. Once out of earshot, I put my finger into my ear. Dry. I pulled it out and looked at my fingertips. No blood. I looked long and hard at my bestie as we walked. He eventually noticed.

"What? My hair sticking up?" Matty then asked.

I breathed out and shook my head. "Is there . . . blood coming out of my ear?"

He looked like I told him I saw flying elephants. "Um, what?"

"B-back on the plane. I got a bad ear ache. Is there blood in my ear?"

Matty tilted his head, scrunching his face. I showed him the side of my head and moved my hair out of the way so he could see. "Uh, no . . . Not that I can see."

"It felt wet."

Matty looked a little closer at my ear. "Nah, your ear looks fine. Maybe it was ear wax or something?"

I blinked. What the hell? Was that a dream or something? I know I saw blood. I know it was on my fingers. Did it dry up by now? No, Matty would've seen traces of it. My ear didn't hurt, though. Not like it did earlier.

"Some sort of pressure problem with the elevation?" Matty asked. "Do you need like a Tylenol or something?"

Maybe I dreamed it. Entirely possible with how little sleep I had gotten. Maybe I . . . Maybe I dozed off on the plane ride. I breathed out and shook my head. "No, I'm—I'm good."

We carried on our way, eventually winding up in the elevator. The back half of the elevator was glass, creating a huge window that showed outside. Orange sunlight lit up the elevator and it was actually hard to see through the window due to the sunset. I could vaguely see a pool and a fancy rock fountain outside. It was through the painful rays of orange sunlight that I could see the exterior of the building. Matty was right earlier. It was cute. Various colors of off-white, various inlays on the walls that looked made of multiple stones, palm trees, tropical flowers. I stared at it as Matty looked at his key.

"I think we're both on the seventeenth floor. I'm seventeen thirty-two. You're seventeen sixteen."

I turned and grinned. "What, not sharing a room?"

"Bitch, I wanna sleep in peace. You stay up at weird hours."

I laughed. "Valid. Can't argue that."

"Mmmhmm." Matty looked outside. As we rose up, the ocean suddenly reflected back at us. Windsurfers were far out, and what seemed like millions of people on the beach looked like ants from this far. "What do you think of that girl Penelope?"

I shook my head and shrugged. "Dunno. Hard to tell, honestly. Why?"

Matty twisted his face. "I don't know. Feel like she's fake as fuck."

I looked over with a lifted eyebrow. "She's a model, of course you do."

"That's not it. Did you hear that laugh? No way that's real."

I shook my head and sighed. "I mean, guess we'll find out the more we get to know her."

"Yeah."

As if to accentuate the end of the conversation, the elevator doors opened. The windowless white halls on either side of us had a red-patterned carpet along with some beach-related paintings on the walls. The lights above were ambient and painted the way ahead in a vacant and lifeless glow. Matty and I stepped out of the elevator, looking around. Matty sighed before handing me my key. "Looks like we're not gonna be close by. I'm going right, you're going left."

"What, they couldn't be bothered to put us near each other?"

Matty gave a look. "This is a luxury hotel, girl. We're lucky to have rooms on the same floor."

"How the hell did Trevon afford all this? Sure as hell can't be his photography."

"Definitely his trust fund. Alright, get showered, do yo thang, meet at the elevator when you're ready?"

I agreed and we split off to our rooms. There was a moment upon looking down the hallway ahead of me that I almost didn't want to go alone. The hallway seemed ever-expanding in front of me, like some long, coiled snake, cramped and spacious all at the same time. The monotony of the red and warm autumn-like colors on the carpet seemed endless, and the slick white walls looked somehow dead despite never being alive. After looking one final time at my key, I started down the way.

"Can't stop, won't stop," I whispered to myself as I trudged forward. I followed the numbers and walked down, passing each brown door with gold lettering. The walk was much longer than expected. It just kept going on and on. "Can't stop, won't stop," I whispered to ease my journey. As I turned another corner or two I began to feel like if it weren't for the door numbers I'd be absolutely lost. I looked at the numbers passing by. 1713 . . . 1714 . . . Then, I turned a corner and saw 1716 next to 1718. I breathed out. Finally. Talk about being far away from the elevator. There had to be a closer exit to downstairs. I put the key in the lock and let myself in.

The room was . . . huge. It had a living room, a bedroom, its own kitchen, and an enormous bathroom. The furniture was a mixture of blue, white, and brown colors. I dropped my bags almost immediately at the door. "Way to go, Trevon's trust fund," I muttered. Blueish late daylight from outside poured in through a large window on one end of the living room. The sound of the ocean was audible in the distance. Immediately, I headed toward the black-tiled kitchen and fridge for some *refreshments*. I found a small bottle of vodka that looked appealing and opened it. "Really, Trevonathy, thank you, so much. You're *such* a good host." I drank as much as I could, as fast as the tiny bottle would allow, and cleared my throat after I had my fill.

I looked around before grabbing my big suitcase and dragging it into my bedroom. I opened it up, searched through my clothes, found a Kiss shirt and some cutoff jeans, and placed the clothes onto the queen-sized bed that was to be mine for the next two weeks. The room was fairly simple, nice even. Had a wardrobe I could stuff my things into, a plant in the corner (pretty sure it was called a Hawaiian ti), and . . . a balcony. My bedroom had a balcony. I opened it and stepped out, getting a whiff of ocean air and looking out toward the ocean. Holy shit, this room was something else. I leaned on the balcony railing, looking down. Jesus, that was a mistake. Immediately I came face-to-face with my mortality by seeing just how high up seventeen stories was. I whistled in disbelief. Below there was a courtyard with a large swimming pool. Still, though, if you were to fall, even into that swimming pool, the impact would definitely kill you. Fall from here? Certain death. I sighed as I looked out before my phone started ringing.

Mom

I ignored it, then sent a text.

`Got to Hawaii safely. Will talk later.`

In moments, like clockwork, she sent me a text.

`OK. Just checking. Love you.`

I texted her back how much I loved her, then took a shower. By the time I stepped out, Dana had sent a mass text asking if we were ready yet. I had just stepped out of my hotel room when the door of 1718 cracked open slightly. I turned to see an elderly woman standing in the entrance. She stared at me, pale skin glimmering in the artificial light. There was a pointed nose in the middle of a face with growths, looking at me with hazel-colored, bloodshot eyes, yellowed from age. Her faded black-turned-gray hair was tied up and greasy, and she stood like a hunchback. Her body was oddly shaped, bulbous. It was almost hard to tell where her neck began and ended with the rest of her body. Her arms and legs, though, were thin. Thin like four toothpicks sticking out of an apple. She looked like every description of a Halloween witch you could imagine, but with a bright red shirt and brown shorts. Every inch of her exposed skin was wrinkled. Her stare was cold, but intensely angry. There was no affection to be found in her bitter, craggy face. She stood there, just staring at me like I had run over her dog right in front of her. The stare persisted, as if she had opened the door for the sole purpose of giving me her dark, hateful look.

I tried my best to be pleasant, offering a smile despite getting a little creeped out by her unblinking stare. "Hi," I said softly as I began to close my door. Her face remained unchanged, almost like she didn't register my greeting. Instead, she remained glaring at me, silent. A dark hatred was in her face as she remained unmoved.

Great, I was put in a room next to a senile old lady. Fantastic. I nodded politely and began to walk away.

"Stupid fucking cunt."

I stopped in my tracks. What the fuck did she call me? I turned around, facing the old woman who was now huffing and nearly frothing at the mouth.

I cleared my throat. She was an old lady, maybe she was having some sort of episode. "Uh . . . I'm sorry, what?"

"You fucking *whore*! Infected *slut*! *S-stupid* fucking *bitch*!"

I would've fired back something, but a wide-eyed look had come over her as she looked me over. Like it wasn't even me she was seeing. Her face dropped, and she quickly pushed the door shut, almost as if in a panic. Her old limbs shook like branches on a tree in a vicious wind.

"It knows! It knows!"

It sounded like she muttered something about the color red before slamming her door shut very loudly and abruptly.

What the hell was that about?

CHAPTER 4

"My God, I could live here," Penelope said loudly after taking a picture of herself. We had walked as a group from Dana and Trevon's penthouse suite near the top floor and now were down on the streets of Waikiki. Whatever expenses Trevon had spent on Matty's and my hotel rooms were apparently nothing compared to what he had spent for Dana and himself. Their penthouse suite looked like the idealized high-rise apartment, with multiple rooms, a large balcony, a large dining table, and even a washer and dryer. Admittedly, it looked big enough to play sportsball in. Apparently, it was fairly normal for some of the rooms to be rented out full time as actual apartments. Pretty sure the only reason that particular suite wasn't was because movie stars would be in a bidding war over it. *That's* how nice it was. If I put my organs on the black market, I still wouldn't be able to afford a month's rent in that suite. No way. I'm sure the same could be said for this area in general.

"I don't know, I hear the housing market here is something else. Plus the H-1 being the main freeway? I don't know if I could do it," Dana remarked.

"That's why you'd get a place downtown, never have to drive unless you want to," Penelope reasoned before sipping the boba she bought shortly before meeting up with us.

Downtown Honolulu, the area we were in that is known as Waikiki, was cute. Matty, Dana, Penelope, and I were walking the streets, and I genuinely couldn't imagine trying to live here. Even in the dusk air, this place didn't look real, it looked like the idealized version of a city. Palm trees, tall buildings, bright lights, greenery everywhere you looked. Even the lampposts and the streets had a charm to them. Then there were the people . . . So many people in swimsuits and summer wear, even as the night grew colder. This didn't look like a place that could exist on our plane of existence. It looked like a city you'd build in The Sims.

"I don't know, Rach, what do you think?" Dana asked me. I blinked and turned to find her pleasant face smiling at me. I hadn't expected to be pulled into the conversation.

"I think if your fiancé weren't paying for this trip, I'd be homeless," I said honestly.

Penelope laughed her weird pixie-like laugh at this. "Word. If I wasn't doing my OF vids, there's no way I'd ever be able to afford this place. Not with *my* employment record."

Dana looked uncomfortable at this mention of money. "Well, Tre really wants everyone to have a good time. That's why he's spending the extra money."

We all went a little quiet at this. Penelope played with her boba straw a bit while looking over the crowd. Matty looked at her with a look of disdain while she remained blissfully unaware. That look alone explained why Matty was so quiet. I didn't share Matty's thoughts of her, but I understood why he felt the way he did. She did kinda remind me of his biggest bully in high school.

I looked around as we walked, deciding to not add to the expense conversation. The flowers were as vibrant as photos that had been deeply saturated and well edited. If I hadn't already reached out and touched one earlier, I wouldn't have believed them to be real. "God, I could take pictures out here for days, though. It's so beautiful."

Penelope smiled at me. "Facts, wouldn't it be great? Do some shoots earlier in the day, tan at the beach at sunset, go barhopping at night here?"

I shrugged. "Y-yeah, I guess. That'd be kinda cool."

"Hey, maybe we can go halfsies on a place out here someday. Buy out Dana and Trevon's suite." I merely smiled at this. No way in hell that'd work. Penelope turned to Dana. "Hear that, Dana? Rach and I are gonna evict you and the hubs. We're gonna be high-class sluts together in Honolulu while you live the *domesticated* life."

Dana chuckled and shook her head. "You're already a slut, P."

"Yeah, but I don't live in Honolulu." Penelope sipped her boba, looking like she was analyzing me. "So I know you do like fashion modeling and whatnot, but like, do you ever go outside of your comfort zone?"

"What do you mean?"

"Like, do you like doing any other types of photography?"

I blinked before smiling. "Uh . . . Yeah, I don't know, guess I . . . Guess I like taking photos of all sorts of things. Just kinda got pigeonholed into what I do by the industry, ya know?"

Penelope giggled. "I'd love to see some of your other work sometime."

Well, she was getting on my good side quickly.

"Oh yeah, she's really good," Dana interjected. "I keep telling her to post more of her other stuff, but she won't listen to me."

I shot Dana a look. I don't remember her ever telling me that. I could be mistaken, though.

"You should post 'em! Oh my God, and there's so many places out here to take photos! Was here all summer last year and I swear, it's *so* cute! Stick with me, Rach, I'll show you all the best sights."

After that, Dana and Penelope engaged in a fast-talking conversation I could barely keep up with. I think it was about a designer-brand purse they saw that I would never be able to afford even if my life depended on it. I wound up talking to Matty, who was still uncharacteristically silent for the most part. It wasn't until toward dinnertime I got Matty to speak up. By then, though, it was hard to get too deep in conversation because there was so much to take in. The restaurant had been partially fashioned to look like a tiki hut, but once you saw the view of the ocean nearby and the fine white sheets on the tables, the illusion of affordability quickly went out the window. We were met with Trevon and his group of boys, which now included a heavier-set white guy than the other white guy that was already part of his crew.

Trevon greeted us with a smile. "Ayy, there's the girls." Dana practically leapt into Trevon's arms and the two shared a passionate kiss that felt a little too intimate for the public. The two connected foreheads. "Y'all have a good time?"

"Oh yeah, I'll tell ya about it later."

I guess I was unknowingly glaring at the two because Matty tapped my shoulder. "Rach . . ."

I turned toward him to see him standing by the cute Polynesian guy from earlier. The guy extended his hand. "I don't think we met yet. I'm Kai."

I looked at his hand, then politely shook it. "I'm Rachel."

As we began to get seated at a long table outside, Kai took a seat near me. Firepits burned nearby, illuminating everything in an orange glow. After we were given menus, Kai said, "So, how long have you known the happy couple?"

I opened a menu, barely giving him the time of day. "Give or take a century. You?"

"Oh, I've known Tre since college. Second or third time meeting Dana, though. They don't come out here too often."

"Yeah, I bet." Let's see . . . affordable food, affordable food . . . As I searched the menu my purse bled tears of blood. Yes, waiter, I'll take the water, maybe a loaf of bread. How much is that? My right foot? Do you think if I threw my other one into the mix I'd be able to afford an appetizer too?

Kai grinned next to me, leaning in. "You should get *that* one. Their specialized Loco Moco."

I looked at the one he pointed out. Seventy-five dollars? What the actual fuck? I merely laughed. "Yeah, right. Cus I could afford that."

Kai merely grinned. "Don't worry 'bout cost, I got you."

I lifted my eyebrows. "*You're* paying for my meal?"

He shrugged. "No sweat."

I nodded then looked at the drink menu. "Stick that super-expensive mai tai-like drink on there and you got yourself a deal, Kai."

He chuckled. "Done." He grinned. "You're someone that enjoys a fancy drink, huh?"

I grinned slightly. "No, it just takes more than throwing money at me to get my number."

Kai burst out with a slight laugh. "Oh boy, that easy to see through, huh?" He sighed. "I guess I'll have to revise my strategy a bit."

"Guess so." I looked around the table and soon met eyes with Penelope, who was watching me with curiosity. I felt a little blood rush to my face as I smiled at her. After a moment, her eyes softened and she smiled back before returning to a conversation with one of the groomsmen.

After we all ordered and ate some of our food, Trevon annoyingly clinked his glass at the head of the table with a fork. I had been munching away at the delicious Loco Moco Kai was buying me (hey, I wasn't gonna say no to expensive-but-free food) and was sucked out of bliss with the sight of stupid Trevon's face.

"Uh, can I have everyone's attention?" he said almost shyly before standing up. The table went quiet, lit by the fires and the ocean sounding behind him. Soft ukulele music played in the background and we could still hear the rest of the restaurant speaking among themselves, but our attention was completely on him.

"I just wanna thank everyone for coming out here on this trip with us. I know it is kinda a big trip, but Dana and I love y'all so much we wanted y'all with us as we got married at one of our favorite places in the entire world." He took a moment, thinking about things. "I thank . . . I thank *God* everyday that she's in my life. I haven't always made the best decisions in my past, and I know for some of y'all being my friend has been a rocky road, especially in my early twenties. But Dana . . . I think we can all agree *she* is one of the best decisions I've made in my life. Cus of that, I wanna do a toast to her, if y'all cool with that."

I stiffened as I glared at Trevon. Dana was too good for him. The way he seemed so genuine, that little wetness in his eyes, that troubled smile. He should get into acting. I knew that kind of behavior much too well. That's how guys like him lured you in. The bad-boy-with-a-change-of-heart type. That's how they tricked you. Making things seem genuine before ripping it all away from you. Seeming like a troubled soul, dragging sympathy out of you, only to mercilessly beat you down with it later. Dana was making the biggest mistake of her life, and there was nothing I could do but watch, disgusted.

"Dana. I love you so much, baby girl. Every day with you feels like a blessing. I don't know where I'd be without you, baby."

I looked over to Dana, who was eating it all up. Completely entranced, completely fooled. My stomach turned as little happy teardrops rolled out of her eyes. Trevon lifted his glass. "To Dana."

"To Dana," the entire table repeated.

"I don't know, Rach. It really seems like he actually loves her," my mom said over the phone. I sat on my bed in my hotel room, looking up at the ceiling.

"Oh, come on, Mom. Don't tell me you buy his bullshit too."

"No, I *am* telling you. I don't think you see the things he posts about her on social media. He's crazy about her."

I scoffed. "I don't care if he writes fuckin' Shakespearean sonnets about her, Ma. That means *nothing*. He's a goddamn liar. If you—if you *saw* how much of an act he made of it at dinner, I don't think you'd buy it either. It's all a fucking show."

Mom sighed. "Look . . . Let's play devil's advocate: What if you're not seeing things clearly and he really does care about her?" I paused. I didn't want to think about it. I huffed, but couldn't come up with an answer. "All I'm saying is, the guy is literally paying for you to be there even though he doesn't like you. He's doing it cus you're *her* best friend. Think you should give him a little respect. If it were me, I sure as hell wouldn't have paid for you."

I twisted my mouth into a tight grin. "Well *you* wouldn't because you're notoriously cheap, Ma. I didn't even have cable growing up cus of you."

"Not the point." There was a brief silence. "Changing subject . . . How have the nightmares been?"

I gulped. "Fine. Dying down as of late. Haven't really had any."

"Rachel . . ."

"I'm telling the truth."

Mom sighed. "Greg was a piece of shit for what he did. I—I would've helped more if I knew what was going—"

"Mom, I'm fine."

Mom paused a second, then sighed again. "I just want to tell you . . . Not every man is Greg, Rach. This hating-men thing you've gotten into . . . Y-you need to be careful. You don't wanna die alone, bitter and old. You *know* me, I'm not one for that wussy crap . . . But I'm starting to think you need to see someone. After what *he* did, I—"

I scoffed. "That'd be the day." I breathed out heavily. "I don't hate men, Ma. Just douchebags like Trevon. I'm okay, trust me."

"Alright," Mom said, retreating. "Well, thank you for calling me. I appreciate hearing from you, and I'm glad you landed safely. Have fun on your trip."

"Thank you, Ma. Love you."

"Love you too."

With that, the phone conversation ended and I put my phone down before looking up at the ceiling. The blank white above me felt oddly comforting as I looked at it, hearing the ocean outside.

Greg.

I kept staring at the ceiling as thoughts of Greg lingered. He'd have some smart-ass remark to say about tonight. He'd agree with me about Trevon. He would . . .

The one who loves the other more is the one who loses.

I huffed, shaking. Greg's face lingered in my mind like some sort of parasite. Once I started thinking about him, I couldn't stop. A sinking hole opened in my chest with overwhelming emotion I could not contain any longer. A mixture of anger, hate, sorrow, jealousy, rage all mixed into an unquantifiable mess that I couldn't properly put into words if I tried.

I'm not sure how long it was before I spoke. "You . . . *bastard,*" I said out loud, whispering to no one but the argument in my head. "You *piece of shit*. You have no soul. No goddamn soul. I did—I did everything I could to make you happy. *Everything,* and it wasn't enough for you." I swallowed, my nose quickly getting stuffed with mucus. The muscle beneath my right eye began twitching. "I *could've* cheated. I had a chance to and I wish I did. I *wish* I took it because then—because in some way, I could've hurt *you*. You'd have deserved it." I began to tear up, and I covered my mouth before speaking again. "But it wouldn't hurt *you,* would it? You don't care. I could be dead in a ditch right now and you wouldn't care." My eyes felt salty, my cheeks soaked. "I loved you with all . . . *all my fucking heart* . . . and you did what you did." I swallowed hard, feeling like there was a lump in my throat. "There's a hell for people like you." My face crumpled as I let out a sob. "There's a hell for people like y—" I stuffed my face into my pillow. "I wish you were dead, you f— I wish you were . . ." I breathed hard and shook, feeling like I was torn apart all over again.

You're not God's gift to men. You were easy to get over.

I wailed into my pillow. I wasn't alive anymore. I was the living dead. My brightest days were clouded in darkness, and no matter how warm it was, the world felt hostile and cold. I was trapped in a frozen hell.

After a bit of crying, I dug out my phone. I couldn't tell you why. Went to Instagram. Scrolled the app and went to the blocked people, down to *his* profile. My heart stopped as soon as I saw his face. His shaved head, his blue eyes, the prominent nose. I shook involuntarily upon seeing him, nausea growing as my finger hovered over the unblock button, my heart thumping harder and harder each millisecond I got closer to pressing that button.

No.

No, I couldn't do it.

I couldn't do it!

A panic came over me as I backed out of the app and curled into a ball, dry heaving. I almost felt like throwing up, but I knew my body by now after a few of these episodes. I knew nothing was coming out.

"Can't stop . . . won't stop. Can't. Won't . . ."

Couldn't tell you what the thought process was. I honestly don't know why I did any of that. I had no ownership of myself at that point. At times like that, I felt like I was barely even a person anymore.

When my heart rate finally lowered and that comfortable numbness that would always eventually come washed over me, I turned off the light then slipped into the deepest depths of unconsciousness.

Doors, opening more doors. Going farther and farther into the depths. Red doors, gray doors, black doors, white doors. Somehow diving deeper down,

down into what I knew was the endless abyss. I felt the pressure equalizing as I dove deeper and deeper down. The doors seemed endless until I opened a white one and found myself in a dark room lit by candles. I recognized the table in front of me. The dining room table he and I once shared. There was a still, lifeless figure sitting in the seat *he* would sit. Comfortable jazz played as I walked forward.

"Surprise!" a familiar but muffled voice said. "Happy birthday!"

I sat at the table and looked down. Some sort of vegan dish made of beans and quinoa, with a glass of red wine to the side. I twisted my face slightly in disdain.

"I know you're still hesitant 'bout the whole going-vegan thing, but I thought you had to *at least* try this dish. I made it from scratch," the muffled, garbled voice said to me, almost as if it was playing on a radio with bad reception. I looked up at the figure, but instead of seeing him, I saw myself. My face looked uncertain, but slightly fuller, slightly healthier than it normally did.

My mouth raised slightly into a grin. "I mean, trying the food is gonna convince me more than those slaughterhouse vids you've been shoving in my face," I said with a chuckle. I began to eat the food in front of me. After a moment of tasting, I nodded, faking it. "Mmm, it's good." I took a moment and sipped from the wineglass, licking my lips before smiling again. "Thank you for making this, babe. I really appreciate it."

"Of course. Anything for my baby girl."

That was when I finally saw him. There was no more jazz playing, and everything was covered in blue. It was not a person in front of me, only a bald mannequin wearing *his* clothes. My hair swished around me like vines as bubbles left my mouth. I sat at the dining table, merely watching as I felt waves rock me back and forth. There was no sound except the muffled rushing of water. The mannequin in front of me floated upward. I looked above as it rose to the surface.

A rattling sound started.

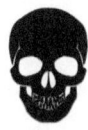

I woke with a jolt in my dark room. The rattling sound was still there. It sounded like . . . grinding. A horrible grinding, hollow sound like two rough and hard objects scraping together. Something like bones. I was barely able to move in my bed. The grinding, it was nerve-racking, and it was coming from a corner of the room. The corner with the plant. My eyes darted that way, nausea twisting in my stomach. Every hair on my body went up. I was . . . being watched. I could feel it. I don't know how I knew, but I knew. Someone was in the room with me. Some primal part of me knew I wasn't safe. I stared at the darkness, and it took a moment for my eyes to adjust. As they did, though, I could make out a silhouette.

It was a man. There was a man standing in the corner of my room, about six feet tall. On his head, a flat-brimmed hat, something like a hat from an old gangster film. I froze. He was staring at me. I couldn't see him very well, but the same feeling I had looking at that faceless corpse permeated. Like something I could never understand or comprehend was observing me. Something malicious. I couldn't look away, even though I couldn't see him clearly. Every muscle in my body froze in place. My heart pounded as he stood there, just glaring at me. There was someone in the room that hated me. Someone that wished me ill . . . and I couldn't do anything but stare into the darkness. I felt small, weak, helpless. It was staring back, the gaze burning through me. *It was staring back.* The walls felt like they were closing in as my gaze transfixed on the corner, working overtime to see the figure better. It loomed before me yet remained perfectly still.

I finally closed my eyes hard, but when I opened them, it was still there. I shook like I was in a frozen lake. The grinding stopped, and I swear I could see the silhouette softly and slowly begin to move toward me.

Finally freaked out enough, I quickly sat up and turned on the light next to me.

As light flooded the room, an embarrassing truth revealed itself: There was no figure. There was no man in the room. Just the Hawaiian plant in the corner. Nothing was weird, nothing was off, everything was just as I'd left it when I went to sleep. A cold sweat drenched me. What the hell was wrong with me? Was that sleep paralysis or something? I breathed heavily, trying to comprehend what was going on. Okay . . . I blacked out on the plane and I just had some sort of hallucination. Maybe I needed to see someone after all. Something was definitely wrong. I breathed out, rubbing my head and catching my breath.

A loud pounding at the door made me jump.

"Jesus!"

The pounding continued, loud and aggressive. I looked at the alarm clock near me; four in the morning. After a moment of gathering myself, I jumped off the bed and rushed toward the front door of my hotel room, shaking off the cobwebs. Thunderous, angry knocks. Who the hell was that knocking on my door at this hour?

I opened my door to be met with an unfriendly face. It was the old lady from next door. She looked almost like a monster, decrepit and craggy, staring at me with those menacing yellow eyes. Her hair was down and long, but still greasy and unwashed. There was a nauseous cat pee-like smell to her and she looked up at me like I was the person she hated most in the world.

I was not in the mood for this bitch. "Can I help you?"

She stood, yet said nothing.

I sighed. "Do you need something? It's four in the goddamn morning." She stood silent, still staring at me wide-eyed. I waited for a moment for a response. None came. "Really?" After another moment, I shook my head, beginning to turn away. "I'mma call hotel staff, they'll deal with yo—"

"Leave," the woman croaked.

I blinked and smiled nervously, stopping. "What?"

"You're not welcome here, *whore*. Leave, and never come back."

I scoffed. "You're a bundle of fun. Where they dig *you* up, hag? Looney bin?"

"You get out of this room, cunt. Out of this hotel! You leave and *never*—"

"Why? Give me one good reason. One *solid* reason wh—"

"*You brought it with you, you stupid cunt!*" she said, now more worked up. "It brought you to *me*! It knows!" The lady's face trembled. "*Get the fuck out of my hotel!*"

I squinted as she breathed heavily. "Know what, I'm not going anywhere. I'm gonna stay right here and finish my vacation. I might even screw some guy's brains out in my room. Screw him loud so you can hear it, and there's not a goddamn thing you can do abo—"

She got more in my face at this, surprisingly quick for a woman of her age. I backed away almost on instinct as her toothless mouth yelled, "*Get the fuck out of here!*"

I slammed the door in her face. The door shuddered again as she continued knocking hard on it. I could feel the violent vibrations, like the sheer force of her knocks was shouting a ghost of itself into my face. There was a click that took me a moment to identify before looking down. It sounded like she was trying the doorknob, but luckily the doorknobs at this hotel were the automatic kind, making keys vital to access the rooms.

That did it.

First thing in the morning, I was gonna report her. I was *not* going to deal with senile shenanigans. Not on vacation. The knocking persisted, seeming almost powerful enough to knock the door off its hinges.

"Fuck off!" I yelled.

Then, as if she obeyed, silence. My heart pounded. I listened for a moment as I heard her heavy steps walk away. I shook my head. What a morning. I huffed as I trudged to bed. "Psycho." I rubbed my head, exhausted beyond belief. I probably should've called hotel services or something right then to complain about the old woman, but I was way too tired. Every bit of my body felt heavy as I sat on the bed, enraged at the encounter I just had. I had just laid down when I heard a dragging sound coming from beyond my wall. A loud one, like the person next door was pulling furniture across a wooden floor. Was that the grinding I heard earlier, maybe? It sounded louder, but I supposed it was entirely possible. It didn't take much for me to figure out that it was from that old woman's room, 1718. What the hell was that old bitch doing?

To be safe from another hallucination, I kept my light on. After adjusting myself back under my covers, I laid my head on my pillow and closed my eyes to go to sleep.

Just then, the TV next door blared. It was muffled, but still loud enough for me to make out words. Some stock Middle Eastern music was playing before two separate voices began to speak, one clearly a narrator, the other some sort of expert.

"The year is 1923. Archaeology has been on the rise in Egypt since the discovery of Tutankhamen's tomb the previous year. The area is a hotbed for many a scholar, but one archaeologist, an ambitious, young aristocrat named Dr. Joseph H. Cartright, has no such interest in finding another pharaoh."

"Cartright was sort of the punk rocker of his field in his time. His belief was that there were grander riches to be found to the east of Egypt, more specifically across the Red Sea. He theorized maybe somewhere in Saudi Arabia or Yemen due to some legends around the area. Now, his stance at the time wasn't necessarily controversial among his contemporaries, but it was odd to them. You must keep in mind it would be another three years before the discovery of the Royal Tombs of Ur. That was the discovery that brought to light the forgotten civilization of Sumer —"

I put my pillow over my head. What the hell, you stupid hag?

I couldn't sleep. Instead, I listened as she switched from the ancient Egypt documentary to the morning news, to what sounded like a cartoon based on what I could make out from the voices coming though the wall. Finally, the TV went off and everything was silent again for about another hour. My eyes felt bloodshot and dry as I lay awake. I huffed as I sat up and threw on some clothes I could walk outside in. I was in a hellfire and brimstone mood. This was the Salem witch trials, and I was Abigail fucking Williams. This bitch was going to hang.

I stormed out of my hotel room, key in hand, but when I closed the door, I noticed a white square on my door. It was a piece of paper ripped out of some small hotel amenity notebook based on the little Tropical Springs watermark. The corner was torn and jagged, and upon further inspection, what held it to the door wasn't tape, but rather . . . children's Band-Aids? They were small and orange and had cartoon characters on them. Cartoons that didn't seem age appropriate for how old she was, being more recognizable and modern. If one had to guess, she had picked them up from one of those ABC Stores that you saw on every corner after accidentally cutting herself or something. They made for terrible adhesives; it was easy to pull the note off my door. In sloppy, almost childlike writing, barely legible and borderline scribbles, only a few words were on the note:

Last chanse: leave NOW!!!

I felt my face curl in either anger or disgust. A sort of fury filled my veins. I glared at her door.

"Thanks for the evidence, asshole."

With that, I began my journey to the lower floors.

CHAPTER 5

The dim daylight of early morning came in through the glass windows of the elevator as I rode it down. My eyelids felt heavy as I leaned against the corner, looking out the window. Everything outside was still a blueish color as I descended toward the ground floor. Tropical Springs really was a beautiful hotel. I almost appreciated it more in the blue light than the warm orange or darkness I had seen it in before. Somehow the blue towers with an even darker blue sea just beyond them felt more real and inviting than the other colors the light had painted them in. It felt more honest. Like *this* was the truth of the Tropical Springs resort. Nobody truly roaming around except for the occasional hotel staff one would see. Everything was naked and bare. A place meant to be filled to the brim with people right now just . . . empty. The way it was before opening, and the way it'll be the day the resort closed. Empty, but grand and cathedral-like. That feeling persisted as the doors of the elevator opened to reveal a comfortable-looking lobby that was almost completely empty. I traversed the warmly lit lobby and walked past a huge, lit fireplace, straight to the front desk, where a woman with a blue suit jacket stood. She had that fake customer service smile on her face as I approached.

"Aloha!"

I cleared my throat and briefly smiled. "Aloha! Hi, uh . . . I need to speak to someone about another guest."

"About another guest?"

"Yeah, I'm getting harassed by my neighbor."

The woman at the desk winced. "Oh, I'm sorry."

I sighed and shook my head. "Yeah, it's this old woman . . . Think she might have dementia or something, but she has made my first night here kind of a nightmare."

"What room did you say you were in?"

"Uh, I didn't, but it's seventeen sixteen. Yeah, it's the, uh, the old lady in seventeen eighteen."

"Got it, I'll look it up now."

I sighed. "Thank you, I appreciate it."

The woman typed away at her computer. Then she gave an odd look. It was almost a look of recognition. "Seventeen eighteen? The woman in *that* room has been causing you trouble?"

I nodded. "Oh yeah. She has been cussing me out, waking me up in the middle of the night by pounding on my door, yelling at me to leave, playing her TV absurdly loud, and, uh, crème of the crème . . ." I pulled the note I found out of my pocket. "She left this on the front of my door."

The woman took the note, then looked at it. Analyzed it before breathing out. "Um . . . That's concerning. I'm sorry about that. Do you, um, do you wish to be transferred to a different room?"

I blinked before smiling. "Wait, the solution here is moving *me* to another room? I'm sorry, but security or *somebody* needs to talk to *her*. I'm not the one knocking down *her* door at four a.m. and threatening *her*. If anyone should be *moved* it should be her."

"Well, there is an issue with that, unfortunately, ma'am."

"Oh yeah, there is?"

"We unfortunately cannot move her from her room. We can speak with her, but unfortunately if one of the two of you is going to move, it *will* have to be you."

My face tightened. "And why's that?"

"Unfortunately, I am not at liberty to discuss the private matters of our guests. Needless to say, we *can* provide you with another room of the same price range, even one on the same floor, if she is harassing you."

I breathed out hard, glaring. "So she does something and I'm the one that has to move? I want to talk to your supervisor. That's bullshit."

The woman took a moment, blinking, before nodding and dialing a number on a nearby phone. There was a moment of waiting before she spoke: "Uh, yes . . . We have a guest that has asked to speak with you at the front desk. Okay, thank you." The front desk girl awkwardly hung up and then smiled at me. "She'll be with us momentarily."

The wait was excruciatingly awkward. I wanted to tell the girl I knew she was just doing her job, but I was in much too foul a mood to do so. Soon, an older woman in a business suit and faded blonde hair walked up. She looked roughly in her fifties. Her facelift was a little obvious and didn't allow her probably the degree of expression she would've liked. Her name tag read *Joan Mitsky*. Yeah, she looked like a Joan. "Hi there, how may I assist you today?"

I explained the situation again and she nodded. Then she tapped the hotel desk girl on the shoulder reassuringly. What the hell? Like I'm the asshole? The manager nodded and thought for a moment. She pulled up a picture of the old woman I was reporting on her phone. "This is the, uh, the woman?"

There she was. Looking at the phone with a weathered face. She looked very stone-faced at the camera. There was certainly less menace than I'd seen in her face, but it was definitely her. Warts, craggy face, and all, that was the ugly woman I had seen just a few hours ago. She almost looked sad, like she had the life beaten out of her.

"Uh, yeah. That's—that's exactly her."

The manager looked again at the phone. "Yeah . . . Um, I suppose I can divulge *some* information to explain the issue a bit here. Ms. Jennings here, she's what you might call a *live-in resident*."

I shook my head. "Live in— Wha—what do you mean?"

"She has a, uh . . . permanent residency at this hotel. Room seventeen eighteen, she essentially lives there."

I tilted my head. What? *"Lives there?"*

Joan nodded. "You see uh, a—a guest, such as yourself, if they were so inclined to, can permanently rent out a room here in Tropical Springs. It's not the standard, and we don't have a lot of guests that do it, but Ms. Mariah Jennings is more or less the exception. She's been here since, oooh, 2002."

I blinked and raised my eyebrows. "She's been terrorizing people here since the 2000s? Since fuckin' *Shrek* came out?"

Joan chuckled. "Well no. Normally she's rather quiet and keeps to herself. In fact, this is the first we've heard of any sort of *negative* incident involving her. She, if anything, was a real pillar to our little community here till bout five years ago when she retired." Joan nodded uncomfortably. "Um, we can talk to her, though. Get her side of things. In the meanwhile, though, would you like a different room?"

"Woooow, that's fucked," Matty remarked from the bathroom in between spits while brushing his teeth. I lay on his bed, rubbing my head, the daylight of the morning more full now as it crept through his balcony glass door.

"Yeah, since she's more or less substantial income for the hotel and has been a darling of theirs for eons, *I'm* the one that will have to either change rooms or just deal with her. Didn't sound like they were gonna do more than maybe give her a slap on the wrist."

Matty peeked in from around the corner after spitting again. "What does she even do to have that much money? To just *buy* a hotel room in Waikiki?"

I shook my head, shrugging. "Think it was implied that she came from a wealthy family or something. She actually sounds like quite the recluse, from what I understand. Only ever comes out when getting groceries. So since she's seen as the quiet, sweet old lady, *I'm* the cunt probably causing issues in their eyes."

Matty thought for a moment. "I mean, you sure there wasn't something you might've done by accident to provoke her?"

"Matty, *I said hi to her.* And I literally only did that cus she was staring at me all weird."

He sighed. "Maybe you're right. Maybe she's gone senile. You should talk to Dana, see if Trevon would be willing to pay for the move to a different room."

I squinted. "You don't think they'd charge me to move rooms, do you?"

Matty shrugged. "Just in case, I'd talk to Dana or Trevon. I know you don't like him, but Trevon's not completely unreasonable. I'm sure he'll be alright with it."

I shifted into a more comfortable position on Matty's bed. "I'd sooner rather die of alcohol poisoning." I closed my eyes. "Why can't the old bitch just croak or something?"

"Hey . . . *Hey!* Look up for a second. Look at my fit," Matty said, getting closer to the bed. I lazily lifted my head. He was wearing a tight crop top and booty shorts.

"You look like the gayest man in Honolulu," I said flatly before dropping my head down to the bed.

Matty sighed. "It's like you're not even trying with compliments anymore." With that, he marched back into the bathroom. "You coming with us on our little tourist journey? We're doing Pearl Harbor memorial, Iolani Palace, and an art museum. Trevon's friend Kai, that guy that was hitting on you last night, he's a local. He's kinda giving everyone a tour. Think then everyone's gonna go to the pool and to a luau tonight."

I sighed, rubbing my head. "I would but . . . that old bitch didn't let me catch *any* Zs last night. Is it okay if I nap in your room for a bit? I don't wanna sleep with her next door."

I closed my eyes and heard Matty walk out from the bathroom. "Yeah, you look rougher than usual. You catch a nap, then maybe when we get back, you join us at the pool?"

"Sure. Sounds good."

Matty said something but I didn't hear it because I was already dozing off. I think he was gone well after I fell asleep.

When dreaming, I dreamed of *the* accident, the one I took a picture of. I was walking through the smoke, past the twisted corpses and chewed-up cars. It was just as slow of a walk as I remembered it being, complete with a high-pitched ringing in my ears. At times, the dream would switch to a door in a dark room with a flashing light behind it. I would see the accident, then switch back to the door, which looked like it was struggling to stay on its hinges as something banged into it from the other side. I realized the light on the other side wasn't flashing, the movement of the door only made it look like it was. Something was trying to break through. As I got closer to the corpse, the door broke open. Finally, where the faceless man should've been on the ground, I saw me lying there, pale and twisted. My face was still attached but I was in the same exact position the man was. I was wearing a white sundress with a small floral pattern on it, something I'd never be caught dead wearing. I almost looked elegant, like a dancer, with how my limbs were placed. As I got out my camera to take a picture, the dead me opened her eyes and looked up at me.

"Rachel? Rachel, wake up, you're missing out!" Matty said, waking me up from my slumber. I lifted my head off the pillow and felt a small bit of drool from my mouth. You know that sensation where you go to sleep and wake up feeling like only a minute had gone by? That was what I felt. My face felt numb as I lifted it, looking at Matty. "Huh?"

Matty laughed. "Oh my God, you look like a little chipmunk with how you were sleeping!"

I threw my head back onto the pillow. "Shut up." I could feel Matty zoom into the room and come over to where I lay on the bed. "Didn't you *just* leave?"

"Girlie, I've literally been gone like half the day. Look at the time!"

I raised my head slightly and looked at the clock. Two p.m. Holy fuck. My face felt numb as I rubbed my eyes. "Jesus . . . How was the tour?"

"My God, Rach. This place is fucking gorgeous. Fuck LA, I wanna live here."

I chuckled. "Not sure rent is any better." I began stretching.

"You gotta see this place in its glory, during the day. It's something else. Come on, get up and get in your swimsuit. Get your camera too. You're gonna want pictures."

I sighed. "Is there alcohol involved?"

"A big fat mai tai with your name on it if you get your ass up and get dressed. First one on me."

I sighed. "You drive a hard bargain." At the promise of drinks, I began to get up. Then a thought occurred to me. "Hey, do you mind walking me to my room?"

Matty chuckled. "Don't tell me the Wicked Witch of the West has you spooked." My face soured and I looked at him with a twisted expression. A look of comprehension washed over him. "She does, huh?"

I nodded. "Just . . . I don't know. Feel kinda unsafe and uneasy around her. Plus, if she acts like how she's been, I need a witness."

Matty nodded in agreement. "Okay. Say less, girlie."

The journey to my room felt agonizing as both Matty and I entered the hall. The hallway felt long and ever winding as we went from one part of the floor to the opposite end. The repetitive pattern in the carpet appeared to stretch for miles before me.

"Can't stop, won't stop," I whispered to myself, gripping my arms. Matty's presence only made me slightly less tense than I would've been. I don't know why, but these halls creeped me out. I felt weirdly naked in them. There was no reason, and when I was tired, they didn't seem to affect me much, but the endless hallway seemed to just stretch on and on before me and that made my hair stand up. Didn't help that the only people I had ever seen on this floor were Matty and that Ms. Jennings woman. It almost made the hall feel like some weird place that should not be. A long human-hamster tunnel with nothing but locked doors and artificial lighting. "Can't stop, won't stop."

When Matty and I arrived at my room, a small bit of relief filled me to see the door of seventeen eighteen closed. I looked at Matty, then looked at my door as I got out my key.

"That's where she is, huh?" Matty whispered.

"Yeah."

I stared hard at her door a moment before Matty opened his mouth again. ". . . Think she's in there right now?"

"Yup, probably carving up children for stew and everything."

"Hansel and Gretel reference, nice."

"I try."

With that, I opened my hotel room. When I did, my mouth dropped. Matty's mouth too. I stepped in, avoiding my panties, which were in front of the front door. Clothes . . . *my* clothes were everywhere. Matty and I walked in.

"Oooh girl, what the fuck?" Matty said after a moment.

I looked on in shock. It was like someone had thrown the contents of my suitcase and carry-ons everywhere. My laptop was open, face down on the floor. My camera was haphazardly stuffed between couch cushions with a few of my lenses on the ground. Various clothes littered the couches, the floor, and the TV.

The fridge was wide open and leaking, and the kitchen sink was running. The bedroom was even worse with one of the nightstand cabinets knocked over, the Hawaiian plant and its dirt poured out onto my bed. In my bathroom, both sinks and the shower were running. To top it all off, someone had crudely drawn some sort of face on the mirror with my ruby-colored lipstick. The head was an oval shape, the eyes were dots, the nose was a triangle, and the mouth was a sharp squiggly line, like some sort of zigzag. It was like a child's drawing. The creepiest part of it all was there were no words on the mirror, no other markings or threatening message, just the face. I quickly went through the hotel room and turned off all the faucets and the shower. It was after I closed the fridge door that I saw Matty looking at me strangely. I sighed and looked around.

"Matty . . . I think she did this . . ." I stared at the wreckage, at all my stuff, before turning to my best friend. "That old lady, *she* fucking did this."

Matty twisted his face. "That doesn't make sense, Rach. How would she even get a key to your room?"

I shook my head. I'm sure that old bitch had her ways. "We're getting pictures, and I'mma bring that note I showed you. I can't stay here if this is how it's gonna be."

The air outside was humid and I swore I was somehow drowning and melting in my skin as Matty and I walked through the crowd. Tropical Springs was big enough to get lost in. You could probably walk through half of it in a few hours, get tired, and take a nap before exploring the other half. It was more than a hotel. There was a fitness center, a spa, a row of shops and restaurants, multiple pools, and of course, access to the beach. If one wanted to spend their whole vacation in the hotel and never go anywhere, they could. That's the kind of place this was. It was the perfect vacation getaway. It was the Disneyland of hotels, and it didn't even have to rely on gambling. Vegas, eat your heart out.

The sun hurt my eyes, even though the pool we were going to, the one I had a view of from my room, was covered mostly in shade. I wore a black swimsuit with sandals and a black shawl. The low roar of the ocean was ever present as we walked past palm trees with bright multicolored flowers. As we approached the pool we found Dana and Trevon sunbathing in the part of the courtyard that still had sun shining in it, right next to the pool. The water looked so nice and inviting, but I had to address something with Dana before any of that.

Penelope, who was in a pink bikini nearby, was taking a pool selfie. She was the first to notice us. "There she is!" she enthusiastically said aloud.

I heard Matty groan, but I smiled pleasantly. "Back from the dead."

Dana and Trevon, almost in unison, looked my way and sat up. She wore a cream-colored bikini and he had black swim trunks. Trevon's face hardened while Dana's sweetened. "Hey, you. Hear you been having some neighbor troubles."

"You ain't kidding." I took a seat on Penelope's big pool-side chair next to her. "I've got evidence." I pulled out the note and showed everyone pictures of my room, recounting the events of the previous night. Matty went to go get drinks. Penelope took the note and scrunched her face. Dana's face slowly lost its sweetness, and Trevon's remained somewhat unchanged as he simply observed the note and photos. "So, yeah. Don't know what to do. She's the hotel's darling, so I feel like if I accuse her of doing that to my room, I'm going to get blamed for it."

"Yeah, if that's how they treated you earlier, I can see that," Dana said.

"How would she have gotten in, though, Rach?" Trevon then asked, somewhat callously.

My lips vaguely quirked upward into something resembling a smile. "I mean, it wouldn't surprise me if she had ways. Stole it off some hotel staff, maybe? I don't know. Point is, they said I have two choices, either deal with it or change rooms, which is something I actually wanted to ask you two about since I don't know if that would be extra money for you guys."

"Lemme see that." Trevon took the note from Penelope. His face hyper focused as he read it, apparently over and over again. "Ay, Dana, I'mma talk to Rach for a second, 'kay?" Dana nodded, exchanging some kind of look with Penelope. With that, the two of us walked a little bit away from the girls. Trevon looked down at the note all the while, studying it, trying to make sense of it. I shifted weight uncomfortably as he looked at the note. "This for real?"

"No, I made it up to make *drama* for you. Yes, it's real," I said uncomfortably.

Trevon looked at the note before looking at me. "And you . . . didn't provoke her in any way to get this from her?"

"The most I said was hi to her before she went off on me. All this stuff she's doing is completely unprovoked. Literally the only thing I could've done that might've bugged her was cry in my room last night."

Trevon's face turned in confusion. "What were you crying about?"

"I cry every night. That's not the point," I said dismissively. "The point is, I'm not making this up. I didn't cause this. I literally feel harassed and possibly in danger, and the only thing the fucking hotel is gonna do about it is *talk to her*. I'm worried about going back to my room cus I don't know what's going to be waiting for me. That's how bad it is."

Trevon looked back down at the note. If he looked any harder at it, he would've found the lost secrets of Atlantis. Then he nodded. "Okay. Aight . . . I'll see 'bout gettin' you a new room."

I blinked slightly in disbelief. "Th-thank you."

"Yeah, just . . . try not to, uh . . ." He handed me back the note, avoiding eye contact. "That better be the extent of drama from you this trip, I guess. 'Kay?"

I glared at him as he walked away. Douche. I followed him, and though Matty gave me the drink I was promised almost immediately, it took a bit before I could finally relax. It wasn't until Penelope offered to help me put on sunscreen that I started to shake off the unease from my ransacked room. When she offered, I blushed at first, getting a good look at her. In her bikini, I could see why she was so successful in her chosen line of work. She had more meat on her bones than I, with curves and the stereotypically attractive feminine qualities most men this day and age looked for. Me, I was a skeleton, some rake-like creature with unhealthily pale skin stretched over my frame. Where she had breasts, I had mosquito bites; where she had thighs, I had sticks; and where she had a well-toned abdomen, you could play the xylophone with my ribs. Even my ass, which I had considered my redeeming feature, was nowhere as nice looking as hers.

"Go ahead, lie on your stomach," Penelope said, rubbing the lotion on her hands. I obeyed and felt her smooth fingers glide over my back. "That's crazy about your neighbor. I'd be so freaked if I were you."

"I'd rather not talk about it, if that's okay."

"I'm just saying, you seem to be handling it better than I would. I would cry."

Dana laughed. "Rachel's tough as nails. Won't catch her crying 'bout that sort of thing."

I sighed. "I mean, don't get me wrong, being around her creeps me the fuck out, but . . . I've met worse people than her."

Both women went silent at this, Penelope's hands still rubbing my back. "Hey, Rach, what's this scar on your ba—"

Dana immediately cleared her throat. Without looking at the two, I could feel Dana giving her a look. I chose to not acknowledge the question. There was a moment of silence as Penelope finished up, and when she was done I sat up and thanked her, looking toward the pool. Matty was in the water, chatting up some guy. What happened to the no-hall-passes necessary, Matty? More than likely just talking, but a part of me did find how he couldn't stop talking to guys funny regardless. Matty will always be Matty. I looked around, not seeing Trevon. "Where's your guy, Dana?"

Dana sighed. "You see the TV at the bar? UFC fight. He, Kai, Scott, and John probably have bets going. He's over there watching."

Sure enough, I looked over and saw Trevon at the bar, watching the TV eagerly. Must be nice knowing where your man was at all times. I sipped my mai tai and giggled. "Boxing, football, hockey, soccer, is there a sport Tre doesn't watch?"

"Golf. Easily. He might play it every now and then, but that and baseball are his least favorites to watch."

Penelope did a cute pixie sort of chuckle. "I'm all about basketball myself. Miami Heat fan all the way."

Dana sighed. "I'd *say* I'm a football fan, but that's only cus of the Super Bowl. And I only like *that* cus of the commercials. Think one time I called the Baltimore Ravens the Crows, and for a moment it looked like Tre was gonna break up with me right there." She laughed.

Penelope leaned a bit between sips of her cocktail. She was staring at me with those . . . *very* vibrant eyes. They felt piercing and admittedly made me a little uneasy. Her face was calm and happy, though. She looked at peace with the world in that smile of hers. "What about you, Rach? Sports girl?"

I blinked and shook my head. "Uh . . . I've been to some Dodgers games, but not my cup of tea. Dragged there against my will." I chuckled.

There was another silence as the three of us lounged in the sun for a bit. Penelope sipped her cocktail audibly. "Oh, that Kai guy was asking 'bout you, by the way, Rach."

In the distance, something caught my eye. It was hard to see among the crowd, but once I spotted her, we were interlocked in a staring contest. Near the entrance of the hotel, I could see the familiar-looking troll woman glaring at me, in those same red shirt and brown shorts. Admittedly it took me a moment to recognize her because she had a big sun hat on, but it was her. On her face wasn't a look of hate this time, but one of panic. She looked at me like I had a gun and was getting ready to shoot her. She breathed heavily and her jaw jittered uncontrollably. If I didn't know any better, I'd have guessed the old girl was having a heart attack.

"Rach?"

I briefly turned toward Penelope, who was expecting some sort of reaction to what she had said. I turned again and Ms. Jennings wasn't there anymore. A chill ran down my spine, but I did my best to hide it. "Uh . . . Yeah." I breathed out and swallowed. "Think I'm gonna go ahead and take a dip in the pool." I got up and walked toward the pool in front of us, looking in the direction I'd seen Ms. Jennings. I searched relentlessly, but the woman had disappeared like a ninja. I searched and searched, but couldn't find anything.

"Rach! Come here!" Matty said, flagging me down.

Before I knew it, I was in the pool talking to some stranger that Matty introduced me to. The conversation was small and forgettable, and in no time at all Matty took control of the conversation again, flirting with the man. I rolled my eyes and let him do whatever the hell he wanted as I leaned backward into the cool pool, letting myself float on my back.

The water submerged my ears and I closed my eyes. After a minute or so, I finally started to feel like I was on vacation. The muted sounds of water rushing by sounded pleasant and I felt as close as I could to peace at that moment. The ambient noise brought my mind to a comfortable void. No pain, no heartache, no anxiety. I breathed out, feeling carried by the water. It rocked me back and forth and I felt my hair swish this way and that. I opened my eyes and immediately got a look at the hotel. Up above, there was some black-haired lady with a bruised face staring at me from her balcony, stories and stories up. She was younger and thinner. I couldn't see her all that well, but she was staring intently. I sleepily smiled at her before closing my eyes yet again.

I don't remember who it was that dragged me out of Shangri-La (probably Matty) but soon I was out of the momentary peace and participating in conversation with everyone. Trevon and his boys eventually showed up, and it was time to get going. The group packed up and began migrating out. We were just passing a rock fountain when Penelope tugged at my arm. "Oooh! Oooh! Rach! Rach! Get a picture of Dana and I next to this fountain!"

I blinked, uncertain. *Uh . . . what about me? I'd like to be in this photo?* was what I would've liked to say in that moment, but Penelope was already dragging Dana away from Trevon. I looked over at Matty, who looked offended at the audacity. I blinked and began to dig out my phone. I looked back over and saw Trevon telling his friends that he'd meet up with them a bit later as Dana held on to him.

Penelope was in fast motion, like someone had pushed x2 speed on a YouTube vid. "Alright *fine*, hubby can be in the picture too! Rach, use the good camera you brought! Think this is a worthy moment."

"You paying her?" Matty said, biting back a bit.

"Uh, Penelope, I don't think that camera is necessary . . ." Dana interjected.

"Hey, why bring a fancy camera unless you're gonna put it to good use? Gotta have some high-def pictures of all of us."

Even Trevon seemed a little hesitant at the ask. As a fellow photographer, to some extent, I felt like he was cringing. He looked at me almost apologetically as the three of them stood in front of the fountain. Matty was telling me with his eyes to not even dare. I breathed out and nodded. "She's got a point, I brought a fancy camera with me. Might as well use it," I said with a smile. Matty scoffed and slowly walked away. I pulled out my camera and looked at the three, who were waiting expectantly, posing with fake smiles as soon as I freed my camera from my bag.

"Alright, ready? Three . . . two . . . one."

I took only a few pictures before they broke formation. Penelope started toward me at lightspeed as Dana and Trevon walked off. "Well? How'd they turn out?"

"Oh, they're good. I'll send you the edits later, 'kay?" I lied.

Penelope smiled. "Come on, don't tease. Let me see 'em."

I smiled wryly, more than a little uncomfortable with how pushy she was being, but it took one look into those vibrant eyes to slowly turn me to putty. This wasn't how I typically did things, but if she *really* wanted to see . . .

"Sure . . ." I smiled at her and went to the photo viewer on my camera. I was trying to look at the photos before showing her when . . .

What?

Staring back at me were not the photos I just took. A lump formed in my throat as I looked at the pictures, or should I say, the same picture multiple times throughout the entire gallery. I clicked on it to enlarge it. Sure enough, it was the picture I thought it was. All color went out of my face as I stared at the familiar photo.

A crimson skull stared back at me as the man with the sanded-off face took up the entire frame. It was the photo I took at the crash. The vacant black eyes stared into my soul as I stared back, bewildered. *What the fuck?*

"Well, lemme see!" Penelope insisted. I could only look up, slack-jawed and wide-eyed. What was I going to say?

I didn't have a chance to say anything. I heard someone rushing up behind me. Before I could turn around, it felt like a rock came down on my head, knocking me dizzy for a moment.

"*Fucking cunt!*" a familiar voice screamed. Multiple hard knocks banged into my skull as someone grabbed my hair by the scalp and began swinging me around. My camera immediately dropped to the ground and Penelope screamed a high-pitched cry. Meanwhile the familiar voice hurled insults. "*Whore! Slut! I told you, motherfucker! I told you!*"

With a freakish amount of strength, I was thrown onto the floor and felt a heavy weight lunge into me. I was face-to-face with Ms. Jennings, who was foaming at the mouth. She wildly swung her fist into my face like some sort of prehistoric beast, primal with rage. I screamed as she pummeled me with bony, wrinkled fists. Parts of my face went numb while other parts felt a white-hot, wet agony.

"*Fucking cunt! I told you, motherfucker!*" At some point, talon-like dirty fingernails clawed at my face. I cried out as they sharply dug into my cheek and forehead, scratching me deep enough to draw blood. It was almost like she was trying to tear my skin off.

"*Security!*" Penelope screamed.

Ms. Jennings stopped beating me for a moment and grabbed me by the chin, forcing me to look at her. The familiar iron taste of blood was in my mouth, seeping into my throat and going down my esophagus. I coughed it out, spraying it a little onto her face. The woman was oddly serene for a moment. I trembled from both searing pain and fear as her hazy, bloodshot eyes stared into mine.

"You don't even know, do you, child?" She breathed hard as I whimpered, afraid. The craggly skin of her wart-covered face trembled, yet her facial expression remained the same. "It's okay . . ." Her grip tightened on my face, nails digging into my skin again as she began to pull something out from her back pocket. She nodded, keeping focus on a part of my face that wasn't my eyes. "It's okay, I'll take it off for you."

It was then that I saw the object in her hands: a long pair of scissors that she held like a knife. I began to squirm and struggle. I couldn't move an inch, though. She was amazingly strong for someone of her age. "N-No! *No! Please no!*" I screamed desperately.

"Shhh, it's okay. Hold still." Ms. Jennings maintained eye contact. It sounded like security or someone was yelling at us, but all I could hear was Ms. Jennings's voice, and watch as she lifted the scissors like she was going to stab them straight down into my face. I screamed until my throat was sore as I struggled against her. She merely stared, talking to me almost sweetly. "I'll take it off for you. Don't worry, I'll take it off for you."

Right as Ms. Jennings was about to stab, security pulled her off. An agonized scream tore from her mouth as she was pulled away, the scissors dropping from her grip.

Ms. Jennings hysterically cried out, almost like she was in physical pain. *"No! Please God, No! No!"*

I breathed hard, shaking, my heart beating through my chest and tears coming from my eyes. Penelope was down next to me in a second.

"Are you okay? Rach? Rach?" asked Penelope in the most normal-sounding voice I'd heard from her.

I shuddered, my face in pain and dripping. My throat hurt from screaming. "Ye-yeah—" I croaked out. "I'm—I'm—" I couldn't voice words as I watched Ms. Jennings get dragged away.

"D-don't look at the red!" Ms. Jennings screamed at the top of her lungs. *"Dear God, don't look at the red! The red!"* she wailed.

I remained on the floor as someone from the hotel began a medical check on me. Throughout every question the first aid attendant asked, all I could really focus on was where they had hauled off Ms. Jennings. More specifically, I was focused on the pair of scissors she dropped before a security person took them away. They had a black handle and looked a little rusted. I breathed out raggedly as I stared. I didn't know what her last words meant, and more than likely they were the delusional ravings of a lunatic, but something about them sent a chill down my spine.

Don't look at the red.

CHAPTER 6

"Once again, if there's anything we at Tropical Springs can do to make your stay more enjoyable . . ." Joan the Hotel Manager said through her heavily Botoxed face. She gabbered on and on and on. I merely glared at her, parts of my face swollen, bruised, and purple. I couldn't muster up any words. This morning I was the cunt that was complaining about a darling old lady; now I was the goddess they prayed didn't sue. Funny how the tables turn. I luckily didn't need any stitches, but once the adrenaline wore off, the agony of the bruises and scratches on my face truly made even talking painful. My lip felt two sizes too big and my nose was stuffed with tissues. My voice was raspy from screaming. I merely glared. My friends were at a luau and I was dealing with this asshole in some hotel backroom that looked two shades warmer than a police investigation room, garage lighting and all.

"You can start by giving me a cigarette."

The hotel manager looked caught off guard by this. "I'll . . . see what we can do. Get a, uh, a complimentary pack of cigarettes and put it in your room. Any brand preference?"

"Marlboro Reds."

The hotel manager got out a notepad and awkwardly wrote down what I just said as I glared, accentuating something with a hard dot. "And done . . ."

Just like that, someone knocked at the door before opening. It was a cop. He was an islander, roughly in his forties, and had a wrinkled face. Officer Aukai, his badge read.

"How you doing, ma'am?"

I nodded bitterly. "We almost done here?"

He grinned sympathetically. "Almost."

I sighed roughly, breathing hard. "Has she said anything?"

He paused and shook his head. "She's unresponsive. I think it's safe to say . . . Ms. Mariah Jennings doesn't seem to be in touch with reality anymore. Her attacking you, if I were a betting man, seems to likely be the result of some sort of delusion. Regardless, you'll be happy to know she's spending tonight in a jail cell. A little time to cool off before being sent to a facility. She was still rather violent last I saw her."

I shuddered, clutching myself. "I gave my side of the story already. Can I go now?"

Officer Aukai nodded. "In a moment. Just wanted to let you know, though, after something like this, it's normal to get jumpy. Happens to the best of us. Now, if you feel you need protect—"

"Not necessary. I'm fine." I looked up at the officer, who looked caught off guard, clearly not expecting to be cut off. I swallowed, trying to ease my aching throat. "It's not my first rodeo being assaulted, Officer. Thank you, though," I said, stone-faced.

Officer Aukai stood in thought for a moment before nodding and handing me a little card. "This is your incident card. If you want updates about the case, you can follow the incident number on there and the instructions." I looked down at the dark blue card as the officer began to walk out. "Have a good night, ma'am."

Shortly thereafter I was brought into a blank hallway where Penelope was waiting. Immediately, she hugged me. "You okay?"

"Yeah," I half-heartedly responded. As we pulled away, she brushed my hair with her nails. "The others already en route to the luau?" I asked.

Penelope folded her lip and nodded. "Yeah."

"Cool. How fast can we get an Uber? It's like a forty-five-minute drive, right?"

Penelope's brow furrowed. "After everything, you *still* wanna go? Don't you wanna lie down or something?"

And be alone with my thoughts? Be lying awake, scared to go to sleep cus that troll lived in the room next to mine? Fuck that. I sighed. "Hell no. I'm not gonna let *this* spoil my evening. Luau, maybe some alcohol, maybe I can turn this day around for me."

Penelope smiled sympathetically. "Okay. If you're feeling up to it, I guess." She reached into her bag. "I, uh, picked up your camera. Surprisingly, best I can tell, it's mostly in one piece."

She held it up and offered it. I looked at the black digital camera warily. I didn't want to touch it. Penelope was right, though. Other than a dented corner, it looked otherwise fine. I'd have to investigate it more later, but that was the furthest thing from what I wanted to do right now. Hesitantly, I wrapped my fingers around it, brushing Penelope's for a brief moment before taking it into my hands. It felt heavy. I could've just been sensitive, but it felt more like I was being handed a gun than a camera. I felt uncomfortable carrying it and stared at it for a moment, then stuffed it into my bag.

"Thank you."

Penelope walked me back to my room to change. When I passed by 1718, I only gave it the briefest of looks before entering my room. Matty and I had picked up my clothes and things quickly before we left for the pool earlier, so housekeeping could do its thing, and immediately upon seeing my room, it was clear they had passed through. The room was back to being the ideal luxury hotel room. Hallelujah. I changed into something more comfortable than a bathing suit while Penelope called an Uber. With very little time or talking we were out of my room and on our way to the big event tonight. Oh, and the best part? They got me my cigarettes.

I smoked and felt euphoria ever so briefly. Penelope didn't judge as we waited outside for the Uber; then again, how could she? She was vaping. Once the Uber arrived, our journey to the luau began. Penelope and I really didn't talk much on the trip. I think she could tell I wasn't in the mood to say much of anything. As the Uber drove I stuck my head out the back window, looking at all the jungle greenery Honolulu had to offer as the sun was setting. The sky was a pinkish orange and I was completely enamored with the beauty as we drove past palm trees and vibrant flowers. It vaguely reminded me of when I had first moved to LA some years back, before the place became tainted for me. Admittedly, though, whatever beauty Los Angeles may have had was nothing in comparison to Honolulu. This place was paradise, I just wish I was happy enough to enjoy it.

By the time we arrived at the luau, the sky was turning a darker purple. The structures at the front looked like some sort of tiki hut and there were chairs and tables all around surrounded by trees and a view of the ocean. Pounding drum music played in the background as torches that were stuck in the ground roared and flickered. Penelope and I were given leis, and when Dana found us her face dropped. *"Oh my God!"*

"Hey, Dana." I smiled, but it hurt. She placed her hands on my shoulders and studied my face.

"Are you okay to hug? Will it hurt you?"

"No, it's fine. You can hug. Face took the brunt of it."

Dana pulled me into a hug. "Dear God . . ." I hugged Dana back as tight as I could. "It's so fucking scary what happened . . ."

"Uh, yeah, I don't wanna talk about it. Let's just enjoy this luau thingy."

Dana pulled away, keeping her hands on my shoulders. "If you need *anything* at all . . ."

"I know. I'm okay."

Dana nodded solemnly, then brought us back to the table. Everyone's faces dropped as they looked at me. Trevon and Matty in particular looked like someone had walked over their graves. Interestingly enough, even though Kai's expression was of concern, he looked more like he was trying to avoid staring. I must've looked pretty bad. Worse than even I thought. It was funny, though. I felt like I've had worse before.

When the show started and we sat down, when Matty stopped checking in on me and got me alcohol, when food had begun to be devoured, I finally felt somewhat at ease. The hula dancers and fire dancers performed to the sounds of percussive music, and it was a site to behold. A little bit of Hawaiian culture felt good to the soul as I sat and enjoyed the show. I must've been more tired than I thought, though, because as the dancers danced I felt a haze come over me. It almost didn't feel real as I watched them twirl in brightly colored garb and spin fire. With the drumming it was hypnotic, and I got lost in the performance while watching.

Flashes of Ms. Jennings's angry, seething face. Her leaning over me, scissors ready to come down. Images of the faceless man at the car accident, the red face sloppily drawn on my hotel mirror. I breathed hard as all of those intercut with the hula dancers. I rubbed my face, trying to get the thoughts out of my head. Bad mistake. It still stung. I must've made a small sound as I moved my hand away because Penelope leaned in and whispered, "Hey, you feeling okay?"

Thoughts of the old woman holding my face in a vise grip rushed through my head.

"Rach?"

I stood. "I'm good, I—I—I n-need a bathroom." I walked quickly through the luau in search of the restroom.

"Rach?" Dana called out. I didn't respond. I didn't even turn around.

"Don't look at the red!"

"Don't look at the red!"

I looked over at the fire dancers twirling and dancing. I felt dizzy, still getting flashes of Ms. Jennings. I finally found the restroom and burst in, kicking the door like it owed me money. I rushed to a bathroom stall, then locked myself in. Immediately, I let out a scream and leaned against the stall wall. My body shook involuntarily and I cried my eyes out for a moment. My breaths came in ragged gasps as I received a text from Dana.

U ok???

I slowed down my breathing and handled my phone, clumsily texting back a lie about how the pork didn't agree with me before putting my phone back. It took me a moment, but I quickly sobered myself up and walked out of the stall. No one else was in the room, thank God. I stumbled toward the mirror and looked back at my beaten, swollen face. I hadn't looked in the mirror back at the hotel room, but now that I did, maybe the others had been right to be concerned. There were shades of purple and cuts all over. You'd think I used my face as a landing pad after falling down a flight of stairs. No wonder it fucking hurt. Still, wasn't as bad as—

I turned on the tap and splashed some water on my face. As the water dripped down a bit, I breathed like I was running a marathon. Then I looked at myself angrily in the mirror. I gripped the sink with a death grip, staring hard at myself, letting the water in the tap run.

I made intense eye contact with my reflection, like I wanted to beat the shit out of myself. "Toughen up. Toughen the fuck up," I said under my breath. I didn't look away. "He did worse. He did worse."

A female giggle echoed in the bathroom, making me jump. Just as soon as it came, everything was silent again. I immediately looked behind me, toward the stalls. No one. Absolutely no one. The hair on my arms stood on its end as I looked around for the source. I even looked back at the mirror and didn't see anyone behind me. After a moment of silence I shook my head. Maybe somehow it was an echo from someone outside; that or I'm fucking crazy. More than likely the latter. I sighed.

"Get help, Rach," I said to myself. When I got back to the mirror, there was no question in my mind that at this point, I needed help. *Professional* help.

I didn't know how much longer I could take the war in my head. The problem was I didn't know how to take down my walls and let people help, though. I was too afraid. Scared whatever was wrong with me would be the end of me. I didn't wanna—

I closed my eyes and breathed in and out. Enough bleeding to the imaginary audience, Rach. Time to get back to the story.

After my mini breakdown, I tried strolling out of the restroom like nothing was wrong, only to see Trevon waiting out front for me. There was something that almost looked like sympathy in his eyes as his brow furrowed, looking me up and down.

"Ay, you alright?" he asked, folding his lip.

I clenched my jaw as I walked toward him. "Pork didn't agree with me," I said simply while beginning to walk past him. "I'm fine."

Trevon began walking beside me. "Ay, I—I wanna talk to you, real quick."

I stopped in my tracks. "Yeah?"

"Away from the others."

I looked around and shrugged. "What? What is it?"

Trevon folded his lip for a moment, looking down and sighing. "Ay, I just . . . I wanted to apologize, I guess. Feel like maybe I been unnecessarily harsh toward ya. An-and what happened today with the crazy old lady? That was messed up. You got my sympathies."

I nodded, looking him up and down. I scoffed. "Your sympathies? Buddy, I have never needed *your* sympathies."

Trevon sighed. "I just can't win with you, can I?"

"You basically made it out like I'm some big drama queen who might ruin your perfect li'l vacation, right before this trip even started. I might be a little salty."

"I *just* apologized for that. I don't know what else I can do." Trevon twisted his face and shook his head. "Look, it's *always* been like this between us. You had a problem with me and Dana from day one, man. And I don't think you have even *tried* to get to know me."

"Trust-fund bad-boy photographer, former junkie. What's there to know?"

"And you're an alcoholic abuse victim who is taking her shit out on me," Trevon said flatly. I curled my face at this. I wanted to claw his fucking eyes out for that. "See, I can play that game too."

I glared at him. "What do you want from me?"

Trevon shrugged. "To *get along, fuck*. Look, man . . ." He closed his eyes hard. "You're very important to Dana. Like it or not, we are gonna be in each other's lives. I love her. I *know* you do too. We gotta get along for her. This ain't about us."

I swallowed. He made solid points. Points I didn't wanna acknowledge. I kept quiet, thinking over what he was saying.

He continued, "Look . . . Today you've had a hard day. I don't wanna fight. Can't imagine what you gotta be going through, getting assaulted like that." He offered out his hand. "Truce?"

I merely looked at his hand, then looked back at him.

He sighed out, seeing I wasn't going to take his hand. "Well, can't say I didn't try." He put his hand back on his waist and nodded. "Look, uh, if you ever change your mind . . ."

"Please just leave me alone, Tre."

And he did. Silently nodding, he walked away. I didn't want to digest any of what he said. Didn't want to acknowledge anything he might've had to say as accurate or correct. The possibility that *I* might be the asshole was just something I didn't have the stomach or the patience for at this point.

When we all got back to the hotel from the luau, I crashed pretty hard on my bed, knocking out as soon as my head hit the pillow.

I had a weird dream that night. It wasn't of Greg, for once. No, in the dream it was my hotel room in the dark. A figure fell out of the ti plant in the corner, toward me. It looked like Ms. Jennings with her face torn off, like the corpse at the accident. Instead of completely blank sockets, though, she still had one of her eyes. An eye that looked blankly at me as her body tumbled forward.

A crash that sounded like glass breaking woke me with a jolt in the dark. I breathed out hard, feeling like someone had slapped me. Immediately, my face felt pain and I slipped into agony. I had been sleeping on it, not my best decision. My lip and cheek felt swollen as I stumbled quickly into my bathroom. As I turned on the light, I looked at my face and saw that parts of it were more purple than earlier, and indeed were puffed up. I found a bottle of Tylenol I'd brought and tried to open it, but my fingers kept slipping.

"Fuckin' thing," I muttered before managing to yank it open. I pried out two and put them in my hand before marching out of the bathroom into the kitchen for water. As I approached the kitchen, however, I noticed my fridge was slightly open and heard a hiss that sounded like my faucet was on. I closed my eyes hard before reopening them and turned on the light switch. After a moment of letting my eyes adjust, I looked down and saw that one of the wine bottles, a light brown expensive-looking one, had fallen from the fridge and its contents had leaked everywhere. I folded my lip in disappointment and put my Tylenol on the counter, deciding I might wanna pick up the glass pieces before walking barefoot to get a glass of water. I knelt down, smelling the white wine as I leaned over the spill.

How the hell did this thing slip out? And what was with the fucking faucet running? Was it some plumbing issue? Were there gremlins in this room? Was I being haunted by a ghost? Yeah, that had to be it, a ghost. One of those ones from Disneyland's Haunted Mansion if they thought this was gonna spook me. Goofy-ass ghost wasting the water bill. I've had late periods scarier than this shit. "Is this room actually stretching?" I said, trying to imitate the theme park ride while picking up pieces. I picked up a big piece of the bottle and read the brand. Some French words I could never hope to pronounce. Shit, the more I looked at the bottle, the more pricey it seemed.

"Hey, Casper, this is going on *your* tab, you dick."

When I finished gathering the pieces of the bottle and threw them away, I put on some shoes before walking into the kitchen, to be safe. I turned the faucet off, wiped up the white wine, and threw the paper towels in the trash. I finally took my Tylenol with a glass of water I poured from the faucet before leaning against the counter and looking at my room. Blueish light had begun seeping in through the large covered window as I breathed out. I looked at the nearby digital clock on the oven. Five a.m. I smirked a little. Went to bed at like nine or ten, woke up at five. Actually got some sleep last night. Progress!

I put my glass into the sink before noticing my digital camera on the kitchen counter. Seeing the camera made me freeze for a moment. Last time I looked at that camera . . . I breathed out heavily as I stared at it, then I swallowed hard, making my way to it slowly. Carefully, I lifted it, handling it like a bomb. Last time I looked at this thing . . . I still don't know how to even explain it to myself. I breathed out hard before turning it on and opening the photo viewer. About five or six photos. All of which were Penelope, Tre, and Dana posing together. Just three people on vacation in Honolulu.

I smirked. Okay, I was just seeing things. Maybe the more sleep I got, the less weird shit would happen. I carefully put my camera down and got out a cigarette, making my way toward the balcony outside my room. As I stepped outside, the sun began to peek out over the ocean. I listened to the waves rock back and forth as I peacefully lit my cigarette and looked out at the freshly orange-looking Honolulu, the world only just beginning to wake up. Maybe I was going to have a nice vacation after all.

"So Trevon's folks come into town tomorrow, and cus of that . . . I wanna move the bachelorette party to tonight, if that's cool," Dana told us as we sat on the little patio balcony of her penthouse suite. My face stung like hell when I moved it, but still it soured at Dana's news. Matty and I looked at each other in puzzlement, both being caught off guard by this. Penelope merely tilted her head, lifting her mimosa to her mouth. Dana continued. "You know, figure we spend the day together, party as much as possible, then when his parents come, we have it all out of our systems."

"Hold on, hold on, hold on," Matty spoke up. "Weren't we supposed to get you for today *and* tomorrow?"

"Well, yeah . . . But—"

Penelope squinted. "Girlie, what's up? Not like you to change plans last minute."

Dana paused contemplatively. She had to have known this decision wouldn't be popular with us. "Well, I know, but . . . Look . . . his parents are already kinda weird with me. I don't wanna rock the boat with them. They're helping fund this whole thing, and I just wanna make a good impression."

I twisted my mouth. "What's rocking the boat? You're a grown-ass adult. You can party if you want. Some might even say it's expected at your fuckin' *bachelorette*."

"Yeah, but . . ."

"But what? How does *you* partying with your friends affect *them*?"

Dana sighed before sipping her mimosa. ". . . It's gotta do with Trevon's past, 'kay?"

"Oh, *come on*!" Matty groaned.

"What? They think you're a bad influence? Gonna make him take up methadone again or something cus you're partying?" I blurted out.

"No, it's just . . ." Dana wiggled her shoulders like a bug had slipped down the back of her dress. "I just wanna be on my best behavior, alright? They make me *so* fucking nervous and they're *such* control freaks . . . I—I don't know, their future daughter-in-law getting drunk when their son is a former addict just doesn't read well. 'Kay, guys?"

"I guess I get the *they're worried he might fall off the wagon* argument, but . . . why's it sound like we *don't* get a day with you tomorrow?" Matty asked.

Dana stared at her mimosa. "Cus when they get here, I don't know how much of my time they will take up." Matty groaned. Dana huffed. "*They're like that*, 'kay?" She sipped more of her mimosa down. "I'm not saying I won't get to hang out with you. I just don't know what crap they'll pull tomorrow."

Penelope nodded her head. "You sound like you're intimidated by them."

Dana wryly chuckled. "Oh girl, you've no idea . . . The thought of them looking at me from the aisle gives me existential dread. I'd rather stick nails in my eyes."

Matty, Penelope, and I shifted glances between each other. This felt kinda shitty. It was understandable, but definitely shitty. We thought we were going to get Dana to ourselves for at least forty-eight hours, but it felt like she was going back on her promises just to appease her in-laws. That's the thing that sucks when your friends are in committed relationships: The deeper in they go, the more you feel like you're losing them. Admittedly, I've wondered if I'd see Dana much after this marriage. It felt like she was being washed away from my life by a riptide. It's something that has made me dread this wedding. The worst part is, I got it. Like, I understood *everything* going on and try as I might, I could not hold it against her. When Greg was my life, it felt like my friends were fading away like specters in the night. I had to fight to hold on as the winds of change pushed us in different directions. Unfortunately, at this moment, it didn't feel like Dana was particularly *trying* to hold on to any of us. And understanding where someone is coming from is not excusing the behavior.

Dana breathed in through her nose, not looking any of us in the eye. "So yeah, bachelorette tonight?" Matty huffed, clearly annoyed. Penelope licked her lips somewhat awkwardly, seeming to weigh out the options. Dana looked between us, searching for a life raft among the doubt. She was quickly finding her decision an unpopular one. Finally, she looked at me. "What say you, Rach? You're the maid of honor."

I breathed out and nodded. She needed to feel like a friend was on her side. I could see it. Well, if I only had so much time left with her . . . I wasn't going to waste it wishing for more.

"Parents come in tomorrow, we got you for twenty-four hours . . ." I looked at her and smiled, even though my face ached. "Let's get you good and fucked-up." Matty grinned half-heartedly, though still looking at me with a tad bit of disappointment, and Penelope smiled. "It's short, but hey, just means we gotta live it up. Twenty-four hours just means we gotta party even harder."

Dana breathed a sigh of relief and smiled sweetly at me. Matty chugged his mimosa and Penelope clapped, laughing.

"Hell yes! I like the way this girl thinks!"

As the girls and I walked through the hotel lobby, chatting a thousand miles a minute about stupid things, the weight I'd been feeling felt a little lighter. We had filled big canteens with juice and vodka like we were in high school, and set loose into Honolulu. Today was going to be a drunken adventure and everything about *that* got me excited. I really started to feel happy. The wet blanket that was my depression didn't seem to currently exist, even if my face was still in pain. My smile felt real, not like some mask I was forcing myself to wear. I didn't wanna think too hard about it, though.

Penelope chewed her gum loudly. "So, Dana, do we have our heart set on the Happening for the clubbing tonight? Cus my fuck buddy back home just—"

"Fuck buddy nine thousand sixty-two?" Matty snarkly interjected. Dana laughed.

"Nine thousand sixty-three," Penelope quickly fired back, giggling. "No—no but, forreal, my fuck buddy was *just* texting me and telling me there's this bitchin' club called the Blue Sapphire. I was thinking maybe—"

"Uh, Penny, let's *see* where we're at when we get there. We have a lot of booze ahead of us today . . ." Dana said with a wide smile.

"Fuck yeah, we do!" I chimed in, laughing. I chugged down a bit of my canteen. Matty watched me a before he followed suit. I noticed his somewhat flattened mood and nudged him slightly. "Hey, maybe we take that T-Rex photo you wanted today?"

He blinked, caught off guard. ". . . you actually want to do that?"

I nodded. "Hell yeah, dude! Let's do it!"

Matty began smiling. "Okay! If you're down! Maybe on a different day, though, cus—"

"What T-Rex photo?" Penny asked.

I blinked, not expecting Penny to butt into the convo. I smiled at her. "Oh . . . at some point this trip we wanna get a photo of us being, like, eaten by a T-Rex at Kualoa Ranch. Matty's gonna photoshop it in."

Penny widened her smile. "Oh, fuck yeah! Let's all get photos like that! Sounds like *so* much fun! Cus of *Jurassic Park*, right?"

"Y-yeah!" I enthused. "Exactly!"

"Yooo, Matty! You think you could, like, photoshop my head off or something? Like it's being eaten by the T-Rex? That would be so dope!"

I looked at Matty, whose face fell as he glared at her. He gave me a look like *really?* before taking another swig. "With how much you give? Sure! Should be easy to take off some head."

I elbowed him in response and telegraphed with my eyes, "Not cool." He only looked back at me and took another swig.

Penny's grin faded a bit as she processed the comment. It returned as she smiled even wider. "Well sick, I'm excited! Hear that, Dana? Wanna go to Kualoa Ranch?"

Dana smiled and shrugged. "Uh, sure! Why not? I haven't been there yet."

I smiled as Matty sighed. I rubbed his back. "Looks like we'll get it today!" I sang slightly. Matty side-eyed me a little and took a swig.

"'Kay, getting an Uber now . . ." Dana said under her breath, looking at her phone. "Sheesh, looks like traffic is gonna be *a lot* to deal with today."

"Oooh, we should play a drinking game in the car!" Penny said, getting pulled into conversation with Dana.

With me urging Matty out of his bitchy shell a bit, the crew talked at a thousand words a minute as we got to the waiting area for the Uber. I kept my eyes open for the car, searching the area as people walked this way and that.

That was when my eyes caught something in the far-off distance. I don't . . . quite know how to explain it. There were people walking all around, so I'm sure in context it doesn't seem all that strange, but there was a woman standing among the moving crowd. Everyone was walking, or otherwise in motion, but she was completely still. I couldn't see her clearly from so far, but it seemed like she was looking our way. Specifically, it felt like she was staring at me. Granted, the most I could really see was an outline far. She was a white skinned, thin woman with long black hair, and she had what looked like a white sundress on. I couldn't make out much more details than that, but I had a feeling similar to when I had sleep paralysis. Like—like there was someone watching me. I couldn't even clearly see her eyes this far away, but I felt like I was being observed. I stared back as the woman stood still among the crowd.

"Hey, Rach, Uber's here," Matty said, grabbing my attention. I looked back at him and saw that a white car had arrived to pick us up. I looked back toward the woman to see if she was still there.

She wasn't.

I thought about it for a moment before nodding and retreating back to the car. I was probably just still jumpy from the attack yesterday. That woman probably wasn't even looking at me. With that thought, I climbed into the Uber to commence bachelorette buffoonery with my friends.

After we got into the car, though, and the Uber started driving, my phone started ringing. I looked at who was calling. The Honolulu police department. I had to tell Matty to shut up before finally answering the phone.

"Hello?"

"Hi there, is this Rachel Hannigan?"

"Ye-yes?"

"Um, hi, Officer Aukai here. I, uh, I was wondering if you had a moment to talk. It's regarding your case and the incident yesterday."

"Okay . . . What about it?"

"Well, there's no easy way to say this but . . . It's no longer an active case."

Immediately I felt terror shake through my body. "*What?* Wh-why? Are you just dropping the case?"

There was a pause as I heard a heavy breath from the officer. "Ms. Mariah Jennings is no longer among the living. She was found dead in her jail cell this morning."

CHAPTER 7

It took me a moment to process what I was being told.

"Dead? H-how?"

The mood in the car completely changed as my friends all looked at me, bewildered.

"Suicide. Best we can tell, banged her own head against the wall until she caved in her own skull. Not before taking off chunks of her face with her nails, though."

My friends kept their gaze on me and I wanted to throw up. What the fuck? I blinked, disgusted, then swallowed, feeling sick. "I'm surprised you're being so forthcoming about that information. Would've thought that kind of thing would be confidential."

"Well. . . normally we would be a little more discreet in interest of the family's privacy. Problem is, Ms. Jennings didn't have any family. Matter of fact, there's no record of her existence before 2002."

I squinted. "I beg your pardon?"

"We can't find any record of her before she stayed at the hotel. She's a regular Jane Doe. If it weren't for the hotel records calling her Mariah Jennings, it's like she never existed."

I shuddered, remembering her wart-covered, menacing face. Who the hell was I dealing with? The police didn't even have records of her? What the actual fuck was going on?

"Anyway, sorry to disrupt your day, ma'am. Just . . . thought you should know. To feel safe and to know . . . you won't have to deal with her anymore."

"Th-thank you, Officer . . ."

The phone conversation ended and there was silence in the car. Dana rubbed my arm. "Everything okay?"

"The old lady from yesterday . . . she's dead."

It wasn't easy recovering the party mood from earlier. How does one feel like partying after news like that? Somehow we managed to eventually find our way back to a good time, though. Kualoa Ranch was a good almost forty-minute drive cus traffic was bad, so after thirty minutes of sipping our "water canteens" and talking about our sex lives, the party began to liven up again. We were definitely tipsy, at the very least, by the time we reached the place. Most of us drank somewhat responsibly, at least; I think we were smart enough to know we weren't sober enough for the zipline tour. Matty seemed particularly plastered, though, and slurred a desire to go; we all laughed it off and went onto the Movie Sites tour instead. We had to be annoying the shit out of the rest of the people on the tour with how loud and obnoxious we were. We posed in front of posters and statues of T-Rexes, skipped along making stupid jokes, Penelope may or may not have twerked in front of an image of the Rock and pretended to kiss it. It was buffoonery at its finest. At one point, when Penny was distracted talking to a stranger, Matty and I snuck away and got our T-Rex photo he wanted to take. It all seemed to go by in moments. Things quieted down a bit somewhere when it came to the bus tour, though. Matty got especially quiet during the ride, either sobering up or feeling the full effects of the alcohol (neither would surprise me).

Once the tour ended, we went to the buffet, where Matty proceeded to disappear into the bathroom. Dana, Penelope, and I sat, eating our food, getting more sober.

"So anyway, 'bout the club tonight . . ." Dana began, catching both Penelope's and my attention. "Can you show me where you thought we should go instead?"

Penelope, who was mid-munching her salad, nodded. "Mmmhmm!" She pulled out her iPhone and typed at lightning speed. "Blue Sapphire. It's fucking awesome. Carter, one of the guys I do scenes with a lot? Buddy of his owns the place. They *literally* had Snoop Dogg there last week. It's killer."

I scanned the details with my eyes and grimaced. "Wait, it says here it's brand spanking new. How the hell we getting in?"

Penelope donned a devilish smirk, pulling her phone back toward her. "So before I even asked, I may have made a few calls. I did say a friend of a friend owns the place, right?"

"You didn't," Dana said, dropping her face.

"Hey, my rank with OnlyFans gets me into places. Places normies couldn't get in."

Dana began laughing. "My God, you *hoe*."

"You're welcome."

"Bitch, I love you."

"And, to top it off . . ." Penny showed us a photo on her phone. "VIP lounge, girlie! Gonna bachelorette in style!"

I smiled, laughing. "Holy fuck! OnlyFans gets you *that* kind of clout?"

Penelope smiled at me, seemingly sincere. "No matter the economy, people are always willing to pay to watch a girl get fucked. It's a business like any other.

The only difference being your body is the product you're selling." Penelope looked deep in my eyes before shrugging. "If ya ever wanted to break in, let me know. I could hook ya up."

I laughed nervously. "Thanks but . . . I think that'd be a *drastic* departure from the pictures I normally take."

Penelope lifted her eyebrows. "Who said anything 'bout taking pictures?"

I had just tried swallowing my burger when she said that and coughed a bit. My face dropped. She meant . . . Oh . . .

Dana burst out laughing. "Penny, you are trouble. Trying to get my girl in the smut business."

Penelope coolly shrugged. "It's not a bad living. Get laid, get paid, see the world. Once you get past how creepy some people can be, it's the easiest gig on Earth." Penelope took a sip of water then swallowed before grabbing her fork again. "Best part too? Since I'm more or less my own boss, I don't have to work with people I don't want to. Makes it better than getting involved with the actual smut industry. Just gotta know how to work social media." Penelope looked me up and down and chomped another bite of salad. "Like I said, I could help ya out if ya want."

I either wasn't sure what to answer, or simply didn't want to. As if by some saving miracle, Matty plopped down, looking paler than usual.

"Jesus, Matty! The fuck happened to you?" I asked blatantly.

Dana winced, putting her hand on his back. "Baby, you okay? You look a li'l green."

"Was just puking my guts out back there. I feel like shit. Like José's-birthday-party levels of shit," he said, looking drowsy.

I winced. "Oooh, yeah, you didn't *seem* like you were pacing yourself today. Too much vodka?"

Matty shook his head. "I dunno. I think I need to go back to the hotel, though, guys."

When the Uber took us back, I was the one taking care of Matty for an hour or two in his hotel room. As I tried to muffle the sounds of him throwing up with the TV, I began to feel pretty bad for him. When he finally emerged from the bathroom after being in there way too long and wearing a purple robe, I knew he was done for the day.

"You good, kid?" I asked, wincing.

"I wanna die." He crept into his bed and curled up immediately. "I'm never drinking ever again."

I grinned. "You? Give up White Russians? Doubt."

"Don't bring my taste in men into this," he said, muffled slightly. "God, I'm going through it."

I nodded and ran my fingers through his hair, then felt his forehead. Warmer than normal. "You're feeling kinda feverish. You don't think it might've been what you ate this morning, do you?"

"God, I hope not. That fish was fucking amazing. No, probably just overestimated my tolerance," he said, almost half asleep. "Hey . . . You and that Penelope girl, you two seem to be getting along . . ."

I shrugged. "She seems cool."

"No, I mean . . . *really* getting along. Is there something you wanna share with the class?"

I chuckled. "The fuck you on about?"

"Do you like her?"

I stopped for a moment. "Wh-what?"

"You know, *like* her. You been looking at her more than you been looking at that yummy Kai. Noticed you checking her out yesterday and today."

I blinked, unsure of what to say. "I— You're fucking drunk, dude."

"Right now I'm sober as the day I was born," he muttered. "Do you like her?"

I thought for a moment how to respond then shook my head. "You're delusional."

"If I am, good," Matty muttered. "She's a snake. She'd use you and dump ya."

"Based on what proof? You don't even know her, Matt."

"And neither do you, Rach. I'm just saying . . . be careful. I have an off feeling about her."

There was a small silence. "She tried to convince me to do porn today."

For a moment, Matty was silent. Then he laughed. "How dare you drop that on me when I don't have the energy to make a joke."

I laughed with him. "I'm being serious."

"No, no, I know you are, that's part of what's so funny." He rolled over, face-first, and laughed hysterically into his pillow. "Oh God, laughing is making my migraine worse, but I can't stop."

I smirked. "I dunno, might be a new career path for me. Go by Evel Apple. Specialize in dominatrix videos and edging. What? Don't think it's a fit?"

Matty lifted his head, still giggling. "I don't know what makes me worry more, you coming up with that name on the spot or the fact you went straight to kinky shit."

I shrugged. "Hey, I'm sexually repressed, not dead." I ran my fingers through his hair. "Safe to assume, though, you're not joining us tonight?"

Matty sniffled. "With how I feel? Hell no. I can't."

"Girls are gonna miss you."

"Wrong. *You're* gonna miss me. Penelope is a two face and Dana . . . Well, she's practically out the door in terms of friendship." I was a little surprised to hear this from Matty. He sighed. "After she gets married, I dunno if she'll stay friends with us. You see how she was this morning? We were barely even an afterthought."

I grimaced and nodded. "Glad I'm not the only one who wonders 'bout that."

Matty rolled over to face me, grabbed my hand with both of his, and rubbed it with his thumbs. "Listen, you go and have fun tonight. If anybody deserves a good time, it's you." He looked at me with an oddly sincere look. "After everything you've been through and after that crazy bitch with scissors, you deserve some fun."

I swallowed and grabbed his hand. "You're gonna be okay, though?"

Matty smiled. "Don't you worry 'bout me. I'll Skype Frankie, and he and I will watch a drag show or something."

I nodded, a grin growing on my face. "You know most people don't use Skype anymore. That stopped being relevant a while ba—"

"Oh, fuck you, you know what I meant. *Videocall!* We all called it Skype back in high school!"

I laughed. "I know, I know."

I dressed in a nice black dress that Matty had convinced me to buy ages ago. It was probably the only other dress I brought besides the official bridesmaid dress I had with me. Never have been and never will be a dress kinda gal. I also added makeup—it stung like hell, but I was able to hide the bruises on my face pretty well. It's something I learned a bit ago, and I've gotten pretty good with it, if I may say so myself. Wasn't able to do much about the cuts, but I felt that was okay. If anything, the cuts seemed more excusable than the bruises. I could lie and say I fell into a bush or something if some guy tried to pick me up. Bruises were harder to lie about, though.

When I finished, I looked over my fit. News headline: *Too-Skinny White Girl in Black Dress Looks Even Skinnier*. The dress was the only thing I had for clubbing, though, so guess this was my outfit. I don't know why being skinny gets glamorized as something amazing. I hate it. I have no strength and I get cold easy. I also have an issue with eating, lately. An issue that is simply the fact that I have no appetite. I never feel like eating. I breathed a heavy sigh before grabbing my purse and heading out of my hotel room. Best I could do, I suppose.

The hallway spiraled ahead of me. I was starting to get used to it, though, so I didn't do my weird li'l motto thing I like doing while heading down. I checked social media on my phone as I walked. Penelope had already started posting photos of the gang on our wild bachelorette express through Kualoa Ranch. I smiled and liked the pictures, spending an extra moment staring a little at Penelope. She stared back at the camera with these inviting eyes that just drew you in, and her smile was infectious. She really was gorgeous. Tanned skin, toned body—

I saw something out of the corner of my vision. Something completely dark. I looked up from my phone to see what the hell it was, and what I saw made me stop.

A man was standing before me, down the hall a ways with his back facing toward me. He was roughly six feet tall and had pale, slightly reddish skin. His head was closely shaved, and his ears stuck out like little dumbo ears. What was odd about him was the clothes he wore. For Waikiki, for Honolulu, for *Hawaii* in general they seemed completely inappropriate. They were all black and heavy looking. The trench coat that he wore looked meant for heavy rain. From what I could see of what he had underneath, he was also wearing a long black suit with a white shirt. There he stood, off to the side of the hallway, completely still with his back toward me. His hands were in his pockets and he was like a statue. With the humidity, he had to be dying of heatstroke in that heavy getup, but not a muscle moved on his body.

He was simply a standing silhouette.

I swallowed before continuing my stride. "Can't stop, won't stop," I whispered. I walked closer and closer, but the man didn't move an inch. It didn't look like he was waiting, and if he heard me, he made no indication of it. There was something . . . *unnerving* about how still he was. I felt my palms grow clammy as I approached him carefully. "Can't stop . . ."

If I didn't know better, I'd have thought the man was dead standing up, or some sort of mannequin. The flesh on his shaved head looked real, though, and glistened in the artificial light. It started to feel colder, and goose bumps formed on my arms as I got closer and closer to him. Still no movement from him, like he didn't sense me getting closer. His trench coat looked weathered and old. Like it had seen better days long ago. I retreated to my phone, only occasionally looking up to make sure he was still in view, pretending I was on social media, mindlessly scrolling through Instagram. I was coming up on him and decided not to look at him as I passed him. I could still see his dark silhouette from the corner of my eye, but deliberately ignored him. The hairs on my neck began to stand and soon I felt again like I was being watched. I started fast walking, ignoring the feeling as I tried to hurry toward the elevator. I stopped in front of it and pressed the button.

"Come on . . ." I whispered to the elevator, really beginning to wish Matty was with me. As I waited, still not looking toward the man, I heard a thud. I refused to look. There was another deafening silence for a brief moment. Just when I began to get comfortable, another thud. My vision zeroed in on the elevator button as I heard a third thud, louder now.

Footsteps.

He was walking this way.

The temperature dropped, and I shivered, reaching into my purse for pepper spray, finding it and clutching it with a death grip in the bag. I refused to look over, but could see in my periphery a dark silhouette getting close and closer. I shut my eyes, waiting for the elevator. "Come on, come on, come on . . ." I whispered to myself, my shivering turning into an all-out shake.

Then, a clicking, grinding sound.

I had heard that sound before . . .

I spun toward the man.

. . .

Okay, what the fuck?

I stared into the blank hallway. No man in a trench coat in sight. Okay, that time I *knew* I saw that guy. I *knew* he was there. I wasn't hallucinating, I'm not fucking crazy. Where the fuck did he go? I searched and couldn't find any evidence of where he had gone. *What the fuck? I felt him.* He was *right there*.

The elevator finally arrived and I immediately got in, afraid. I closed the doors just as quickly too. Although I was starting to feel the humidity again, my arms were still covered in goose bumps. I leaned against the glass window, breathing hard. That man was there, and then he wasn't.

That man was there, and *then he wasn't.*

I breathed hard. Somehow, even though nobody was around, I felt like I was being watched still. I crossed my arms and dug my nails into them.

The grinding sound began again.

I looked around frantically, as if my life depended on finding the source of the sound. I couldn't figure out where it was coming from, though. It was like . . . someone playing with bones, rubbing them together frantically. No matter where I looked, though, I couldn't see anyone else around. I was the only one in the elevator. It wouldn't stop, that sound. I didn't know what it was, only that I didn't like it.

"Stop!" I finally shouted, against my better judgment.

With that, it did.

The elevator doors opened and a family with a little boy that couldn't have been older than four came in. The mother greeted me with a pleasant smile as

I tried to hide how freaked out I was and politely nodded with a forced smile that probably looked more like I had gas than anything pleasant. As soon as she turned around, my face dropped as I searched the elevator cab again before closing my eyes entirely. When I opened my eyes, I noticed their son, who they were holding hands with, looking up at me. I forced my smile again when I realized he wasn't looking at me, but rather above me. I slowly began to follow the track of his eyeline into the upper corner of elevator behind me. I stared at the blank corner, shifting my gaze between the boy and the corner. He was looking straight at *something*. I kept my eyes glued to the empty corner of the elevator. To the point where I almost completely ignored the ding that symbolized the elevator was at the bottom.

"Miss?" an unfamiliar, nasally male voice then said. I turned and saw it was the father of the boy. He was holding the elevator door. His face looked less than pleasant, but sympathetic. The kind of look you would give to a homeless person on the street that clearly wasn't all there. I didn't like the look. "You getting off? We're going up."

I looked over at the mother, who was giving me a similar look. I looked again at the little boy, who was still just staring at the upper corner of the elevator behind me.

I swallowed. "Y-yeah. Yeah, I'm getting off." I quickly began walking into the lobby, and looked behind me to see all three family members staring at me, their faces deadpan, if not a little hostile. As the elevator doors began to close, though, I could've sworn I saw a black-haired woman standing directly behind the mother. It looked like she was smiling at me right as the elevator closed.

I rubbed my head.

What the fuck was wrong with me? Was I seeing things that were there, or was my mind finally out to fucking lunch? I breathed hard, noticing the people walking by were staring at me.

Nails pressed on my flesh and I jumped.

"Hey, girlie! We've been looking for ya!"

I looked back; it was Penelope. Penelope and Dana. They were in dresses and heavy makeup as well, ready for clubbing. I stared at them, bug-eyed.

"Whoa, girl. You okay?" Penelope asked, brow furrowed.

"Yeah, you look . . ." Dana added, scanning me up and down. "Uh . . . *Not okay.*"

I felt clammy and feverish. How would I even begin to describe what just happened? I swallowed. "Yeah, I'm fine, let's just go." Dana tried to press on, but I more or less ignored her. The sooner we got away from Tropical Springs, the better.

I didn't feel less tense by the time that we got into the Uber. My leg shook up and down as I searched outside the window, scanning the night-lit streets of Honolulu for anything unusual. I didn't know what I was looking for, I was just painfully aware that I was looking for something I wasn't finding. I rubbed my forehead.

I'm not crazy.

I'm not crazy.

What I saw was real. I *know* it was.

"Rachel?" Penelope said after a bit. She was sitting right next to me in the Uber. I turned toward her.

"Mmm?"

"You seem nervous."

I scoffed lightly and chuckled. "No—no I'm not. Just jumpy, I guess."

There was a moment of silence, and even though she was on the other side of Penelope, I felt Dana's gaze. Penelope nodded. "Well . . . if you want . . . I brought Scooby Snacks for tonight. Might take off the edge for ya."

I squinted. "Scooby Snacks?"

Dana cleared her throat. "Penny, I don't think that's—"

Penelope shot a smirk her way. "She's a big girl. Clearly stressing out . . . I don't know. Maybe she might like a Scooby Snack. Hell, I'm for sure gonna have one. Going clubbing? It's gonna be fucking amazing. How 'bout it, Rach, you roll?"

I looked at Dana, who looked annoyed. Penelope stared at me with a devilish grin and showed me the inside of her purse. A small bag of pills. I blinked and licked my lips. "Just what is 'Scooby Snack' slang for?"

Penelope chuckled. "You know: candy, beans . . ."

Dana looked at the Uber driver then mouthed "molly" to me. I lifted my eyebrows. "Oh . . ."

"Aunt Mo?"

I thought about it and looked at Penelope. Something about her was so vulnerable yet so inviting. There was this sweetness in her eyes that she had probably learned how to use over time, but I didn't care, I was sucked in. Her light brown eyes looked into mine and I felt my heart skip a beat. I swallowed. "I've never done it before but . . . couldn't hurt."

Penelope laughed. "Fuck yeah! Thatta girl!" She got out a pill and gave it to me. "What about our bride-to-be?"

Dana shook her head. "You know I don't do shit like that . . ."

"Come on, it's your party!"

"I hate the comedowns. Hard pass. I'll get plastered, maybe do a hit of snow, but I do *not* mess with Aunt Mo anymore. Last time was not a good time."

Penelope smiled at me. "Guess that just means you and I are gonna have the good time."

I blinked, looking at the pill in my hand, then at her. A smile grew on my face. "Count of three?"

Penelope got hers in her hand, her grin turning into a full smile to match mine. "One . . . two . . ."

The world was sex and I was fucking it. Everything felt amazing, even the water Dana made sure to get me to stay hydrated. The flashing lights of the club seemed to glow just that much brighter, the music was that much louder, and I felt more horny than I had in a long time. I wanted to fuck. I wanted to be fucked. Everything around me was fucking. Penelope, Dana, and I passed through the crowd, hardly able to think, let alone hear each other because the music was so loud. The world was fast and slow at the same time. I felt like I would be happy forever. At some point while dancing, some guy groped me and was grinding on me, and very unlike me, I actually went with it. I felt him press into me and it took impulse control to not fuck him on the dance floor then and there. Penelope was actually the one who pulled me away from him. She didn't lecture me like Dana would, though. No, instead she pulled me closer, putting her hands on my hips and leading me into her. Before I even knew it, we were forehead to forehead, our hands caressing each other's bodies.

"You're so fucking cool, you know?" I tried to speak loudly.

Penelope laughed. "What?"

"You're so fucking cool and beautiful and I want you in my life. I just . . . I want you in my life," I said loudly.

"Dude, I literally can't fucking hear you," Penelope said with a laugh. She grabbed me by the hand and began skipping through the club. Everything seemed to be happening faster than I could keep track. In moments, we were in the VIP lounge. Dana was with us, but it almost didn't seem like it. I was laughing about something Dana said, but amid the red and blue lights, Penelope had almost my entire attention.

"Dance with me!" Penelope shouted, leading me back to the dance floor.

I don't remember how we got there, or why, but soon, our mouths were intertwined. I tasted her cherry gum-flavored mouth as her tongue danced with mine. In the red lighting, in blue lighting, in pink. Our hands moved through each other's hair. She grabbed my head roughly and put her forehead to mine.

"I wanna fuck you so bad right now," she said through her teeth.

I blushed all over. "I'd like that . . ."

"So bad . . ."

Fast forward and I was sitting in the VIP lounge, her hand up my skirt. Her fingers worked overtime and fireworks went off all over my body. She leaned in toward my ear. "You and I should do a video sometime."

I smiled. "Yeah?"

"Yeah . . . We could make a lot of money together."

I laughed a little. "I'd like that. I'm broke as fuck."

Penelope smiled and laughed. "So much money . . ."

Somehow we wound up in the bathroom and seeing even more of each other than expected. I . . . don't wanna get too deep into that for obvious reasons. Needless to say, at some point during what we were doing, my mood dropped.

It was like a dark cloud suddenly weighed me down out of nowhere, and no matter how I tried to keep myself in a good mood, I just didn't have the energy. It all came crashing down and I was crying. I just— I couldn't handle things anymore. Penelope pulled away.

"Hey . . . you okay?"

"Yeah, I—I don't know . . . I don't think the molly is agreeing with me. I just—I just feel so . . . small." I broke out into sobs.

"Hey . . . hey . . ." Penelope pulled me toward her breasts and hugged me. "It's okay . . ."

I closed my eyes hard, feeling her warm embrace. "I—I don't wanna be alone. I don't wanna fucking die alone."

I opened my eyes and she was gone. My mouth was dry, and she was gone. It was only me in the stall.

I shook a moment. Where was . . . Where the hell was Penelope? I shuddered. She was just here. Just in this stall with me. I rubbed my face. What? Suddenly I felt cold, naked, and exposed. I pulled the top of my dress over my chest and properly made sure none of my bits were showing. As I stumbled out of the women's bathroom, I awkwardly tried not tripping on my heels. Lights flashed and I walked out onto the dance floor. What was once a wonderland of mystery and joy was quickly turning into one of dread and agony. The music was too fucking loud, the colors too fucking bright, and I felt nauseous. I closed in on the bar and saw Penelope and Dana talking excitedly. I marched over, best I could. I looked over at the crowd and thought maybe a black-haired woman was smiling at me, but couldn't quite tell. Everyone and no one seemed to be looking at me at the same time.

Finally, I got up to the bar where Penelope and Dana were talking. That was when the two finally saw me.

"There she is!" Penelope shouted.

"We've been looking all over for you."

I swallowed and sniffled, glaring hatefully at Penelope. "Why'd you leave me in the bathroom?"

Penelope looked caught off guard, doing a double take. "What?"

"You left . . ." I could feel Dana's concern as I tried to make sense of their puzzled faces. "You left me *alone* in the bathroom. Why would you do that?"

Penelope chuckled nervously and looked over toward Dana. "Um . . . girlie . . . I've been with Dana this whole time."

Dana shook her head. "Yeah . . . We last saw you dancing with some guy, then completely lost track of you." I blinked. What the fuck? I was *just* having sex with Penelope in the bathroom. What? My face dropped.

"Uh . . . you need water, Rach?" Penelope asked sheepishly.

I soured, glaring at Penelope. She was lying. She had to be. Molly wasn't hallucinogenic. "I don't . . ." I curled my mouth and looked at her, shaking my head. She knew. *"Fuck you."*

I stormed off back toward the bathroom. That couldn't have been a hallucination. It couldn't have been. And it *was* her. It was definitely Penelope. I thought I heard someone call out over the crowd but couldn't be sure with the music. Flashes of Ms. Jennings beating me passed through my head as I tried to get through the maze of people. It was real. I know it was real. I tried getting through the crowd, which seemed thicker and thicker by the second. Suddenly, a bald man turned around to look at me.

It was Greg. He stared at me in the red-light glow with those piercing blue eyes. I backed away a step. What was Greg doing here? He looked at me, clueless, dressed up in a white dress shirt. Then I blinked, and it was some guy that didn't even look like him.

You were easy to get over.

I felt like throwing up, and pushed my way frantically through the crowd. I could still feel hands all over me, even if none were there. Hands feeling me up and down, hands hitting me, giving me pleasure, giving me violence, doing the unthinkable. Hands. Hands. Hands. I burst into the bathroom, into a stall, and puked. My head swirled. I felt like shit. Absolute shit. What was going on? Where was I?

Knock knock knock.

"Rachel?"

It was Dana's voice.

"Rachel? You in there?"

I shuddered and sniffled. "Yeah . . ."

"You okay?"

My lips trembled. "No."

I flushed the toilet and came out to see Dana looking at me, brow furrowed. Clearly worried. "Rachel, what the hell's going on?"

"I don't . . ." I shook my head. "You . . . you don't think Penny's molly was mixed with something else, do you?"

Dana shook her head. "Not Penelope's stash. Knowing her, it's pure."

I sighed and walked over to the sink, Dana placing her hand on my back.

"Talk to me. Tell me what's wrong."

I huffed, turning on the sink and getting water on my face. "I just . . . I don't know if I can handle everything anymore." Tears slipped out of my eyes. "It's just too hard and—and I don't know how to be a fucking person anymore since Greg. And I just—and I just . . ."

Dana pulled me into an embrace as I cried out into her. "It's okay, Rach. It's okay. You've been through a lot." I embraced her tightly. It was a good, long, solid moment. Dana pulled away and handed me a water bottle. "Drink this. You need to hydrate. Molly dehydrates."

"Thanks."

I sipped down the cool water. As I drank, Dana's smile changed. She was smiling at me lovingly. She almost looked like she was chuckling, like someone said something funny.

I pulled the water bottle away from my mouth and blinked. "What?"

Dana shook her head, still chuckling. "You know you're the most *pathetic* person I know, right?"

I stopped. What?

Dana smiled fully. Not with any malice. Just like she was posing for a photo. "Everyone knows you're worthless. I only invited you cus I felt bad. Truth is, though, you liked what Greg did to you. Didn't you?"

I stared at Dana, beyond shocked. What the fuck? Dana's face fell into something more serious. She blinked and her brow furrowed, her jaw moving side to side. The grinding of her teeth sounded as her jaw moved. She shook her head and blinked. Then she stared at me, wide-eyed. "I don't . . . I don't know why I just said that . . ."

Then there was a crunch. It was like she suddenly punched herself in the mouth with how fast her own hand moved to her jaw. She reached into her mouth with her fingers, wincing in pain. In moments, she pulled out one of her back teeth with relative ease, blood dripping past her lips. She looked at the tooth in shock, then at me.

Dana's head violently slammed into the bathroom mirror, cracking it. She staggered, bleeding from the forehead.

"*Dana?*" I called out.

She inhaled sharply, holding her bleeding head. There was a sickening crack as one of her legs suddenly bent the wrong way. She screamed out, now using the bathroom counter for support, but then her head slammed downward, as if pushed, into the counter, sending her down to the floor, sprawled out.

"*Dana!*" I screamed out, stepping toward her. In moments her body had been dragged across the bathroom floor, something unseen controlling her. She convulsed on the ground, her chest moving frantically up and down. I rushed immediately to her, dropping to the floor. "Dana? Dana!" She clutched me desperately, twitching this way and that. Blood poured out of her mouth and through it she began wailing and screaming, all the teeth in her mouth missing. She convulsed violently as suddenly, with a loud crack, her shoulder was pulled out of its socket. Small things started to poke out from under her skin, breaking the surface as they pushed their way through.

"Dana, please!" I tried touching her but cut my palm trying to do so. Shards of what looked like was glass were now tearing out through her skin like someone was pushing the sharp shards outward from inside her body. She screamed and wailed, her eyes rolling into her head as I watched helplessly, unable to help my friend. Her other arm slowly twisted and the broken bone at her elbow broke free of her flesh. Her foot on her unharmed leg began twisting the wrong way. I stood up and rushed to the exit of the bathroom. Dana's body continued to move like she was having a seizure. The blood from her mouth mixed with foam as her screams turned into moans.

"*Somebody! Somebody help!*" I yelled out into the loud club. I couldn't hear my voice over the music. *"My friend's dying! Help! Please!"* People looked over as I kept screaming for help.

I heard a familiar grinding sound and immediately looked beyond the crowd, toward its source. The hairs stood up on my neck. Something was watching me again. Among the crowd, somewhere among the flashing lights . . . I saw the shadow of a flat-brimmed hat.

CHAPTER 8

I hate hospitals. They reek of death. Doesn't matter how nice and cozy they are, there's always a stench of old people and sickness. The agents of mortality, the grim reaper itself, it lingers over these places. At any given time, loved ones shut their eyes forever. People lose children, people lose parents, people lose families. My mom almost died from appendicitis in one of these places. Dad *did* die from his motorcycle accident. I hate hospitals.

Having to wait in one for hours was absolute torture. The police came and went, and instead of seeing how my friend was doing, I was waiting in the hallway. Not that there was anything I could do. I had stood there helpless as something attacked my best friend. As she gurgled, glass stabbing through her skin, I was helpless as a newborn babe. I felt like a fucking joke.

What was I supposed to do?

The story I gave the cops wasn't what I perceived as the truth. I gave a story about finding her that way. I genuinely didn't know what else I could've said that would've made sense. I still didn't quite know what happened. What I could've done to stop anything. I looked at the cut on my hand, analyzing the crevice still throbbing in my palm. It wasn't a deep cut, and I didn't seem to need stitches, but it ached and throbbed all the same.

Penelope rushed down the hall, the most serious face I'd ever seen on her as she walked more smoothly in heels than I ever could. She breathed out, "Haven't been able to reach Matty."

I twisted my mouth. "He's probably out like a light. With how sick he's feeling? We ain't hearing from him till morning." I leaned back rubbing my eyes. "What about Trevon?"

Penelope folded her arms, leaning against the nearby wall. "He's on his way." She sighed, shaking her head, her eyes red and wet. "I don't . . . I don't understand how she could end up like that," she said, her voice shaking. Heavy labored breaths and sniffles escaped her, but my gaze didn't linger on her. I was too busy thinking about Dana. "Every limb broken like that, glass in her skin. B-before she even has a chance to get married . . . this happens." I felt her eyes linger on me.

"Yeah."

"Rachel . . . how *did* she wind up like that? You had to have seen something . . ."

I merely stared ahead, not answering. I shook my head. "I'm not going through the story again, Penny. I don't have the energy."

"I get it, it's just . . . so fucking weird. I mean, the way she's mangled up . . . you'd think—" I merely gave her a look. She twisted her face. "It's like she fell through a window or something."

Penelope turned toward me and must have finally noticed the harsh glare I was giving her. She seemed to squirm as my eyes locked onto hers, unflinching. I finally closed my eyes hard. Like I said, didn't have the energy. I put my hand on my head and massaged my brow. What the fuck even happened back there? My head still couldn't make sense of it. The effects of the molly had worn off by now, but I felt like absolute shit on multiple levels.

"Trevon!" I heard Penelope call out. I looked up and saw Trevon looking absolutely wide-eyed with all the color drained from his face. He was rushing down the hallway, almost stumbling over nurses while he chaotically made his way toward us.

"Wh-where is she? *Where is she?*"

Penelope held him back with her dainty little hand. "She's in surgery right now. They rushed her in immediately, told us to wait here."

I looked away, breathing out. I didn't wanna be here.

"How . . . I . . ." Trevon seemed to be stumbling on his words. "Wha-what . . ."

"Shhh, it's okay. You should sit down. Your breathing is out of control."

"Ay, Rach. *Ay!*" I hesitantly looked his way. He was breathing fast and hard. "The fuck happened to her, Rach? Who did this?"

My eyes strained, beginning to water. "I, um . . ." I shook my head. "I didn't see."

Trevon looked on the verge of exploding "Y-you didn't see? *You didn't see?* Penny told me you were with her! What do you mean, you didn't see?"

"Tre . . ."

My face crumpled. "I'm sorry. I just, I—I didn't—"

"Sorry ain't good enough!"

"Tre, calm down," Penelope tried to interject.

"*That's my fucking wife in there!*" Tre yelled, glaring at me, his voice breaking. His eyes were red and his lips quivered, and he pointed somewhere to the side. "That's my fucking . . ." He put his hand over his mouth and shook his head. "Fuck."

Penelope pulled him into a hug as he began to sob. "Shhh, it's okay. Everything will be okay."

She led him to a seat, where he buried his head in his hands. His pitiful sobs unleashed in full fury as he wept like his heart was breaking in front of me. Did he *actually* love her? Was it possible he actually gave a shit about her? I . . . didn't know what to say. "Dana . . ." he said between sobs. "Dana, no baby . . ." Penelope wrapped her arm around his shoulders.

I *wished* I had an answer. I *wished* there was something worth saying. I wasn't lying when I said I didn't see what attacked Dana, though. That was the worst part of all. I knew what I saw, but what I saw was Dana bending like a pretzel due to *nothing*. There wasn't any explaining what I saw without sounding like either an absolute asshole or a crazy person. Still not convinced I'm not both.

I stood up, swallowing. "I, uh . . . I think I need to go back to the hotel. You staying here?"

Penelope nodded, looking briefly at Tre. "Yeah. Think so."

"Good. Uh . . . If there's any updates—"

"I'll let you know."

I nodded, taking one last look at Trevon before looking back at Penelope. "Later."

"Get back safe."

I turned around. Started to walk.

"Stupid fucking whore."

My ears twitched. On a dime I turned back toward Penelope. "Huh?"

She looked up from Trevon. "Mmm?"

"What'd you say?"

Penelope looked at me like I was an alien. "I didn't say anything . . ."

I stared at her hard, not trusting her at this point. She didn't seem to notice my glare; too focused on taking care of Trevon. I huffed out as I began the lonely trek outside. The difference in the air was jarring, from the icy halls of death to the warm, humid air that is Hawaii. I ordered my Uber and waited on a bench in front of the hospital.

God, I needed booze.

I wanted to cry my eyes out but no tears streamed down my face. A part of me I thought was numb and dead stung. It was the part that cared if I cared about other people. I didn't know how to handle it. I didn't think anything else could hurt me . . . But that did. As I sat on that bench just outside the hospital, a wave of disbelief ran through me.

My best friend might be dead.

I sat with that.

My best friend might be dead . . . and all I wanted was booze. I was a piece of shit. A friend was dying and I just wanted to get fucked-up to forget about it. Even that robot Trevon had more emotion than me.

I was fucking useless.

"'Scuse me, miss . . ." an unfamiliar voice said. I looked over and saw an older man walking toward me. With the rugged state of his clothes, it wasn't hard to piece together he was some sort of vagrant. His face was hard and craggy, his skin dark from hours of being in the sun. His hair was brittle, looking ready to fall off at any second. He was wearing a tank top and had long, skinny arms. In his hands, he had a pack of cigarettes.

"You got a light? Forgot my lighter on my way here."

I swallowed uncomfortably, trying to not look at him. I pulled out my lighter from my purse while eyeing my pepper spray. I handed him the lighter and then turned my head back to the side, still watching through my peripheral vision. A lighter is like one to three dollars total at a gas station. I was broke as fuck, but I could get a new one. "Keep it. I'm trying to quit."

There was a sound of a cigarette being lit and air being blown out. "You know what they say, hun, no one ever quits."

I refused to acknowledge or look at him. I heard him shuffle, then chuckle.

"So I used to knows this guy, right? Big-time smoker. Had this girl. Almost as pretty as you. Almost as pretty as you. She was a knockout, man, top dollar . . ."

I looked at my phone, trying to see where the Uber was. Five minutes away. Ignore this guy for five minutes and I'm safe.

"Yeah?"

"I think they got married in Alameda, California, or something, I don't remember. But they shack up, right? Get themselves a nice li'l place in Haleiwa town. She tells 'im—she tells 'im, hey we got this nice fuckin' house, I don't want yah smokin' no more, right?"

I stared at the phone. "Yeah."

"So, my buddy—my buddy he obliges. Anyhow, one day this guy he—he comes home from work . . . there's fuckin' blood everywhere. He walks in, and there's blood on the floor. He walks to his room to find his wife dead, chopped to pieces. He finds his best friend buck naked, covered in blood, carrying an axe in one hand, a fuckin gun' in the other. Bam, best friend blows his own brains out. So my buddy gets blamed for it. Double homicide. Sentenced to the chair. You know what his last request was on death row?"

I furrowed my brow and turned my head to the man. I almost had to do a double take. The man next to me was not the man I gave my lighter to. At least, not as I had just seen him. He still looked homeless, but this one wasn't even the same ethnicity or height. His bone structure was completely different. He was a chunkier fellow, shorter, maybe a few years younger. No visible hair, just a beanie. He smiled at me, round face, big, deep eyes. He smiled big. "A fuckin' cigarette."

I stared at him in awe. What . . . what the fuck?

Then he winked at me. "Your ride is here, miss."

I turned to the road and saw that my Uber had in fact arrived. I stood up and got into the car as fast as I could, closing and locking the door. I looked back at the homeless man in wonder as the car drove. He merely smiled back at me, chuckling, smoking his cigarette. As the car drove farther and farther away from the hospital, it still seemed like he watched me until we disappeared from view entirely. I blinked and swallowed before rubbing my head. It was starting to feel like something was fucking with me. I couldn't make sense of what was going on. Either I saw what hurt Dana and my brain was faulty, or there actually was something weird going on here. Either way, I was getting real sick of it. I frowned as I looked out into the night. What the hell was going on?

The streetlamps were cold, and aside from buildings, at this time of night, the beautiful Honolulu looked more or less like any other city. Capable of being just as sadistic, just as evil, just as cold as any other place at nighttime. The shadows brought by streetlamps were just as dark no matter where they were.

Thoughts of Dana twisting on the ground flooded my mind. Convulsing, contortions, eyes rolled back. *Something* was in that room with us. The more and more I thought on it . . . the more it made sense. People don't just . . . *break* the way she was breaking. It was like someone was snapping her bit by bit, like a twig. And the way the glass just came up through her skin . . .

What the hell was that?

I breathed out uncomfortably as the Uber to drove me to Tropical Springs. By the time we got back, it was four a.m. and the sky was turning a dark blue. I had gone an entire night without sleep. I rubbed my eyes, but somehow didn't feel overly exhausted despite my mind working overtime trying to figure out what the hell was going on. I trudged through the mostly empty hotel, completely preoccupied as flashes of Dana passed through my mind. People didn't just bend and break for no reason. And they certainly didn't have shards of glass pop up through their skin spontaneously either. No matter how I tried to justify it was all in my head, it didn't make sense.

But if it wasn't just in my head . . . What did that mean?

When I got to my hotel room, I got a good look at myself in a mirror. Dear God. I looked like *that*? My eyes were sunken in, my hair was all over the place, and most embarrassingly, there were puke stains on my dress. I was disgusted with the woman in front of me and marched into the bathroom. First order of business, before bed or anything, I was taking a shower. There was hot mess, then there was just mess. I was the latter. I stripped off my clothes and looked briefly at my bony, naked body before climbing into my shower. The warm water felt womb-like, and I began to feel like I was being hugged.

Warm water was a godly embrace to the damaged and frail. I wrapped my arms around myself, feeling the water drip down my face. My face crumpled as I felt tears silently fall out.

Dana was dying.

Dana was *dying*.

I put my hand to my face and a sob or two escaped and my nose became runny, but honestly I felt too tired to cry. I huffed a bit and shook my head.

I ran my hand through my hair. When it got to the back of my skull, I felt a sharp pain. I pulled my hand away and as I did, a clump of my black hair came with it, wrapped around my fingers like little snakes. Did I . . . did I just pull my hair out?

Panicking, my hand went to the back of my head again. This time it felt like my fingers went *inside*, like there was a hole. I froze, eyes widening. My fingers felt the edges of the hole. It was hard, like bone. I pulled my hand away, even more hair on my fingers. I turned my head toward the shower head and immediately felt pain as the water hit the back of my scalp. I ran my fingers through my hair more, and bigger and bigger clumps came out. Blood and hair leaked onto the floor, past my toes, and drifted down the drain. The back of my head was in agony. I immediately rushed out of the shower and twisted to looked in the mirror at the back of my head.

It was a bloody mess back there, missing bits of hair, and skin and muscle exposed. I pulled at some of the hair that was still there and it came off easily, stretching like it had some sort of goo attached. I pulled more and more, beginning to see the face of a bloody skull on the back of my head.

I opened my eyes and screamed. I sat up in my bed and immediately felt the back of my head in the dark.

. . .

It was normal. No blood, no holes. I breathed a shuddered breath, lying back down. I swallowed, my throat dry.

I was in my hotel room. That I could deduce, even though it was dark. I looked over at the alarm clock. Four a.m. That couldn't be right . . . I got back to the hotel at four. I looked around. I didn't even remember going to bed. I quickly grabbed my phone.

April 19.

Went to the club yesterday, which was the eighteenth. It was the right day. Looked through my messages. All still the same. Dana in the hospital and all. I rubbed my head. Was that a nightmare? That couldn't be right. I breathed hard, tossing my phone aside. I rubbed my eyes. A sound like the faucet turning on came from the bathroom. I looked toward where the sound of water came from.

Right when I did that, the grinding noise began again. I felt the hair on my neck stand up.

It was here.

My attention, on instinct, went to the corner of the room where the ti plant rested, even though I couldn't see it very well. It was over there, whatever it was. My pulse quickened and my body froze.

Thump.

I jumped on instinct. Soon, another thump. Followed by another. I saw the tall figure with the flat-brimmed hat. Another thump. More of the figure became noticeable through the dark. He had a black coat and the back of his head was shaved and white. His back was facing me. He took an awkward, stiff step backward. It was like someone was moving an inanimate object. He seemed almost dead as he slowly and awkwardly jerked, taking another step backward, toward me. The grinding was getting louder. I breathed hard, the air icy cold despite it being fucking Hawaii. He got closer and closer with every step.

Then he stopped and turned his head toward me. I closed my eyes hard, the grinding getting louder and louder, covering my ears because it sounded as loud as a fucking 747.

Just as suddenly as it came, the sound stopped.

Hesitantly, I opened my eyes. From the shadows, I could see the silhouette of the man with the hat looking at me, and through the dark I could make out some of the details of his face. It looked like a bloody, dripping skull was staring at me, partially covered by a hat. Then the man lurched forward and wrapped his hand around my throat and pushed me down. Instead of falling into my bed, I fell into water. It was like my bed was suddenly a bathtub as my sheets and hair swirled around me.

I couldn't—I couldn't breathe. The salty water seeped into my nostrils, down my throat. I fought as best I could, struggling against his iron grip. My arms splashed and thrashed this way and that to no avail. Through the surface of the water I could only see his hat-wearing silhouette as I tossed and turned. Bubbles flew out of my mouth as I swished around in what tasted like sea water.

There was a sudden shift in pressure and I immediately rose out of the liquid, drenched. I looked around. No man with the hat. I breathed hard, feeling behind me. Nothing but bed. Solid bed. My hand felt the sheets. They weren't even wet.

I coughed, shivering.

Suddenly, something unseen pulled my head to the side, and a man's voice whispered angrily in an unrecognizable language. I could almost feel the harsh, hot breaths on my neck as whoever or whatever it was whispered in my ear.

And just like that, it was done. The room was quiet again.

"*Matty, open the fucking door!*" I yelled before pounding hard on his hotel room door. After several rounds he opened his door finally, looking like utter shit. His hair was sticking up.

"Rachel, what the fuck?" he complained.

"Where the *fuck* have you been?"

"Asleep . . . Why are you all wet? You just take a shower?"

I rushed into the room. "Did—did you see any of the texts Penny and I sent you? Get any of the calls?"

Matty looked at me, confused. He put up a finger and marched sleepily to the side of his bed. He picked up his phone and noticed it was unplugged.

"Oh fuck . . ." he muttered. "My, uh, my battery died. Lemme plug it in . . ."

I walked up to him and grabbed him by the arms. *"Matty."*

He looked at me, puzzled. I shivered and shook. "Dana . . . Dana is in the hospital. Getting surgery. Right now."

He blinked. "Wh-what? What the fuck happened?"

I shook my head. "If I tell you, you have to promise me not to tell anyone else what I saw."

"What?"

"Promise me."

"What the fuck did you see?"

"I said *promise me!*"

Matty blinked, breathing hard. "Alright, alright, I promise. The hell, Rach?"

I blinked, walking away, shaking my head. "You're gonna think I'm crazy." I looked back at my best friend, who looked at me very seriously. "Something—something attacked her. It was—it was like she was possessed or something.

First, she began losing teeth— Then her head slammed into the bathroom mirror. Glass started—started *coming out* of her skin . . ."

Matty's sunken facial expression made him seem utterly lost. "What?"

"It was like—like something I couldn't see was breaking her apart bit by bit and making me watch. There's something *very* wrong going on here, Matt."

"Wh-what are you saying, Rach?"

"I feel . . . I feel like something is *hunting* me. Something not fucking human. It's been hunting me since I got here, and I don't know what to do . . ."

Matty gave me a look.

"I'm serious, Matt."

He blinked, folding his lip. He thought for a moment and clutched me kindly, softly leading me toward the bed. "Um, Rach, honey . . . I think you need some sleep. You look terrible."

"I'm—I'm *not lying*. I *don't need sleep*. Something is—something is after me, Matty. There's—there's something I didn't tell you."

"Rach, come on. You should lie down."

"I—I need to tell you! I don't need sleep!"

"Lie down."

"Matty, I mean it— There's something going o—"

"*I said lie down!*" Matty said loudly, forcing me to sit on the bed. He looked me deep in my eyes. "Listen to me, Rachel Hannigan. I don't know what you're on, but you are going to sleep this off. I am going to watch over you, make sure you don't OD or whatever the fuck—"

"*Look at your fucking messages, Matt! I'm not lying!*" I yelled.

He stopped, breathing out. He blinked, before nodding his head. "Fair enough. I *haven't* checked my messages. I'm going to check them right now . . . but whatever is going on, you need to calm down, 'kay?" I blinked, breathing out. He continued. "You've clearly been having some kind of night. You *need* to rest. Just, humor me. Lie down, close your eyes. When you open them again, we'll talk, 'kay?"

My eyelids *were* heavy. I was too scared, though. My face contorted. "I—I don't—I don't wanna sleep. Please, Matty. I don't wanna sleep."

"It's okay."

"It attacks me when I go to sleep, please."

Matty gently pushed me till I was lying down. "I'm going to check my messages. You get rest, 'kay?"

Almost as soon as I hit the pillow, I felt like I was falling. My world entered an eternal void. Somehow, it felt like I was going deeper and deeper down into an endless trench. My hair swirled all around me and the breathless depths got colder and colder as I fell through water.

Eventually the darkness swallowed me whole.

Faces.

A wall of faces.

One on top of the other on top of the other, slightly covered and glistening with water.

The faces were all a porcelain white, like some sort of mask, stacked evenly atop one another, eyes closed, carved out of the same material. I hovered over them endlessly. I couldn't count how many faces . . .

When I opened my eyes. I saw Matty's back facing me, looking out the window. Daylight was peeking into the room. My head felt ten pounds heavier. I breathed out and coughed. This caught Matty's attention.

"You're up . . ."

"Yeah, I guess . . ." I said with a voice deeper than I thought my voice could go.

Matty's face twisted. "You were out for a bit. Didn't wanna wake you."

I ached as I lay in his bed. "How *you* feeling?"

Matty blinked, grinning slightly before the smile fell and he answered, serious. "Better, considering everything happening. Don't even feel sick anymore. What about you?"

I swallowed and looked down at my cut hand before sighing. "You read the messages?"

Matty nodded. "Yeah . . . and I got off the phone with Penny 'bout an hour ago."

I breathed out. "Did you tell her what I told you?"

Matty thought for a moment and shook his head. ". . . No. I—I made a promise, right?"

Well, at least only one person thought I was for-sure crazy. "What'd you tell her?"

Matty twisted his mouth. "Just said you were breaking down crying and upset 'bout what happened. Didn't say much else."

"Do you believe me?"

Matty looked deep in thought. "Would you blame me if I said no?"

I breathed out hard and frowned. "Figures."

"Look . . . Penny said you saw what happened. If that's what you believe you saw, then I believe that's what you believe you saw. Crazy demon shit, though, is a little outside of my realm of belief, sweetie."

I scoffed. "You believe in tarot cards and horoscopes but not this?"

Matty shrugged. "It's just wild and far-fetched, you know? I know you're not the type to just *say* stuff like that, but you gotta admit . . . what you say happened is kinda insane."

I soured my face. "Matty . . . I-I've been seeing things. Like, *weird* things. Things I can't even begin to describe." I breathed out, shaking my head. "Ever since the accident." Matty looked confused at this. Right. I didn't tell him about that. "The day before we left for here? I was late to the photoshoot cus there was this . . . this accident outside my favorite coffee place. It was a head-on collision. There was this guy whose—whose face got ripped off . . ." Matty was listening intently. I studied him a moment before continuing. "And I've been seeing that same ripped-off face ever since. It's been following me. I don't know what's going on, but I feel like it has something to do with that accident . . ."

Matty looked at the ground for a moment.

"I know you think I'm crazy. Maybe I am." I began shivering. "But th-that old woman said I brought something with me. What if—what if she wasn't that crazy? What if she was right?" I looked up at him. "What if something I brought with me is what hurt Dana?"

Matty thought for a moment. "Not saying I believe in it but . . . Well, devil's advocate, if there *is* some sort of entity or whatever following you around . . . what do you wanna do? See a psychic or something?"

"God no," I said solemnly. It was a fair question. One I hadn't even considered. Suppose there *was* something following me . . . just what the hell was I going to do about it? I mulled it over a moment. "I think . . . I think I need to go to a—a library or something, I don't . . ." I looked up at Matty, who looked at me with a question. I nodded. "I *need* to know what I'm dealing with and . . . I don't wanna be here, in this hotel." I looked up at him and shook my head. "I don't wanna be here."

It wasn't long after that conversation in Matty's hotel room that he and I set out to go to the Waikiki-Kapahulu Public Library, the closest library in town. Bless Matty. I could tell he didn't believe a single word that came out of my mouth. But he was being a good friend. For better or worse, he was a true ride or die.

Did I really think I was going to find what I needed at the local fucking library, though?

I mean, it was a start.

I just needed information. I needed information for whatever I was facing. A little jingle from an old animated TV show ran through my head about the joys of having a library card. The odd things that run through your head in times of stress, am I right?

We entered the hotel lobby when I felt what was starting to become a familiar sensation by this point. The feeling of being watched.

I slowly turned toward where I thought someone was watching me, ready to face anything.

Almost.

When I turned, though. It was not a man with a hat looking at me. It was . . .

Me.

I studied her . . . me. I studied me. She was staring directly at me, black hair down, standing still. She wore a white sundress with a flowery pattern. Her skin was slightly paler than mine, though. And her eyes . . . Her pupils were bright yellow. Like she was wearing yellow contacts. But she stood there, among the crowd and people walking, just staring at me. A big, toothy, cheesy smile on her face. Her eyes didn't blink. She looked almost fake. She didn't breathe, she didn't move. Just stood like a mannequin, a mannequin with a stupid smile. Nobody else seemed to notice her, standing like a statue. The crowd simply walked around her, but nobody else acknowledged her, like she wasn't even there. Slowly, fist clenched, I began walking toward her. Still, she didn't move. Her eyes just stared into mine.

"Rach?" Matty asked.

I turned around. Matty was looking at me with an eyebrow raised. "What're you doing?"

I looked back over to the other me. She wasn't there anymore. I grimaced as I searched for her, with no success. "Let's just get going."

CHAPTER 9

On a good day, I could barely suffer fools. On a day like that day? Day after my friend wound up in the hospital? Day I was having weird supernatural bullshit happen to me? I wasn't having any of it.

"So you guys honeymooning here, or what?" the Uber driver asked Matty and I. He was an older man with a baseball cap, a devilish smile, tanned skin, and blue Hawaiian shirt. Matty and I looked at each other awkwardly.

"No, just, uh, just friends," Matty responded politely.

"Ah, I gotcha, one of *those* deals. Know that one," the driver said with a suggestive smile and a dumb chuckle. "You know, there's plenty of great deals out here in Honolulu for *just friends*, great places too. They got Manoa Falls, for example. Beautiful view. Perfect place to take pictures and stuff in front of."

Matty must've been able to tell I was about to say something cus he tapped me and shook his head.

"Yeah, they got plenty o' restaurants for friends out here too. Best of the best. And have you been to Waikiki Beach yet? Absolutely magnificent. Perfect place for a lovely couple of kids like yourselves."

"You the fuckin' ad campaign?" I said under my breath. Matty elbowed me and shook his head.

The old man went on, like he didn't hear me. "Honolulu is the best place I've ever been. Absolutely beautiful, even in the rainy weather. Ain't ever been a better place. The wife loves it here. Say, where's you all from?"

"LA," Matty said.

"Oh, LA, I've been there once or twice."

"Really?"

"Oh yeah, saw Farah Fawcett eating at a diner at a table next to me off Hollywood Boulevard. She was hot shit! That was a time when movies were movies, ya know? Nowadays you got all that woke fairy bullshit. But movies in the '70s and '80s? Those were *real* movies. Don't make 'em like that anymore."

I looked at Matty and winked. "Yeah, those gosh-dern *fairies* ruined everything, huh?"

Matty rolled his eyes and huffed. The old man tried to backpedal a little.

"Well, I—I mean I got nothing against nobody. How they choose their life is their choice, ya know? Anyway—"

And the Uber driver continued his little speech about Hawaii like a preprogrammed fucking robot. I could've been bitchier. Part of me wanted to tell him I fucked a girl last night, but that'd raise too many questions from Matty. Questions I wasn't sure how to answer. Two stars, maybe even one, though. Fuck this guy.

I went quiet as I began thinking about where we were going and what we were doing. A library? Most people would just use Google. Hell, I'd be lying if I said it was a bright idea to go all the way to the public library for info. In fact, it was probably weird, outdated, and dumb. The truth was, though, I didn't wanna spend another minute in Tropical Springs. None of Hawaii felt safe at that point, but especially not the hotel. I dreaded going back to my room. I *suppose* I could start looking things up on my phone, but . . .

Actually, not a bad idea. Start looking things up. Give myself an idea of what to look up while at the libra—

Oh. As I looked at my phone, thoughts of doing just that deflated. My battery was at 15 percent. Leave it to me to not charge my fucking phone. I hate to say it, but typical Rachel move.

The building that was the Waikiki-Kapahulu Library looked almost like a little brown hut with large reflective windows. Type of place that had like three books on the bookshelves and had the audacity to call itself a library. Needless to say, I was less than amused.

"So, Rach . . ." Matty started.

"Yeah?"

"I have a very important question."

"What is it?"

"I get you wanted to not be at the hotel but . . . couldn't we have just looked up what you wanted on my laptop at a café? Did we really have to come here?"

I blinked and sighed without looking his way. "Shut up, Matt."

Lucky for me the inside of this place was bigger than the outside made it seem. Though still, it did seem rather small. I twisted my mouth before heading over to a computer. Matty sat beside me and I could feel an intense gaze from him. Immediately, I began a frantic search. Folklore involving skinned corpses, cryptids, real-life supernatural encounters—I searched them all and began grabbing books haphazardly off the shelves.

By the time I got back to my desk with a pile of books, Matty was looking at me with wide eyes. "You take a whole shelf?"

I plopped the books in front of him. "You're helping. Start searching."

"And what am I even looking for?"

"Ghosts with hats, demonic possessions, myths about skinned people. Top three topics."

Matty twisted his face. "I have ADHD, you really expect me to read?"

I nodded. "Yeah. Yeah, I do. It's life or death, Matt."

Almost immediately after saying that, I dove into the pile. I sped through each book in front of me as fast as I could to try to get as much information as possible. The thing about this search for information was I was quickly finding myths that were close to what I was experiencing, but not exactly. There was a hat-man ghost, but he seemed more likely to be just a shadow or a Benadryl hallucination (certainly not a man with a ripped-off face). There were doppelgänger and glitch-in-the-matrix stories, but I bought those about as much as I bought Matty's Vegas story. (The one where he hooked up with Adam Lambert? Sure, Matty, sure.) Finally, there were also stories of demonic possession. Looking at those objectively, though, most just seemed like abuse and mistreatment of the mentally ill. It was just dead end, after dead end, after dead end. The only thing that even remotely caught my attention in the search was a god in a book about various mythologies.

Xipe Totec, Aztec god of spring, agriculture, disease, and death. It was the face that caught my attention first. The art was oddly graphic for a mythology book. A meaty red body poorly hidden by flayed skin. According to the descriptions, he would wear other people's skin over his skinless body. Apparently this god required human sacrifices and there were explicit rituals where people were flayed all in service of this god. I was just beginning to read about him when Matty called my attention.

"Rachel . . . if there *is* an afterlife . . . why do you think some ghosts would wanna stay here?"

"I dunno," I said callously before turning back to the book.

"No, really. I mean . . . I guess I get the heaven-and-hell thing and wanting to avoid judgment but . . . I'm inclined to think here, our world, *is* hell."

I smirked up at him. "What are you on about?"

Matt shrugged, moving his jaw back and forth. "I dunno, think about it. Hell is supposed to be eternal suffering, right? A place where we're in an endless loop of torment. How much worse can it be than here on Earth? Like, why would a ghost wanna stay here?"

I lifted my eyebrow, then did my best to ignore him.

"You have genocides, *child bone cancer* is a thing, any day we could blow everything up with nukes. Don't even get me started on—"

I sighed, frustrated. "Matty, where is all this coming from?"

Matty shrugged. "Reading some of this stuff gets ya thinking."

"'Kay, well, think somewhere else. I'm trying to focus," I said gruffly before returning to my book.

Matty yawned, tossing his book on the table rather loudly. "Don't mind if I do," he said before standing and stretching. "Hey, I think I'm gonna walk around a bit. Maybe tan in the sun a bit outside. Give me a call if you need me?"

I glared at him. Whatever, he wasn't helping much anyway. "Sure."

"Good luck with . . ." he began before gesturing his hands toward the books. "This." With that he left. I sighed before looking at the book he'd tossed. He put it down so loudly earlier I was almost sure a little librarian lady was going to angrily tell us to shush. I sighed, staring at it, when I realized it wasn't a book I picked up at all.

The hell?

I looked up and couldn't find Matty anywhere. What the hell was he doing with this book? I picked it up and studied the cover, which had some sort of stone face carved into a wall with moss beside it.

Forgotten Worlds: A Shortlist of Archaeological Finds and Artifacts.

I tilted my head. Was he even searching for what I fucking told him to? I cursed Matty under my breath before quickly flipping through the book. The book was a regular British museum of ancient artifacts. Bowls and crap. I shook my head and was about to put the book aside when I saw something . . . interesting. Or rather, I should say I felt pulled to it. It was a similar sensation to . . .

I opened up the book and sprawled it out on the desk in front of me. It wasn't a photo that took up a whole page. If anything, it barely took up a corner, but I felt drawn to it all the same.

It was an ancient statue of a woman. A pregnant woman standing, completely naked. She looked like she had hands for feet, her arms were missing, and her face looked completely sanded off by time; the yellowish stone where her face should've been was an odd orangish-red. A chill went up my spine studying the picture. I looked at the caption below.

The Red-Faced Madonna - Discovered in modern Yemen back in 1923, this statue was found in an underground tomb by Dr. Joseph H. Cartright. To this day, the civilization of origin for this artifact is unknown.

I stared at the statue in bewilderment. There was a . . . a sense of familiarity, though I had never seen it before. I felt like, through the pages, the thing was almost staring at me.

Don't look at the red.

I blinked, mesmerized by the picture. After a moment of staring at the strange statue, I finally gathered up the courage to turn the page. Nothing about the statue. Just about forgotten civilizations and artifacts from them. It quickly became rather clear that the articles within the text had nothing to do with the statue. Frustrated, I turned to the computer I was sitting in front of and searched the Red-Faced Madonna statue in Google. Immediately, I was brought to multiple sites detailing the statue, which was currently in a museum in Oxford. I skimmed through the information. The red on the statue was apparently a strange effect that was believed to be caused by oxidation, but archaeologists weren't entirely sure. Supposed symbol of fertility, yada yada yada. I sighed as I kept looking through the article. Basically, there was next to no info on the statue that archaeologists knew other than it dated back to very early civilization, almost caveman days. Dead end.

Don't look at the red.

The words Jennings shouted to me as she was being dragged away rang through my head.

Don't look at the red.

What the hell did that mean? I looked at the images of the Red-Faced Madonna in front of me. It took me a moment to get there, but I think the runner with a bad hip in the race was just about to cross the finish line. *Don't look at the red* . . . Red-Faced Madonna. The crimson skull face.

Red.

The color red.

On my mirror . . . there was a crudely drawn face on my mirror . . . done in my *red* lipstick.

Had Jennings known something?

I looked at the book again and stared long and hard at the picture of the statue. What did this have to do with anything?

At that moment, there was a sound like smacking lips. It was a gooey sound, like someone taking a bite out of a big juicy burger. It was followed by a soft "mm" by a woman. Was someone . . . eating something? I looked around, no one . . . no one was eating anything around me. The sound went on, though, a second moan sounding more sexual in nature. I looked at the people around me. Some students were studying at the desks nearby, an older man with gray hair was searching through the romance section, a heavyset librarian was looking at her computer. Nobody was looking at me, and certainly no one was eating. My eyes lingered on a sign that said *No Food or Drinks Allowed*, but I kept hearing the sounds . . . sounds like a woman was eating something tasty, and messy.

I felt a pinch on my ankle, like a bug bit me or something. Immediately I looked down, under my desk.

Another me looked back at me from under the desk, face covered in blood, yellow eyes staring at me, the tendons of my ankle wriggling from her mouth as her jaw relentlessly chewed and pulled flesh from my bones.

I screamed as loud as I could, falling out of my chair.

Within a blink, the other me disappeared. I immediately grabbed my ankle, panicking. It was . . . okay.

I was okay.

I breathed hard, looking into the dark corner that was under the desk I was just sitting at. My eyes searched the shadows. Where was that thing? The room was quiet overall. None of the library patrons had seemed to notice or care that I fell down screaming. None were paying attention. The older man was still looking through the romance novels, the librarian still stared at her computer, and the students still studied. The library was just . . . quiet.

I breathed out. That was . . . weird . . .

Then the older man in the romance section of the library began chuckling, still looking at the shelves. Eventually, those chuckles turned into laughter. He looked barely able to contain himself, at one point even bending over from the laughter. The librarian at her desk began laughing too, still looking at her computer. Her hand went to her forehead and she turned red, and she gasped like she was having a hard time breathing. The students at the desks nearby began laughing soon after too, still looking at their studies. Soon, other voices of laughter joined in. I got up, looking all around, terrified. The entire library was laughing, and it was *loud*.

Then just like that, they stopped, and the library was quiet again.

My phone was out of battery, so I couldn't call Matty to get the fuck outta there. I simply bolted as fast as I could and made my way out of the library. I fast walked into the Hawaiian sun, hyperventilating so badly I needed to lean against a nearby trash can and catch my breath.

"Matty?" I called out, looking around. The area around the library was mostly just fields of green grass. I searched with my eyes; I didn't see him. "Matt?" Now that I got a good look around, I realized this library was nowhere near the tourist trap parts of Waikiki. A bird cawed somewhere. I searched all around, frantically. No Matty in sight. For being in Waikiki, the vibe at the moment was oddly quiet. Only the soft wind and birds chattering could be heard, with the occasional car passing in the distance.

Where the fuck was Matt?

After searching a little more to see if Matt was indeed gone, I walked out and began walking down the long, long street. How was I gonna get back to the hotel? I was stranded without any battery in my phone to get an Uber. I didn't even know where to go or how to get back to the hotel if I used public transport. Despite this, the first chance I could, I hopped onto a bus, not even knowing where the hell I was going to end up. I rode it awhile, watching Hawaii from the window. In the bright sunlight, the vivid colors of Honolulu had an odd plasticity to them. None of it felt real. The people on the bus seemed wary of me, like I was an odd, dark cloud in their bright and chipper lives. Every time they looked at me, I looked back until they looked away, appearing deeply uncomfortable.

I supposed I just had that effect on people. The bruises and cuts on my face helped, though. I was okay with people not talking to me. I didn't have energy for conversation. And even if I did, what would I even say? *Lovely day we're having*? Yes, I'm having an absolutely lovely trip here in Hawaii. I'd have found the hypocrisy funny if I was in any sort of mood. I scanned the streets, half expecting to see the other me or the man with the hat at any corner. They were everywhere. I couldn't see them, but I knew they weren't far at any point.

It didn't take long to eventually find my way back to the hotel. After a bit of traveling downtown, I was able to figure out the route, and based purely on sunlight the whole trip probably took an hour. I slumped through the lobby of Tropical Springs, feeling woozy at this point from a lack of anything to eat. I thought I saw Trevon get hugged by what looked like two older versions of him, one male and one female, probably his parents. I was eyeing them when I caught another unrelated pair of eyes were watching me. The hotel manager, that Joan woman, stared at me from afar. Her eyes were transfixed on me, face cold and robotic. Her eyes followed me all the way to the elevator.

Once I got to the elevator, the gravity of going back to my room began to hit me. Would the man with the hat be up there? "Can't stop, won't stop," I muttered to myself, watching the elevator go up. "Can't stop, won't stop. Can't stop, won't stop." An abnormal dread filled me as I waited to reach my destination. I really didn't wanna go. I *really* didn't want to go. My eyes wet a bit. The elevator seemed like a slow crawl up to my floor.

"Please God, please," I whispered to myself. "Please don't let it get me. Please, please, please." My body shook as I watched the ground grow farther and farther away, the elevator climbing ever closer to my floor. When the doors opened. I braced myself. "Can't stop, won't stop." I got a grip on myself and walked out, every step feeling heavier than the last.

Unlike usual, the hall wasn't silent.

A low hum of a vacuum cleaner filled the air.

I breathed a little easier as I walked the spiraling, cramped hallway. As I did, the vacuum sound got louder and louder. By the time I got to my room, I could see the wire plugged in nearby for the vacuum cleaner. I looked down the hall to see a husky Latin woman in a maid outfit. She was minding her own business, vacuuming like she didn't even hear me. I breathed out, staring at her, then turned to my door and began fiddling with the knob, before taking one last look at her. This time she was not focusing on her work, but rather looking at me. I studied her, now that she was. Round face, a lot of makeup, hair tied back, and a name tag that looked like it might've said something like *Rosa Hernandez*. I politely waved and she nodded before returning to her work.

Normal. Cool. Nice change of pace.

When I got back into my room, I hooked up my phone and let it charge for a few minutes before turning it on. When I turned it on . . .

Seventeen missed calls.

I blinked. Holy fuck. They were all from Matty and Penelope. I squinted, looking at the time. I had been gone for at least two hours. I shook my head, passed all the angry/worried texts from Matty, and just gave him a call.

"Rachel? Rachel, what the fuck!"

"Hello to you too."

"Where are you, are you okay?"

"What? I walked out of the library and you weren't there. Phone was dead, had to take the bus."

"Okay, you're at the hotel, though?"

"Yeah. Just got back and charged up my phone a bit."

"That's a relief . . ."

There was a pause.

"Have you . . . Have you seen my texts yet?"

"No . . . Why?"

Matty paused. "Uh . . . Fuck. I don't know how to tell you this."

"What's up?"

"It's—it's Dana, she's . . ."

At that crushing moment, I knew. I knew what Matty was going to say. "What about Dana?"

"She, uh, she had an aneurysm and . . . Doctors say that her brain isn't showing any signs of activity. Rach, only her body's alive. Dana's gone."

My heart sank like a ton of bricks. What? I blinked in disbelief. Dana? My beautiful friend Dana? Gone?

"They're, uh . . . They're gonna keep her alive long enough for loved ones to say goodbye. Then they're gonna pull the plug."

I felt my tongue lodge in my throat.

"Rachel?"

I breathed out, processing the information. "Um . . . I'm here," I said, my voice shaking. "Um . . . Wow."

". . . Yeah."

My eyes teared up. "We have to find out what this thing is, Matt."

"What?"

"The thing that attacked her. I have a lead."

There was a silence on the phone.

"L . . . lead?"

A sort of static-like noise sounded on the phone.

"Yeah, a lead. I think I have an idea what might be behind this."

"Wha . . . re yo . . . alk . . . out?"

The noise began to get louder, breaking up Matty's voice.

"Matty, are you in a tunnel or something? It's getting hard to hear you."

"Ra . . . can . . . you . . . elp. I love you, bu . . ."

The static sound was getting louder and more aggressive, hurting my ear.

"Matty? Hello? Can you hear me?"

"Rach?"

The phone call dropped. I looked at my phone and it said, *Call Lost*. I winced. What the hell? I had full bars. Maybe it was something on his end? Immediately I tried calling him again. Rather quickly I was met with an automated message.

"I'm sorry, but the number you dialed is no longer in service. Goodbye."

I pulled away and called him again, frustrated. Again, met with the same message. I tried maybe a few more times before I eventually threw my phone onto the bed to let it charge.

Fucking service. Probably didn't pay his phone bill, knowing him. I rubbed my eyes, the hunger headache truly beginning to set in. Know what I needed? A fucking cigarette. I went to my purse, curious if I still had a lighter, but I found the one I handed to that weird homeless person the night before. I tilted my head as I pulled it out. I don't remember buying two, and I definitely gave him the lighter. The hell? Too tired and frankly overstimulated by the weird at this point, I didn't question it for long.

Screw it.

I pulled out my cigs and headed toward my balcony, opening the door. A light oceanic breeze hit my face as I stepped out and lit my cigarette with a little trouble. I swore the bright beauty of Honolulu was mocking me. The building I was in cast a long shadow over the courtyard with the pool down below. Down below, I could hear some ukulele music on some speakers faintly in the distance.

Dana was brain-dead.

I had to sit with that for a moment.

Dana was brain-dead, and I was directly responsible.

If I wasn't here, Dana would be getting happily married tomorrow. If I wasn't here, Dana would be enjoying this beautiful scenery. If I wasn't . . . here. I leaned on my railing and put my hand on my face. Something resembling a sob came out of my mouth, but it felt blocked up. Like somehow, I was emotionally constipated. My face crumpled on its own, but I didn't feel like I was even in my own body.

She had so much going for her.

"Dana . . ." I whimpered. My face felt numb, and my fingers came away wet from holding it.

She had everything.

I began breaking down right there, but it didn't even feel like me. I knew I was supposedly feeling the emotion, but I felt too numb to properly feel the pain. I pulled my hand away and put out my cigarette, then I noticed something in the pool below.

Among the crowd of people in the pool, a black-haired lady in a black bikini was lying on her back. She was floating in the water and smiling at me.

I . . . I knew that face.

A chill began to creep over me as I watched the lady smile at me, and giggle at something. She was bone skinny but looked at peace at that moment. Her face was clear and serene as she seemed to stare directly at me, before she closed her eyes and continued relaxing. I stared in bewilderment, backing away into my hotel room.

Just then a loud scraping sound came from the wall next to me, causing me to jump and scream out, "Fuck!" My attention quickly turned toward the wall, when I realized: That was the same wall that Jennings had been making sounds behind. The harsh sound reminded me of someone moving furniture behind the wall. In theory, Jennings shouldn't have been in there, though, right? She was dead. Tried scraping off her . . .

That's when I finally put two and two together.

She tried scraping off her face, but slammed her head into the wall to cave in her own skull. Claimed I brought "it" with me. It *found* her. She killed herself because it found her. It found her and was trying to take off her face.

I brought it. And that was why she tried to kill me. She knew.

Steadily, I approached the wall as what sounded like a TV turned on in the other room. I squinted as I stepped toward it. There was a thin sheen of something on the wall; it looked like it was glistening. I reached my hand out to touch it and felt water over my fingers. That wall was completely wet. I pulled away and looked at my hand as droplets of water dripped from my fingertips. I had to get over there. I had to get into Jennings's apartment.

Without thinking, I headed for my front door like a bat out of hell. I opened it almost as fast as I could before being met with the cleaning lady from before. *Rosa Gonzalez*, her name tag read. She was standing directly in front of my door.

"Oop! Just caught ya as you were heading out. Thank goodness!" She smiled with a too-huge smile.

I blinked. "Um . . . I-I'm sorry?" I asked, caught off guard.

"I've been wanting to talk to you. Been hearing all about you, mija. I heard you were the neighbor of that *nasty* lady!" she said in her most HR-appropriate, overly friendly way.

It took me a moment to process that there was someone in front of me, let alone a weirdo that was blocking my doorway. "Uh, yeah—"

"None of us liked her, you know. She was a . . . a *nasty* person. Never let us help her or nothing. Never let us in. Just a—a very *dirty* person."

"Uh . . ."

"Never really fit in around here, ya know? . . . Was just *strange*." The woman reached out and lifted my chin "Oh, *pobrecita*, she did a *nasty* job on you, huh? Ya know, my cousin, she has a cream she sells. It'd heal that lovely skin right up!"

I blinked as I stared at her, slowly removing my head from her hand.

"Thanks, I'm good, though . . ." I said, backing away a little. She stared at me unblinkingly. She was . . . too pleasant. She moved her jaw side to side, grinding her teeth. I blinked. I cleared my throat. "Um, ya know . . . I'd *love* to talk about this more some other time, but actually, I *just* realized I have to call my friend and see how he's . . ."

I stared at her and realized she wasn't making eye contact with me, but rather above me, at my forehead. I squinted as I stared at her. She was completely still. Not even breathing. I slowly began backing away.

"Housekeeping. Housekeeping," she began saying to no one as I started to close the door on her. "Housekeeping. Housekeeping." I managed to close the door completely. Even as I did, I could hear her still saying, "Housekeeping." With that, I backed away from the door.

Alright. Okay . . . The thing attacked me in the library. It stopped me from going out my door. I swallowed hard. It was trying to keep me from finding information about it. That had to be why. There was *something* in Jennings's apartment that would give me answers. The truth was in her hotel room. I was sure of it. That was why it blocked me just now . . .

"You don't want me to know something, do you?" I said under my breath to no one. "You're keeping me from something . . ."

I glanced at my balcony and began heading toward it. Outside, I looked at the barrier that separated my balcony from the room next door. It was a relatively small wall. Not very thick. As a trial, I reached around it and found that I was able to firmly place my hand on the other side.

I gulped and looked down.

Fuck, that was a long way down.

I froze for a moment and felt the wind on my face. Fall from this height and I was a goner. Was I really thinking about doing this? I stared down below for a moment. People from this height looked like ants. If I fell from here, I wouldn't survive. My skinny body shook as my eyes widened. "Can't stop, won't stop. Can't stop, won't stop." I pulled the chair to the corner of the balcony. Hesitantly, I stood on it and began hugging the wall. My foot felt like it might slip as soon as I put it on the edge of my railing. "Fuck me. Fuck me."

You know that thing where they say to not look down when doing something dangerous high up? Yeah, I couldn't help but look down.

There was a booming sound coming from inside my hotel room. So loud it almost made me fall off.

"*Housekeeping!*" the cleaning lady screamed from outside my door, now sounding much more hostile. "*Rachel!*" the voice said, dropping by octaves, like it was turning from feminine to masculine. *"Come wash these fucking dishes like I fucking told you!"* The voice was definitely male now, and familiar, slightly distorted. I breathed hard as the door knocked hard again. *"Ungrateful bitch!"* Something in me kicked into gear, hearing that voice. I wrapped my leg around that corner wall, hugging it for dear life as wind blew through my hair.

I closed my eyes hard as I tried to get around it, my back to the wind. A fall backward and I was done for.

The knocking on my hotel room door became more frantic, like it was about to make the door come off its hinges, and the sound of the voice deepened and distorted. *"Raaaaaacheeeeel! Raaaaaacheeeeeel!"*

By the time I got both feet on the ground of the neighboring balcony, the knocking completely stopped. I backed away from the railing as fast as I could, breathing ragged breaths. I listened for a moment. No sound. None at all. Just the faint music in the distance and the soft breeze. I wiped my forehead, which was covered in sweat, and closed my eyes hard. That was arguably the dumbest thing I had ever done in my life. I thought about what I just heard the thing say . . .

About the dishes.

How did it—

How *the fuck* did it know about that?

I hyperventilated as a plethora of nasty memories flashed through my mind. No.

I didn't want to think about that. Not the dishes conversation. Never the dishes conversation. Not even my nightmares dared.

Somehow, this thing knew intimate details. Things I never told anyone. There was only the two of us in our duplex when he said that. There was only . . .

It took me a moment to snap myself out of falling down the mental rabbit hole that was Greg. My heart pounded hard in my chest as I put a hand there and caught my breath.

This thing played dirty. Very dirty.

I turned to the glass door that would lead into Jennings's apartment. I could only see my reflection in the glass, the way the light refracted off it. I swallowed hard, stepping toward the door, grabbing the handle, and opening it with relative ease.

The first thing to hit me was the stench. It was pungent and putrid. Like rotting food and feces. I gagged, taking a breath outside before taking a deep breath in and covering my nose.

Trash littered the floor. Papers and food containers mainly. There wasn't anywhere in the hotel room that you could reasonably step without stepping on some sort of trash. Any space on the floor that you could see was faded, long-outdated carpet, or carpet that had been ripped out to reveal concrete. There was no bed, just a disgusting-looking armchair well past its heyday. Judging by how the trash around it was tossed, it was safe to assume *that* was the piece of furniture that had been dragged so obnoxiously. The light leaking in through the open balcony door was more or less the only light seeping into the room, since the windows had curtains drawn over them. The walls were completely covered in red writing that looked like it might've been done with Crayola. Phrases like **Don't look at the red** and **the red** and **fear the red** were written in sloppy childlike writing all over the walls in a haphazard and chaotic manner. There were shelves and shelves of VHS tapes, mostly seeming home recorded with handwritten labels just as illegible as the notes on the wall. The TV was on but it was playing some old black-and-white movie I didn't recognize. On another part of exposed wall I saw a bunch of sloppily written notes, held up with Band-Aids, centered around an old black-and-white photo of a portly man with a white hat holding the Red-Faced Madonna statue surrounded by workers with shovels; standing nearby was a taller, thinner man with a gaunt face in darker clothes.

I tried reading the notes, but for the life of me, I couldn't read what the hell they said. One definitely said *Cartwright*. Then another said something about water. This woman had such sloppy handwriting that I could not make out what the hell any of it meant.

I ventured farther into the hotel room to find a pair of orange construction buckets (and thus the primary source of the stench). Flies buzzed around them as they stood next to a wall, and it only took a quick glance to confirm my suspicions and gag. I quickly looked away, noticing a shelf in front of a door that would've been the bathroom. I took a brief look at the kitchen and noticed that the sink was completely taped off with bright yellow tape, like someone was trying to prevent usage of the sink at all.

"What kind of life were you living, Jennings?" I asked under my breath before heading to the room with the TV again. I scanned the shelves with the VHS tapes before running into something I wasn't expecting.

It was . . . a Polaroid photo of Dana and I, just lying on the shelf. We were smiling at the camera and holding beers with one hand, while our other arms were around each other. I tilted my head and lifted it. I didn't remember ever taking such a photo. It was us, though. Without a doubt.

How the hell did she even get this?

I breathed out, trying to keep my cool. This was just getting weirder. I put the photo down, trying to shake off the eerie feeling it gave me, and chose one of the VHS tapes at random. I kicked some of the trash around to make myself a place to sit on the ground. Carefully, I turned down the volume on what I now realized was an older television and put the VHS into the VCR. I looked at the screen, which was blue, and pressed play. Immediately it looked like some *Ancient Aliens*-type documentary. Some guy with glasses that looked like George Lucas minus a few pounds was on-screen.

"Cartright and Franklin, they were inseparable." The camera zoomed in on a black-and-white picture of two men, one portly and one gaunt. "To the point where when the accident with the train happened, Cartright was absolutely devastated by his friend's sudden death. All of the sudden, he had to enjoy his archaeological success ultimately alone, and according to his close friends, it never sat right with him. He went to his deathbed in his eighties still grieving his friend."

The screen transitioned. This time to some sort of talk show from the '80s or '90s. A Latin woman spoke gleefully into the camera. "Up next, we have a father with a boy that believes he is being haunted by a malevolent spirit."

The screen flicked, revealing a teenage boy sitting in an arm chair next to the woman. "It—it all happened so fast, ya know. This guy got— He got his face like torn off by the boat. And for some reason, like, I was shocked but— I just, I had to get a picture. I know I was raised right and it, uh, it ain't like me to do things like that. But I did it, and um . . . ever since, I've been seeing weird—"

The screen flicked, still in the 1980s. This time it was a pair of news anchors: "Our top story tonight, a teenage girl murders her parents before committing suicide in a particularly disturbing manner. Authorities say she scratched off her own face with a kitchen knife after brutally butchering her fam—"

The screen flicked again. This time it was some sort of old evangelical program. Some middle-aged guy was talking to a very old man in front of a cross. "Yes. You can call me crazy, Reverend. Lord as my witness. I know what I sound like, but I've *seen* the devil. He's got a red face, no horns or nothing, just . . . bone. Like a skull. And I need salvation, cus he's coming to get m—"

Screen flicked again. This time the footage looked more 2000s. An Indian doctor was standing over a screaming little girl, the whites of her eyes a frightening red. The deepest shade I'd ever seen. She was being held down by her scared, crying parents. The documentary cut to the Indian doctor talking to the camera, his voice dubbed over by an English speaker.

"Her case is one of the worst I've ever seen. Nadia's parents have run out of options. Even with the best in modern medicine, we can't figure out what's wrong and her condition is only getting worse. She keeps scratching her fac—"

Now there was a middle-aged woman, her eyes wet and red from crying. The camera filming had to be old and low tech. "I—I keep seeing this man with a hat. He's got a—a red face. I don't what he wants from me. I don't know what he—" The woman began breaking down crying.

The TV flicked again to the teenage boy on the talk show. This time he was being held down by security and his father. The boy was screaming and crying:

"He's behind you! I'm behind you!" His face was planted into the ground as he squirmed, his face completely distraught. *"I'm behind yoooo—"*

The TV flicked one more time, and I saw something I didn't expect. I saw . . .

My stomach did a somersault and a lump formed in my throat.

I saw me.

I was sitting in what looked to be a police questioning room. It looked like it was from a camera feed. I was in different clothing than I was wearing at the moment, but it was definitely *my* clothing. Gene Simmons was on my black shirt from what I could make out. I also had nasty bruises on my face—different bruises, though—and my eye was swollen shut.

"Tell us again, what happened the night of the tenth?"

Wait . . . This was familiar . . . How did . . . My heart sank as I recognized what this was.

The me on the screen breathed out, shaking my head. "Greg, he . . . he made me some—some vegan meal. He keeps doing that, even though I'm not vegan." The me on-screen paused for a moment and shook her head. "So anyway, I just got back from a long day at work. I didn't even feel like eating. He, um, he knew I had a rough day, promised he'd make me a nice meal. When I get home, though, he, um he demands I do chores. Like, not asks. He starts demanding. Not his first time he's done this, but . . . I had a bad day . . . I—I refused."

I closed my eyes in shame. I remembered this. The me on-screen started crying.

"I—I don't think he meant . . . I don't think he meant to hurt me . . . I don't think he . . ."

My eyes watered and I put my hand on my forehead. I was such a fucking idiot. An absolute fucking idiot. To think, I had tried to go back to him after this. I would never forgive myself for that. I would never forgive myself for letting him do what he did. My lips trembled in shame.

The tape stopped playing sounds, but it took me a moment to look up. How the hell did Jennings even get this? This wasn't . . . I breathed hard and looked up. The screen was frozen.

The me on the screen was looking at me and smiling.

The oh-so-familiar grinding noise sounded behind me. I slowly turned around, trembling.

The other me was sitting behind me, her yellow eyes staring into mine, a big shit-eating vacant grin on her face, grinding her teeth but otherwise perfectly still.

Before I could even tell what was happening, she violently pushed me down to the trash-covered ground. The other me pinned me down, putting her hands over my arms, moving all the while not unlike a stop-motion figure. The skin of her hands was rough like sandpaper, almost like the skin of some creature at an aquarium. I screamed as she shook violently, jittering her head from side to side, all the while staring at me with those horrible, wild, yellow eyes. There was something horribly lifeless yet frantic about her movement. Like someone animating a doll or something. Her cheeks puffed out like she was about to vomit and her body lurched accordingly. I screamed bloody murder and tried my best to get out from under her, but it was like trying to move concrete.

She opened her mouth, and another lily-white hand attached to a full arm extended from between her lips. That hand went over my mouth and gripped my face with an iron grip. It began to squeeze, the pressure of the grip feeling like it was crushing my bones. The other me seemed to continue smiling at me, even with an arm jutting out of her mouth. Her eyes began rolling back into her head.

I awoke with a jolt, somewhere outside. The sun was shining bright, so bright it made my eyes hurt. The sound of waves crashed nearby.

"Jesus, you wake up like you were in a war." Penelope's voice, laughing.

I looked around. Penelope and I were on plastic chairs near the beach. We were dressed in sun hats, sunglasses, and bikinis. I took off my sunglasses and breathed hard, hearing the commotion of all the other tourists around me. Families, surfers, all sorts of people. How the hell did I get here?

"I wasn't gonna wake you. You looked like you needed the sleep. You get a good rest, babe?" Penelope asked, sipping what looked like a piña colada.

"What're we doing here?" I asked raggedly, sitting up.

Penelope giggled that pixie giggle that she did. "Getting some R and R. What else you supposed to do on a Hawaiian trip?"

"But, Dana . . ." I started, twisting my face. "Wh-what about Dana?"

Penelope thought for a moment and shrugged. "There's not much we could do. I mean, all we can do is wait for her to heal up, then we can enjoy times like this with her too."

I took offense and sat up. "H-heal up? Sh— Penny, what do you mean *heal up*? She's *brain-dead*, remember? You don't *heal* from being *brain-dead*."

Penelope stared at me long and hard, completely caught off guard. "Is—is that supposed to be some kind of joke, Rach? It's not funny."

"It's not a joke. Remember? She had an aneurysm and she's gone. Our friend is *dead*, more or less." Penny only stared at me in response. I continued, "W-we have to go visit her. Before they pull the plug, we have to say goodbye."

Penelope leaned in, looking over her sunglasses, analyzing me for a second. "Rachel, what're you talking about? We *just* got back from the hospital. She was fine, remember? Doctor said she was in stable condition."

I blinked. "What?"

"Rach, you're kinda freaking me out, girlie. We were just at the hospital, remember? Visited Dana. Doctors told us she was in and out of consciousness but on the mend. Then we decided we needed some beach time to cheer ourselves up. *You and I.* We decided to have girl time. You just had a nap and woke up all . . . *weird* . . ."

I blinked, stressing out. "Bu . . ." I started. I couldn't scramble any thoughts together. "But Matty *told me* she was . . ." My throat felt as dry as sandpaper. "Wh-why would he tell me that she was brain-dead?"

Penelope scrunched up her face. "Rach . . . Who the hell is Matty?"

CHAPTER 10

I stared at Penelope for a solid ten seconds before words crept their way out of my mouth.

"M . . . Matty. You know . . . *Matty*."

Penelope squinted, a dumbfounded expression written all over her usually wise face. "I . . . I don't think I've ever met this Matty . . . Is he a friend of yours? Is he here in . . . Waikiki?"

I searched her eyes. She seemed . . . serious. Like she genuinely didn't know who I was talking about. I licked my lips. Something was off. I assessed my situation. The way she continued to look at me . . . Something was wrong.

"Um, I'm sorry I . . ." What do I say at a moment like this? "I guess . . . I woke up kinda . . ." I looked up and saw Penelope's eyes staring deep into my soul. "Confused."

Penelope grabbed my hand and caressed it. She looked at it for a moment. "Um, Rach . . ." She thought deep for a moment, eventually sighing. "It's—it's okay." She stared at me with those beautiful hazel eyes. I couldn't help but get caught in them. They had an old, soulful wisdom to them. I could look at her eyes for days. Even in my vulnerable, confused state, those eyes felt safe. "Before what happened, Dana and I talked about what you have been through in the past . . ." She shook her head, lifted my hand, and kissed it. Then she put it to her chest, over her heart. "I am so sorry you went through that, Rach." My heart fluttered. Her skin was warm underneath my fingertips. She used the fingers on her other hand to brush my hair out of my face before placing it on my shoulder. "I just . . . I want you to know, I'm here for you. We haven't known each other for long, but . . . I'm here for you and I care for you. Okay?" I stared hard at her, processing what she was saying. "Whatever you're going through . . . You've been brave *enough*. You don't have to fight your battles alone. Okay?"

I stared at her eyes, completely vulnerable. My heart fluttered. I blushed slightly, politely pulling my hand away. "Y-yeah . . ." I nodded. "O-okay . . ." She pulled me into a tight hug as my mind began to ask questions.

Why was she acting like she didn't know Matty?

It wasn't long after that conversation that she and I went to a beachside bar. Once there and ordering a very alcoholic-friendly drink, I pulled out my phone from my purse and looked at my messages.

There weren't any from Matty.

That was . . . odd. He'd tried to text me a half a billion times about Dana. I *knew* he did that. I was completely cognizant and aware that he did. The next thing I tried to do was give him a call. Quickly, I searched for his number in my phonebook.

The only person under "M" was "Mom."

I blinked. "The fuck?" I muttered under my breath. Matty had been my best friend since high school. We survived Burbank High together. His number had been a mainstay in my phone for a very long time. Even during our worst fights, I never deleted his number. I scrolled the rest of my contacts to see if he might be under any other name, with no such luck.

What made me start to panic was when I checked social media.

Not a single photo of my best friend to be found. I looked at our Europe trip together, through my high school years; all the photos that ever had him were *gone*. I searched his usernames, but according to social media, no user had ever had those names. I even searched his boyfriend Frankie's social media and found Frankie in the same couple photos he had with Matty but with a different, completely unfamiliar man altogether. This man was named José, and other than his relationship to Frankie, there was nothing else he and Matty had in common based on what I saw while stalking his social media.

I didn't imagine over fourteen years of friendship with my best friend. There was no fucking way. A pit formed in my stomach as I tried every method I could think of to find my friend via my phone. It was like . . . he was gone. Not in a kidnapped sort of way. Gone, like he never existed. A deep sense of dread came over me as I relentlessly searched my phone. The fuck happened to my dear, dear Matty?

As I was frantically looking over my social media and Penelope chatted at the bar with the bartender, I felt a tap on my opposite shoulder.

A pretty, young blonde thing with big eyes and a blue bikini was looking at me, all doe-eyed. She couldn't have been older than eighteen.

"Excuse me, miss. You're Eveline Apple, aren't you?"

I merely glared at her in response.

"I'm a—I'm a huge fan. I follow your Instagram religiously."

I didn't answer, merely taking a sip of my cocktail.

"I, um, I'm actually trying to break into modeling myself. I have a bit of a following on Instagram and, uh . . . I was wondering if you wanted to collab or something sometime? You know, do a shoot, maybe out here on the beach or something. Whatever you're comfortable wi—"

"Right." I spewed a chuckle at the end. It took me a moment before my mouth slid into a wry grin. "Un-fucking-believable." I breathed out, shaking my head. "No. No, I really fucking don't."

The blonde youngster looked caught off guard by this response. "Uh . . . O-okay—"

"Do you see me right now? Here at a bar, in a bikini, getting wasted? Does it look like a time to try to approach me about business? Does it *look* like I'm trying to work here? Half naked, tits out."

"Uh, I-I'm sorry if I offended you, it's just—"

"You know, I should be *fucking* vacationing right now. But I'm not. And you know why I'm not? My friend is in the hospital. My friend is in the hospital, and another one— I don't know where he fucking is! I'm not exactly in the mood to be approached by the long-lost Olsen twin."

"I—I just—"

"*You just—you just?* You're just another pretty face that will become faceless in the algorithm. One with the gall to approach me *out of the blue on my vacation* to do something for *you* cus all you care about is yourself like every other Insta model. Fuck you. Fuck you, and fuck off."

I turned and drank some more of my cocktail. Turned back to see her still standing there, absolutely shocked.

"Do you mind?" I added.

With that, she turned away and walked off, almost in a daze.

"Don't you think you went a little overboard there?" Penelope asked by my side.

I shook my head and sipped my drink, unable to come up with any proper reply. Penelope walked off, and I heard her say, "Hey, wait a second!" to someone.

Was it fucked-up of me to chew the model out? Yeah. But my best friend in the world just disappeared off the face of the Earth. Another one is in the hospital, *and* I have some weird ghost thing haunting me. Weep me a goddamn river with that Instagram model's woes. God forbid people have real problems. I continued searching for evidence online of Matt until we eventually left that little seaside bar. Still no sign of him.

It was only once I asked the hotel desk if my friend Matthew Vasquez checked in did I know for sure he had disappeared.

"I'm sorry, it doesn't appear anybody by that name has checked into this hotel."

"You sure? Not in room seventeen thirty-two?"

The person at the front desk shook her head, staring at the screen. "That room is completely empty. Doesn't look like we have anybody by that name scheduled to be in there either."

My heart felt a sort of hopelessness as I tapped the desk and thanked the clerk.

As I rode the elevator, I really began to think about the implications of Matty's disappearance. Clearly I didn't just imagine fourteen years of friendship. There's no way. The only logical conclusion was . . . somehow he was erased from reality. The idea of that felt like a stab to the gut. Penelope really seemed like she had no idea who I was talking about. My mouth twisted. It was the feeling of dreaming of someone you swore you thought was real, only to wake up and realize the person you dreamed about never existed. But Matty *did* exist. He was my crazy best friend. The one that drove cars fast and told tall tales and was a fashionista that had more clothes and hair products than I would ever know what to do with. And he was gone. I looked up at nothing. "You give him back," I muttered under my breath. "You fucking give him back." When the elevator arrived on the seventeenth floor, I turned right instead of left, down Matty's hall. I rushed it like a raging bull, arriving at his door in what felt like seconds. I was about to knock hard when a thought occurred to me.

He wasn't going to be there.

Shaking this thought off, I banged on the door.

"Matty?"

Silence.

I banged on the door again. "Matty, come out. This isn't funny." No answer still. I aggressively knocked on the door. "Matty!"

Nothing.

There were no sounds behind the door, no life in the halls, nothing to indicate that there was a resident in there.

My eyes strained as I looked at his door number. I leaned my head against the door. "Matty, please . . ." It was a crushing weight. It felt like the knowledge one gets when someone close to them has died. That sinking feeling that you will never see them in the flesh again. The horrible feeling that all you really have left of them were memories. To say it was awful would be an understatement. "Matty, come back to me . . . please." I put my hand on the door. "I need you."

It took a lot of strength to peel away from that door. I backed away too, keeping it in view in case Matty ever poked his head out. No such luck.

When making my way to my own room, the walk felt lonely. Not scary this time, just . . . like I had no one in the world. A tear managed to sneak its way out of my eye as I continued to look back, even though his door was well out of viewpoint. I walked the winding halls, the trip long and tedious. Eventually, my room door came into view. But of course, because my room came into view, so did room 1718.

The door to 1718 was . . . open, though. The door to Jennings's room was open.

That was enough to make me stop, dead center in the hall. I licked my lips. Jennings's room. The room I was attacked in, the room that held the secrets of the thing that was hunting me. As if my feet could think before my head could, I walked straight for 1718. After taking a moment of mental preparation, I leaned forward and pushed open the door with my hand.

. . .

. . .

What?

The room was . . . *blank*. It looked like a normal hotel room. Matter of fact, it didn't look any different from the one I stayed in except my stuff wasn't in it. I walked in farther to investigate.

No trash on the floor, no writing on the walls, the sink wasn't taped up, and most damningly, there were no VHS tapes on shelves. It was . . . a hotel room like any other. The biggest tell that something was very different was the smell. What was once a smell that rivaled the dump or sewer in its aroma was now a lemony clean smell. A smell that might even be considered nice to some. The kinda smell that cleaning products produced and at times could be overpowering. The carpet was newer and neat. The walls had wallpaper that matched mine. It was . . . *a pleasant* room to be in . . . and it had no evidence that Jennings ever lived there. I frowned as I looked around, putting two and two together. I quickly pulled out my phone and typed up "the red madonna" in the search bar. Only images of the pop singer came up. Some images were scary, sure, cus Madonna . . . but no ancient statue was among any of the pictures. What the hell was going on?

Suddenly, I heard the front door behind me creak open. I turned, half expecting something horrible, but instead of another me with yellow eyes and a white sundress, I laid eyes on a familiar cleaning lady. It was the one that the thing took had taken the form of, but I looked at her name tag and it said *Rosa Hernandez*. Her heavily made-up face was considerably less pleasant than it was yesterday, bug-eyed and full of terror. "What're you doing here?"

"The, um—the door was open, so I—"

"You're not allowed in here. You need to go."

I felt slightly slack-jawed. "Um, okay but what—what happened to the tapes that were here?"

"I don't know what you're talking about. You need to leave."

"Jennings left stuff behind. *Where* is it?"

"I'mma call security if you don't leave this room, mija!"

"I just wanna know—"

"Get out! Now!"

"Fine! Jeez, I'll go!"

She began cussing at me in Spanish as I passed her, managing to take one final look at the room before Rosa slammed the door. Jennings's room, cleaned out overnight? I didn't buy it. Something weird was going on. Something very weird. I hurried into my room and shut the door. Okay . . . Matty was gone.

So was any information about the Red-Faced Madonna and any proof that Jennings lived next door. Did the thing that was after me have that much control over everything?

I passed a mirror in the hotel room and had to stop. I looked closer at my face. No purple marks, no cuts, my face was . . . perfectly fine. I thought for a moment, staring at my bruise-free face. No proof Jennings existed either. Could something have that much control? Could something just . . . erase people and information from the universe? I knew I wasn't crazy. I didn't imagine yesterday. I hadn't been imagining getting attacked by Jennings. I definitely didn't imagine an entire friendship. I knew what was real and what wasn't.

This thing . . . it was *trying* to convince me everything was a dream. That had to be it. It was *trying* to convince me this entire trip had been some sort of strange nightmare. I didn't buy it. When I got showered and changed, though, nothing happened. For a few hours I waited in my hotel room, watching TV, waiting for some sign of the entity to show itself. But it never did. No grinding. No thumps. No other me staring at me with a vacant smile.

Nothing.

It was almost more unsettling now that nothing happened, rather than something.

If the entity had the power to just completely erase people from existence, what else could it do?

After quite a bit of frustrated waiting, I decided to take an Uber back to Dana's hospital room. The trip there was actually quite beautiful. The sun set in a beautiful orange glow that painted Honolulu in what looked like the most beautiful lighting I had ever seen. A lighting that Matty would never see. I grimaced thinking this, as I looked out the window. It seemed like Honolulu only got ever more beautiful, but I could never fully appreciate its beauty. Flowers were vibrant, the town looked quaint and cute. It was almost an insult that such beauty be paired with the dread I felt. Nothing felt real. Nothing except this strange sense of doom that I couldn't quite place. I searched frantically for either the other me or the man with the hat, but somehow deep in my gut I knew searching for them was pointless. *They* weren't showing themselves.

The Red wasn't showing itself.

When I finally got to the hospital, I only had to wait in the waiting room for just a moment until a nurse brought me back to see Dana.

It was heart-wrenching to see her on her bed. Arms and legs in slings, wrapped in bandages. In a strange way it was altogether both a comfort and devastating to see her in such a way. On one hand, it was definite proof that the entity was out there and I wasn't completely crazy. On the other hand, one of my best friends was in the hospital, *like this*. The heart monitor beeped as she lay there, unconscious. I pulled up a chair beside her, watching her chest heave up and down. She looked damn near like a mummy with how much wrap was around her body. I frowned as I stared at her. "Dana . . . Dana. I—I don't know if you can hear me. Hell, I don't . . . I'm barely sure what's real anymore." I waited a moment, looking at what I could see of her cut-up face surrounded by the bandages. "Whatever did this to you took Matty. Like . . . he disappeared off the face of the Earth." I searched around the room a moment, a tear leaking from my eye before I stood up, taking steps closer until I was almost standing over her bed. "I—I don't know what the hell this thing is I'm up against. I don't know if I can survive it. I promise you, though . . . I'm gonna do everything I can to make things right." I carefully leaned in and kissed her forehead. "I promise."

There was a moment of silence as I stood by her bed, watching her sleep what seemed like an endless sleep. I spent a good chunk of time there. I didn't even turn when what I assumed was a nurse opened the door behind me. I kept fixated on my wounded friend.

"*The fuck* . . . are you doing here?" a familiar voice called out. I straightened and turned toward the voice. Trevon was standing in the doorway. He seemed . . . not okay. Obviously his eyes were red and watery, but that wasn't it.

He looked . . . clammy too. The skin under his eyes was slightly discolored, he had the sniffles, and he looked . . . jittery. Like a frightened cat.

"I said . . . the fuck you doing here?" he said again.

I swallowed, thinking for a moment. "Just . . . just paying my respects to Dana. That's all."

Trevon did something like a stiff nod and sniffled a bit. "Right." He moved around the room, toward the seats, never once taking eyes off me.

I blinked, taking an uncomfortable breath in. "Is there a reason you're looking at me like that?"

Trevon smiled this strangely accusatory smile. "Just thinking about the story you gave to the cops. 'Bout how you didn't see who did this to my precious Dana. I mean . . . it sounds like it was a hell of an event to just . . . not see."

"It's true. I didn't see who did this to her."

Trevon scratched his head. "Cops been asking all sorts of people at the club that night if they saw anything. Even wanted *my* fucking alibi." He shook his head, then carefully stood up. "See I was . . . at my bachelor party with my boys, thinking I was gonna get married this week." I turned away, looking at Dana, not him. He got close enough that I could practically taste his hot breath and loomed over me. "Penelope even had a solid alibi too. Knew exactly where she was, who she was talking to. *Everyone* has a solid story. Everyone . . . except you." He grabbed my arm, hard. "This time for real, tell me who did this to Dana."

I felt myself shrink a bit. "Let go of me."

"Tell me who did this."

I tried to pull away but couldn't. I folded my mouth. "Tre . . . you've clearly been hitting the methadone again . . . but just let me go and I'll forget—"

"You're hiding something. You tell me *right now*. You tell me right now or I'll—"

"If you don't let me go I will fucking scream," I said, turning toward him. He was staring at me with a pure, unbridled hatred, practically foaming at the mouth. His eyes were bloodshot, snot and drool coming out of his nose and mouth. I stared at him back, with an equal amount of hatred. "Let. Me. Go."

After a bit of a stare down, he finally let me go, a look of sarcasm on his face as he practically threw my arm back to my side. He sniffled. "Aight. Okay . . ." He chuckled, stepping back. "That's how you wanna play, okay." He swallowed angrily, looking feverish. "I'm gonna find out what you're hiding from me one way or another." His face twisted with a sort of gleeful malice. "But if you ain't gon' tell me. Get the fuck out." He licked his lips. "You don't *deserve* to be around Dana."

I quickly grabbed my purse and backed out of the hospital room, keeping eye contact with him the whole way.

Fucking creep.

Lying in my bed that night was impossible. I stared at the ceiling for hours. The waves rocked back and forth outside, but they never managed to lull me to sleep. I didn't know what was going on. I didn't know what I'd experienced. My mind was a rabbit hole and instead of solid questions, I merely had fragments of answers that didn't make sense no matter how I tried to put them together.

Matty was gone.

He was gone, and a part of me knew he was never coming back. He was taken by what Ms. Jennings had called "the Red." My best friend was taken by the Red. I closed my eyes hard.

What. Was. The Red?

It was clear that it took many forms. The hat man, the other me, and whoever else it wanted to be. It was also clear I had an enemy out there. An enemy I couldn't fight, an enemy I could never see coming nor predict, an enemy that could have been watching me right then, at that very second. So far, I had no way of predicting its comings and goings. No real motive for why it plagued me other than the fact I took a photo of a corpse. I knew that it lurked in every shadow and that it knew my darkest secrets. I didn't know why it wanted me.

But it did.

And if it was able to erase people off the face of the Earth and change the narrative of the world around me, what else was it capable of?

What the hell was I up against?

I started to imagine. Not dream. My eyes were open, staring at the ceiling. All the same, what I imagined felt like a dream. I imagined being down in the courtyard with the pool, in the middle of the night. I imagined walking forward, through bushes, and seeing the other me smiling at me, pushing someone's face into the water of the pool. It was hard to tell, but it looked like a man. Both figures' features were colored in the blue glow of the water below. The man with his head in the water struggled and struggled, water splashing everywhere. I walked to the edge of the pool, on the other end of it from the two figures. The man tried to get free of the other me's iron grip. Her yellow eyes never blinked as the man's arms slowed, more and more. Eventually the splashing and the bubbles stopped. The man hung limply, his upper half remaining buried in the pool. I stared a moment at the man who was now floating in the middle of the pool with his back breaching the surface of the water. Oddly enough, I didn't feel anything seeing his body. Just . . .

I don't know.

Apathy.

The other me stood up as if in fast motion. Her arm moved in stop-motion to her face, where she began to peel herself.

In real life I sat up and put my face in my hands.

I didn't know what was going on.

The world around me felt like it was losing all logic. Suddenly, it was trying to tell me things that never happened, and that scared me on a deeper, more primal level than I'd ever known.

I looked at the clock beside me. *4:30 a.m.*

I had been up this whole time, and even though I was tired, not an ounce of sleep had yet made itself available to me. Cursing myself, I got dressed and decided that if I could not sleep, I'd tire myself and force myself to sleep. I dressed and walked out. For once, while walking the halls, I almost dared something to happen. This time I'd be ready, I told myself. This time, I was prepared. Whether I truly was or wasn't remained to be seen.

Nothing popped out at me while roaming the halls. No eerie visions. No feelings of being watched. It was . . . just me. Me and what wound up being the lonely uninhabited streets of Waikiki. The ocean roared in the distance as I began to walk the sidewalk beside it, the morning air giving off a chill that made me thankful I had been smart enough to wear a hoodie. Wind blew through my hair as the lonely street lights painted my way forward. The sky above slowly lightened as I walked, looking out toward the sea, and I breathed in the sea air as I leaned against a nearby railing that separated Waikiki Beach from the sidewalk.

I looked around; not another soul in sight. I took off my shoes and hopped the railing, landing in the cool sand. I trudged through the sand toward the ocean and turned to make my way along the beach, carrying my shoes. The wind blew harder and I clutched myself. The world started to become blue.

It really was beautiful out here. I stood and enjoyed the scenery for a moment, taking in everything Waikiki Beach had to offer. After waiting a few minutes and allowing myself a moment to enjoy it, I decided it was time to head back.

Before I could, I saw someone in the distance.

What?

It was a rather familiar figure standing in the ocean, his back to me.

Matty.

That couldn't be right. What was he doing out here? Surely I was just imagining things. As I got closer, I saw his familiar back, the bougie jeans he'd wear, the very WeHo haircut he sported. He was just . . . standing in knee-deep water. He began turning around, looking at me. It was definitely him. He waved at me, smiling pleasantly.

It probably wasn't him. A part of me knew . . . but that didn't stop me from starting to run toward him. "Matty?" I called out. He merely smiled at me before turning his attention ahead of him and walking out, deeper into the ocean. "Matty!" I cried, tossing my shoes and hoodie with my phone and valuables aside onto the sand. I ran out into the ocean toward him, as he ventured farther and farther in. "Matty!"

Waves crashed down and he dove in, his head breaching the water before he turned and looked at me with a smile, almost like he was daring me to come after him. I began dog paddling in the water, trying to keep afloat as he swam farther and farther out into the water. I dove through the waves too, salt water burning my nostrils as I breached the surface. "Matty, come back!" I yelled, trying to swim through the ocean. The distance between us only widened. I frantically swam toward him, trying to catch up.

Suddenly, something gripped my ankle and pulled me down. I fought to get back up to the surface, getting a quick breath of air. "Matt—"

The thing dragged me back under the surface. I looked down and saw the other me down below, tugging at my ankle, that shit-eating smile. I also saw what looked like millions of disembodied white hands attached to long white arms headed straight for me, like some strange body of kelp. I kicked and screamed as they tugged at me with sandpaper-like skin, grasping onto arms, legs, clothes, whatever they could get their hands on. I struggled as hard as I could, briefly breaching the surface again before being pulled down. I saw Matty, just before going under again, get pulled down by hands as well.

Underwater, I watched as the hands tugged at either end of his body before hearing the awful sound of a rip and watching the top half and bottom half of the blurry figure sink down below, a cloud of dark red in the water forming ahead of me. Bubbles flew out of my mouth as the white arms tugged and tore at my clothes, dragging me deeper and deeper down into the dark. I twisted and turned my body viciously before the grip of the hands seemed to slip away. I shot up to the surface of the water, coughing as seawater spewed from my mouth.

I was . . . drowning.

My arms were tiring and I was having trouble keeping afloat as a wave pushed me down. A man's distorted voice whispered angrily in an unfamiliar language anytime my head was underwater. I breached the surface, fighting as the waves seemed insistent on dragging me farther out to sea.

I—I couldn't . . .

I couldn't breathe.

My arms and legs were getting sore and numb as they hopelessly dragged through the blue-green water, trying to get me to shore. Black crept in around the edges of my vision as I began to lose consciousness and fought tooth and nail to survive. I didn't want to die here. I did not want to die here.

As fate would have it, I felt sand underneath my fingertips and had to fight the waves trying to drag me back out. I coughed rigorously, gasping for air as I stumbled to my feet, my clothes dragging behind me. My movements were awkward as I finally stepped onto the beach, the surrounding sky fading to more a shade of purplish orange rather than the blue I started out this misadventure with. I dragged myself to the dry beach, seaweed and kelp tangled around my feet as I stumbled. Once I felt I was far away enough from the water, I fell onto my hands and knees, desperately fighting for air as my lungs burned.

A woman giggled somewhere and I looked toward the ocean to see the top of the other me's head peeking out from the water, staring directly at me with those horrid yellow eyes.

Yet again I felt the strong sensation of being watched. The familiar grinding sound joined it too. I looked behind me and the man in the hat was in the distance, his red skull face staring my way from the beach.

And that was when I passed out.

CHAPTER 11

"Do you think she's alive?" an awkward, high-pitched voice asked in the darkness.

"Dunno, she ain't breathed yet," another one, a little deeper, answered.

Something poked me in the boob.

"Hey miss . . . you alive?" a third voice, somewhere in between the two tonalities, asked.

"Yo, what the fuck, Bry?"

"What? I'm not touching it if it's a corpse."

"Dude, that's like mad disrespectful if she's dead."

"Yo, you think she's actually dead, though? Maybe we should call the police or somethin'."

Another poke. It jabbed a little harder this time. Ow. Fuck.

"Dude, she hasn't moved. She looks hella nasty too."

"Yo, stop filming!"

"What?"

"You're gonna get Logan Pauled!"

"Only if she's dead."

"We don't know yet!"

"Bruh, sto—"

Another jab. I sucked in a breath, and immediately began coughing.

"Oh, dude! Dude! She's alive! She's alive!"

I grit my teeth, still having trouble opening my eyes. "If you little fuckers don't stop poking my tits, I'll end you." I tried to say, though admittedly, it was probably too quiet to hear. Finally, I opened my eyes to see three dumb-looking preteen boys standing over me. They had tanned skin and shaggy hair. All three had shirts on but bathing suit shorts. One had a stick and a blue shirt on, another with a gray tank top was aiming his phone at my face, and the third, who was wearing yellow, was leaning in the closest. It was still early morning if the orange daylight was anything to go by.

"Oh shit! Yo, she's awake!"

I pushed the stick away from me. "Get that fucking thing away from me!" I sat up and kept coughing, shivers skittering over my body. I was still soaking wet and covered in sand.

"Yo, lady, you need like a hospital or something?"

I looked at the boy who asked it: backward hat, yellow shirt, long dangly brown hair. His face looked stupid and like a baby's. I rubbed my face, my head aching and my throat dry. I looked farther up the beach. There were people around now . . . and I couldn't see the clothes I'd tossed on the beach when chasing Matty. I scanned the beach in both directions and I couldn't see them anywhere. Shit. "Have you boys seen a black hoodie and some VANS shoes somewhere on this beach?"

The boys looked at each other. Shook their heads.

I sighed. "Forget it. I'm fine. No hospital."

My hotel key, my phone, and my wallet were all in that hoodie. If I lost it, I was fucked. My body shook like a leaf as I sat there for a moment, considering.

"You sure you don't need a hospital? You look . . . sick," another of the boys asked.

"Yeah, you were like, pretty dead-looking there a sec, Miss."

"No, no hospital . . ." I breathed out. "But I'll take a twenty-dollar bill if any of you got any to spare."

One of the boys reached into his wallet and pulled out a ten and a five. "It's, uh, it's all I got . . ."

I snatched it out of his hand before he had a chance to think about it too much. "Thanks." I greedily looked at the money, crumbling it up in my hand and deciding against putting it in my wet pants pocket just yet.

It wasn't too long before the boys eventually fucked off. (I'll spare you/myself the details of the idiotic conversation they tried to have with me). Then I was left wandering the beach, alone. I felt homeless while desperately searching for my phone and shoes. My clothes were ripped up and barely hanging on my body, and my hair was an absolute mess. I'm sure I didn't look good, though I didn't have a mirror to tell. The way the hapless beach tourists looked at me, though, was like I was some sort of parasite. Like I was the dead body of a cheap hooker left out in the sun too long. Stinking and rotting. When I finally gave up searching after a few hours of scouring the beach and realized bits of my bra were showing in the tears of the ripped-up shirt, I sat under a palm tree, desperately grasping the fifteen dollars in my hand.

I had no shoes, no wallet, no room key, no phone. It'd be a long walk back to the hotel, one that would surely tear up my bare feet if I decided to hazard the many concrete sidewalks and asphalt streets it would take to get there. I cursed myself for aimlessly walking so far from the hotel. Then, of course, would be the matter of getting my room key from the front desk and the nightmare proving my identity would be. Didn't even want to think of finding a way to cancel my credit cards and cell phone service. It was too much.

I watched the ocean roll back and forth in the distance, frowning at it as I tried to figure out what to do next. I was baking in the sun and eventually took off my ripped shirt, though I knew I was going to wind up with even worse sunburns. I sighed, afraid to step anywhere near the water to try to cool down. It looked so inviting now in its bright greenish-blue. Were it any other day, I might've gone for a plunge into its crystal-clear depths.

But no. I knew better.

Let alone the fact that I was getting thirsty in this sun and the salt water of the ocean would make it worse, there was something about water. The Red had some sort of connection to water. That's why it lured me out there.

Matty.

I knew somehow, though not the exact details, that Matty was no longer among the living. I felt it in my heart. Before, I knew he was gone, but now? Now, from every fiber of my being, I knew he was dead. Whether it was because he was ripped in half like I saw in the ocean or some other more perverse paranormal way, he was dead. A heavy, familiar blanket of grief washed over me as I sat and felt like I was rotting.

The Red had killed Matty.

I frowned at the ocean, just staring back as it rocked back and forth. Matty was *dead*.

Eventually, I spent the fifteen dollars on a large bottle of water and relatively cheap flip-flops that cut into the space between my toes. At the end of the transaction I had mere quarters, not even a full dollar. With that, I began the journey back to the hotel. Hunger was beginning to set in, though, and my belly was furious with me. A layer of drowsiness washed over me, and the soreness in my limbs from fighting drowning made every step feel like I'd fall at any moment. My eyes glazed over as I walked through the sunny and beautiful Honolulu, where everyone seemed to be doing their best to avoid my gaze. I thought I saw the man with the hat in the distance, a shadowy figure among the otherwise bright colors.

"Come get me . . . you fucker . . ." I whispered to no one but the dark figure I wasn't sure was actually ahead of me. "Come get me. I'm . . . not . . . scared . . ."

"Rachel?" a voice said, far off from somewhere.

I walked forward in a daze. Toward what I thought might've been the man with the hat. My fists clenched. "Come . . . get some."

I heard footsteps hurrying behind me. "Rachel!"

I didn't turn until fingers brushed my arm, which made me jump.

"Rachel!"

A vaguely familiar face was looking at me. He almost stepped back when he saw the ugly look I gave him. "Whoa!"

I blinked for a moment, processing who was in front of me, every movement of mine feeling sluggish. "K-Kai?"

"Wait, so *how* did you end up in the ocean again?" Kai asked as we sped along in his black Jeep. He had a surfboard in the back and black aviator sunglasses on. His shirt was dark green and he wore full-on jeans as he sped through the streets. The bright green trees rushed beside and over us as we rode back to Kai's place. He drove without abandon, but I didn't feel anxious with him at the wheel. It was damn near like he was a race car driver with how well he handled the faster speed.

I chewed on the McDonald's burger he'd bought me like my life depended on it. "Would you believe me if I said evil spirits?" I said with my mouth full before I swallowed and took another huge bite. I was famished.

Who knew drowning worked up such an appetite?

Kai chuckled. "What, the Night Marchers drag you out there?"

"The what?"

"Ehhh, old Hawaiian ghost story. Spirits that lead the dead to the afterlife. Not the point, though." Kai looked in his mirror. "Nah, but for real. Why were you swimming in the ocean without a lifeguard? The waves are supposed to be rough all day today. You could've been killed. I—I mean, sounds like you almost were."

I shrugged. "Ever heard of a night swim?"

Kai gave me a look with a grin. He knew I was full of shit. "I have a sneaking suspicion the pool might've been safer."

I shook my head. "I'll keep that in mind next time." I chewed my burger. "So these Night Marchers, though. What's their deal? Like, their forte?"

Kai chuckled, then looked at me. "You're serious?"

I shrugged. "What? Sounded interesting . . ."

Kai sighed, his black hair being tossed by the wind. "I don't remember the stories that well, to be honest. Buuut I guess they're like a group of ancient warriors that pound drums in the middle of the night, and if you look at them, unless you have an elder that can vouch for you nearby, they drag you to hell. You're supposed to try to ignore 'em. Looking at them pisses 'em off, I guess."

"Why's that?"

"I . . . Who knows? It's a ghost story. Who knows what the logic is behind the myth." Kai laughed.

I blinked, twisting my mouth. "Ya know, that's a lot of things I've been finding when looking up ghost stuff, though. It's weird." I chewed a fry. "Certain entities you're not supposed to look at or something bad happens to ya. Like, just seeing these things is like enough of a reason for them to kill you or something. It's weird how unforgiving these things are in myths."

There was a slight pause as it looked like Kai was trying to figure out whether to continue the conversation or pay attention to the road. Finally, he chuckled. "So ghost stories your thing or something? You sound like an expert."

I grimaced. "Nah . . . just have taken an interest as of late."

There was a momentary silence as Kai drove. I looked out as Kai drove farther and farther away from the parts of Honolulu I knew. After a few minutes of silence, he said, "So, I know its kinda a taboo subject but . . . you were there, weren't you?"

I scrunched my face. "I was where?"

"When whatever happened to Dana happened."

I blinked. He was looking over at me. I swallowed and shook my head. "No . . . I mean—I was . . ." I stared at my own lying face in the reflection of his sunglasses. "But I didn't see it."

Kai seemed to analyze me, then sighed. "Fair. Crazy, though. I mean, what happened to her . . . that was outta nowhere, ya know?"

My lips tightened as I looked out the window. "Mmhmm."

"Trevon is in pieces. Never seen him this broken up."

I kept my mouth tight as an airlock. That's right. Kai was one of Trevon's besties.

"Fucked-up that someone would just . . . *assault her* like that. Do they know yet who might've done it?" Kai looked over my way. I avoided his gaze.

"N-no."

Kai looked forward again. "They really messed her up, whoever did that . . . It's gonna take a long time to heal from all those broken bones."

"How much longer till we reach your place?" I asked, trying to change subject.

"Eh, like, ten more minutes?" he stated. Then Kai continued, almost off in his own world. "But yeah, life's just . . . short and crazy like that though, ya know? We think it'll go on and on, but . . . truth is, for all we know we can be gone tomorrow."

I nodded. "Yeah. Yeah, I guess."

"Have you ever wished for . . . something more?"

I grinned wryly. "What?"

Kai watched the road. "Rach, when was the last time you truly felt alive?"

I was speechless and shrugged. Where was he going with this?

"I mean, we're all just slaves at the end of the day, right?" Kai gripped his wheel a bit tighter, adjusting his jaw a little. The car seemed to go just a little faster down the road. "It's all one big joke."

I squinted my eyes, giving him an uncertain look. "Um, I don't follow."

He smiled softly. "Sentience. Knowledge of our existence. Who knows how long any of us are here? Life is short so we have to live in the moment. Seize the day. Take risks."

I looked around, noticing the speed of the car really was slowly increasing. I looked at him more as he kept his eyes forward. My heart beat a little faster as I looked forward too, at the road in front of us.

"Our existence is nothing but a blip in the universe. We are the most supreme species on this planet, but we are alone in the universe. Given just enough sentience to be aware our existence is futile. *We* are one big joke."

He passed some cars rather quickly. The wind blew our hair more furiously. He swerved between cars, almost knocking into one or two and avoiding them by hairs.

"I think you should slow down."

"*Slow?* To what? Enjoy a second longer? To hold on to what little life we have left? What good will that do, Rach?" He looked at me over his glasses, a wild look in his eyes as he smiled. *"What good will that do?"*

A car honked as we swerved and cut them off. I clutched my seat. "Kai, seriously, you're freaking me out!"

"You scared?"

"Yes! Yes, I'm scared, you fucking nut! Slow the fuck down!"

Kai stared at me through the sunglasses. I couldn't see his eyes, but I felt the look pierce me. It was only for a moment before his face eased into a smile. The car slowed a little, then smoothly pulled into a driveway and parked. We were at a one-story house surrounded by greenery, to the point where one couldn't tell where the house began and ended. He chuckled, pulling the keys out of the Jeep. "Got you."

I breathed heavily. "What. The fuck. Was that?"

"Oh man, you should see your face." Kai laughed. His face rested for a bit and he moved a piece of hair out of my face. "Relax, babe. Was just fucking with ya."

"That was *not* funny!" I hissed, slapping his hand away. Kai only laughed harder. I felt like hitting him. "Seriously, dude. *Not cool.* That was fucked!"

Kai seemed to sober up a bit at this. "It was—it was a joke, Rach. Bad taste, I guess. But a joke."

I immediately began to undo my seatbelt. "*Yeah, very* bad taste." I reached for the door.

"Wait, Rach."

I stopped, looking at him with the meanest glare I could muster. He seemed at a loss for words. "I'm waiting."

"Just . . ." He thought for a moment, blinking. Then he sighed. "Look, I'm . . . I'm sorry. Guess I . . . wasn't thinking. It *was* a fucked-up joke."

I folded my arms, mad. "Yeah. No shit."

Kai sat, seeming to think over his actions and maybe even regret them, a halfhearted wince on his face. "Look, uh, in retrospect, dickish thing to do . . . I understand why you're mad. Let me . . . I don't know, make you dinner. To make up for it."

I glared at him before shaking my head, sighing. "Look. I'm . . . just *not interested in you*, man. Okay?" His face was unreadable to this, so I continued. "I'm just gonna use your phone to make a few calls when we get inside, then I'm getting an Uber, alright?"

He nodded, looking down and looking sincere.

So sincere, in fact, I didn't see his elbow to my face coming. My world fell into darkness.

The first thing I heard was a fly buzzing somewhere.

When I woke up, my head was spinning and I could hear my nose whine as air struggled to move out the nostrils. A tiny bit of drool sat on the corner of my mouth as I raised my head off what felt like pillows. Ahead of me was a TV that was showing some sort of racing movie. The characters were in cars, including an actor I didn't know the name of but recognized by face. If I had to guess era, maybe 2000s?

My head throbbed as a barbecue-like smell vaguely crept into my nostrils.

I was . . . in a house. In a house and on a couch. The floor underneath was wood, and a blanket covered my body. I was also wearing a T-shirt much too big for me. Every muscle throbbed. I was dizzy, dehydrated. I struggled to sit up, not sure where I was.

Last I remembered I was with Kai. We stopped in front of his house and—

My eyes widened as I began to put two and two together. What the fuck?

Did . . . did he knock me out and take me into his house? At that point, it seemed the only logical conclusion. I quickly looked around. There was a kitchen and dining room next to this room. To my left, it looked like there was a back door. Quietly, I began to sit up even though everything in me ached, moving the blanket off me as carefully as I could. Okay, I was going to quietly get out the back door. I didn't know where Kai was, but hopefully I could get away from this place undetected before he noticed. I didn't know what he wanted from me, but I didn't want to find out.

I planted my feet on the ground carefully, trying to not make a sound. My eyes darted around, searching for where he could be as I began to stand. Right before I could make a quick getaway, though, Kai entered from the back door, carrying a plate. I stopped, meeting eyes with him. He had a smile on his face.

"Hey! You're awake!"

I gave him a look. A very harsh look. Words hadn't found their way to my mouth yet, either because I was too scared or too angry. At this point I couldn't tell.

"It looks like it's getting ready to rain out there. Got these ready just in time."

I looked down at the plate in his hands and saw he made something like a stack of kebabs. I couldn't tell what exact meat they were, but they looked like red meat, without any vegetables on the sticks. He had cooked a pile of meat. *Just* a pile of meat. He closed the door behind him and locked it with his free hand.

I grit my teeth before looking up at him. "W-why?" I croaked out. It was like I had a frog in my throat, and all the feelings I was feeling simultaneously could only accumulate into that one word. Adrenaline shook my insides as I stared, wide-eyed.

"Why? Why what?"

I breathed hard. As it was now, if I tried to make a run for it, he'd catch me immediately. I was on the smaller side, sure, but this house wasn't big at all. If anything, it was tiny. I swallowed and shook slightly, but tried to keep the fear on my face hidden.

"Why . . . did you knock me out?" I struggled to say.

Kai did a double take. "Knock you out? Here I thought it was exhaustion that got you to pass out in the car. Didn't know my conversation was so dull." He laughed it off, then gestured with his head. "Come on, let's eat some dinner and make those phone calls."

I stared at him. Was this motherfucker gaslighting me? He gestured again with his head. "Come on, let's eat at the table." I hesitated. He was standing, making sure I got up too. He knew, didn't he? He knew that if I tried to run for it, I was a grasp away. He knew that I was one hundred pounds soaking wet, without an ounce of muscle, and he knew he could probably do whatever he wanted to me. An overwhelming but far too familiar sense of dread took hold of me. I knew this feeling. Kai had me right where he wanted, and at the moment, there wasn't much I could do but play along.

"I, uh, I'm still kinda full from the McDonald's. Thanks, though."

Kai smiled. "Come on, that was hours ago. I'm sure you're probably hungrier than you realize."

"Kai, I'm—I'm not hungry—"

"Sit at the table," he said, face still calm but with a tad bit of bite to his voice. What, was he going to drug me with whatever he made? What kind of play was this?

Deciding not to incur his wrath, I stood up and uneasily kept eye contact, for the most part. The table in the kitchen was small and unimpressive, just big enough for the two chairs on either side, both sides set with plates to eat off and bottles of beer. There was a bar, and at the back of where I was to sit looked to be a window with shades slightly open. Behind the bar was a refrigerator and a sink and not much else but a food pantry.

Kai directed me to my seat and practically sat me down himself. Then he sat down across from me and put the plate of meat kebabs in between both of us. Immediately, he took one of the kebabs of meat and began tearing away at it like it owed him money. When he wasn't eating, he slurped down his beer like it was water in a desert. I looked around. Right behind Kai was a hallway that looked like it led to the front door of the house. Trouble was, Kai was practically sitting guard right in front of it, preventing exit. The window behind me looked like it was nothing but plant life past the partially open shades, and the kitchen window above the sink looked too small for even a child to fit through. Best bet was to somehow make a run for it toward the back door. I'd still have to pass Kai, but—

"You gonna eat?" Kai asked, mouth full, eyes occasionally giving me some sort of brief but knowing look. I half-heartedly smiled and picked up a kebab.

I bit into a tiny sliver of it. If he was going to drug me, it was at least going to be a frustratingly longer process.

"Good, huh?"

I merely nodded my head.

"Old family recipe. My grandma used to make us this as kids."

I simply chewed and fake smiled. "What kind of meat is it?"

Kai smiled. "Cow."

I nervously chuckled. "Most people call that beef."

"Yeah, well I'm . . . not most people."

I awkwardly smiled as I carefully bit into the meat. Kai still tore away at his like someone starving. Another strange silence. I'd have made the move, but Kai kept his eyes on me. Almost never moving them, even as he ate.

"So, you girls been hanging with someone new?"

I squinted. "Uh . . . no."

"Who's the girl in the picture Penelope took, then?"

I breathed out. "Girl?"

Kai pulled out his phone and scrolled for a moment. I looked again toward the room with the back door. It was all too brief a moment, though, as he showed me his phone.

"This girl."

I studied the phone a moment. It was an Instagram post Penny made of her with that Instagram model that tried talking to me. They were both looking cute in their bikinis and smiling at the camera. The picture had at least a hundred thousand likes. I shook my head. "She's just some girl we met. Instagram model."

Kai looked at his phone. "Damn, she's cute." I eyed the door yet again for a brief span. "Annnnd followed."

"What, new wank material?" I fired back.

Kai's eyes immediately darted to mine. He gave me an icy glare. "You're cuter when you don't give lip."

I blinked, feeling my heart drop at the cold statement and the look he shot at me. He went back to his phone and put it away. I looked down. "S-sorry."

I continued to eat, carefully biting off a centimeter at a time. How the fuck was I going to get out of here? I was contemplating my escape plan when I felt something in my mouth that wasn't part of the meat. My tongue swirled around in my mouth, having trouble getting a hold of it.

"Don't make movies the way they used to anymore."

I looked up, puzzled. "Mm?"

Kai was staring at me, taking a big, long swig of beer. He put down his bottle and wiped his mouth with his hand. "Movies. I would take you to one but I don't like *the crap* that they put out anymore."

"Fair, I guess . . ." I began to dig into my mouth with my finger, searching for the thing that felt so off.

"Everything is just a copy of a copy. No originality. No *gusto*. Nobody has any *fucking balls* anymore."

Finally, I was able to dig it out.

A long, dark blonde hair.

I blinked in confusion. Kai and I both had black hair . . .

Kai took another vehement swig. "It's all the same diluted crap as ever. Where's the fucking grindhouse? Ya know, stuff that gets under your skin. The *Cannibal Holocaust*-type shit? The exploitation genre. *That* was a real genre of movies, cus they weren't fucking around. Movies try so damn hard to not upset anybody they appease nobody, it's fuckin' pointless."

I tuned out Kai's peculiar rant about movies and focused on the hair. Where the fuck did this come from? Was I not the first girl he knocked out and forced to have a date with him? Was there something worse going on? I didn't know, but I knew I needed to get the fuck out.

Kai burped, taking me out of my trance. I looked at him as he lifted his beer bottle. He was smiling. "Uh, I'm a little light, babe. Mind getting me another one?"

I stared at him as if he were from another planet. What the hell was going on? What was I going to do? I hadn't angered him yet. I would make my move when I saw I could get away. Yes, that is what I would do. I'd be patient, then make my escape. I swallowed as he stared at me. "Is it in the fridge?"

He chuckled. "Shit, I hope so. I hate warm beer."

I searched around with my eyes and nodded, beginning a trek toward the kitchen. His gaze followed me. Somehow the steps to the sink felt like they took forever and weighed tons. As I got closer to the fridge, my gut swirled, tightened. I felt a sense of doom as Kai's gaze all at once ripped my clothes off and tore me apart. I felt hopeless, until I saw a glimmer out of the corner of my eye.

My eyes had settled on a knife in the sink. A very sharp, long kitchen knife underwater, under soap suds.

Alright.

Now we were cooking with grease.

I quietly sighed and continued walking to the fridge. The counter partially covered my waist at this point. If I wanted to grab the knife and hide it, I'd have protective coverage. Keeping this in mind, I opened the fridge door.

. . .

. . .

What?

"Everything okay in there, babe?" Kai called out.

My jaw went slack as I breathed hard, feeling like puking. Wh-what?

. . . *What?*

She wasn't her usual vibrant self. That was evident by her facial expression. The cold air hit me as I stared at a pair of blank eyes. They were eyes I had considered pretty. Captivating eyes. Eyes that even still held my gaze, as Penelope's decapitated head sleepily stared back at me, blood-splattered foil at the base of her neck. Her face looked serene, maybe even beautiful, save for the small trickle of blood coming from her mouth, and frayed hair like someone had grabbed it. Vomit scratched the back of my throat as her head just sat there, top shelf of the fridge. I wanted to scream, but I think it was trapped behind the vomit trying to come up. My hand went to my mouth in silent horror.

Play it off.

Play it off, don't react.

I had to play it off. I grabbed a bottle of beer and closed the fridge door.

"Hey, you okay?"

I immediately straightened up my back. Kai stood nearby, blocking my only real exit out of the kitchen. My heart fluttered in my chest uncontrollably and I shook like a dying leaf. "Yeah, fine." I stepped forward, beer outstretched in my hand. He took it and smiled. I gulped, staring into his eyes. "I think I should . . . make those calls and—and get going."

"Yeah?" He stepped toward me, taking a swig of his beer. I backed away, winding up with my back at the sink.

"Y-yeah, the meal is . . . fantastic but, uh, I really should get stuff squared with the hotel, and—"

"Cut the shit," he said with a laugh, putting his beer down.

I froze. Was he referring to the head in the fridge? "What?"

"We know why you really came. You don't gotta play coy."

He leaned in over me. My back ached, I leaned away so far. I let my hand dive into the sink behind me covertly, hoping he wouldn't notice. He moved some hair out of my face. Softly, he lifted my chin. "I knew how you felt about me the moment you laid eyes on me."

My hand felt the knife. Not the handle, but a bit of the blade. I awkwardly grabbed it as hard as I could, causing the sharp edge to dig into my fingers. I winced in pain but tried to make it unnoticeable.

"I know how much you wanted me." His face came closer, and he kissed my lips. "Why deny . . ." he said between kisses, kissing me more fervently, even though I didn't return any. ". . . what you want—"

There was a soft sound. A sound like cake being cut. A sound you would have to really listen for in order to hear, but it was there.

Warm liquid rushed over my hand as I held on to the knife's handle with a death grip. Kai took a moment, pulling away, looking at me with wide eyes. He breathed hard. "Wha—"

He stepped back, off my knife, looking at the fresh wound in his gut. I had stuck a hole right into his abdomen, and he looked surprised that I could do such a thing. Dark red leaked out of him. "What did you—?" He stumbled backward. Seizing the opportunity, I stabbed him in the gut again and again. He let out something in between a groan and a scream and fell backward to the ground, grabbing me in the process.

He was screaming, carrying on while he gripped my shoulder in a tight death grip. I desperately pulled myself away, but not without falling on my ass. I scrambled to run away, but he was on his stomach, grabbing my leg, getting absolutely covered in blood.

"What did you do to me? What did you do—"

I kicked him in his bloodstained face as hard as I could. Did so twice before his hand let go. He reached out for me as I ran toward the hallway, my feet slipping slightly on the blood that was pooling on the floor. The small hallway was narrow and dark. Immediately, I fumbled with the locks on the front door that I couldn't see well, not wasting a moment.

"Rachel! Rachel, get the fuck back here!" Kai called out. I looked behind me to see him crawling around the corner. I fumbled harder with the door, eventually prying it open and running out to the front porch.

Right as I was exiting the house, a very familiar Jeep pulled up to the driveway. I stood there in the doorway as the headlights hit me. *"Rachel?"* an equally familiar voice shouted. Without turning the car off, Kai exited his Jeep. I froze, watching him rush up to me, perfectly fine, not covered in blood. A bewildered look was on his face. "What were you just doing in my house?" he said, his voice breaking.

I blinked. Confused. "K-Kai?"

"Answer me, what were you just doing in my house?"

I looked back into the house. It was just dark in there. "Wh-what . . ." I struggled to get out, turning back to Kai. "I—I . . ."

Kai looked absolutely petrified, looking at me wide-eyed. "Rachel, did you just—did you break into *my house*?"

Just then—I heard a grinding sound. A grinding sound I was coming to know all too well. And it was coming from behind me. My face crumpled, tears falling from my eyes. I knew what that meant. "No, please. No, no, no . . ."

Kai seemed to study the situation as I blankly looked forward. "Hey . . ." He put a hand on me that I immediately shook off. The grinding was getting louder and louder. I thought Kai might've said something like "I'll call somebody, okay? It's okay, Rachel," but I couldn't hear him properly.

I looked behind me to see the man with the hat in the doorway, his dripping red face pointed directly at me.

"*Get the fuck away from me!*" I screamed at the top of my lungs to the figure. I backed away quickly, leaving Kai looking at me confused, unaware of the man in the hat standing behind him. "*Get the fuck away!*"

I ran. Fuck if I knew where to. Just . . . away. Away from the entity. Away from Kai's house. Just . . . away from it all.

It wasn't long before the rain began falling, and falling hard. Falling as I kept running.

What do you want from me?

What did I ever do to deserve . . .

Where am I?

What is going on anymore?

"Can't stop, won't stop. Can't stop, won't stop," I repeated under my breath. I lost one of my flip-flops at some point; the other was folded under my foot. The rain drenched my hair and my shirt as I eventually ran out of steam. Dusk had started to settle and I breathed raggedly as I walked and walked. Eventually, I wasn't too far from the freeway. I had cried hysterically on the run, but now I was too tired to cry. The sidewalk shifted into a ramp that led to an overpass bridge over the freeway. The rain pitter-pattered and the sky grew darker. The streetlamps and car lights were what lit the world at this point. I dragged my feet lazily as I climbed up to the overpass.

"Can't stop, won't stop. Can't stop, won't stop."

I couldn't stop if I wanted to. My feet drove themselves. I didn't know where I was going. It didn't matter. Nowhere was safe.

"Can't stop, won't stop. Can't stop, won't stop. Can't . . ."

It took me a moment to register that there was a woman in the distance in front of me, leaning on the railing of the overpass. The dim light from below highlighted her features as she watched the freeway underneath.

I couldn't believe my eyes at first. Was that . . .?

My pace quickened. I kicked off my remaining flip-flop and hurried through the rain toward her. She wore a minty green dress with white dots. It was sleeveless and showed cleavage, but looked really comfortable. Her light brown hair was wet and she had pointed her head up to the sky like she was taking in the rain with a look of bliss over her face.

"Penny?" I asked, my voice quivering. *"Penny, is that you?"*

Penelope turned to look at me, a good-natured, huge smile on her face. "Rachel? What're ya doing out here?"

I rushed to her and hugged her tightly. Tighter than I ever had hugged anyone before. "I thought . . . I thought . . ." was all I could stutter out. Penny hugged me just as tight.

"Okay, okay, I surrender . . ." Penny chuckled. I backed away, still clutching her. Her smile quickly turned into one of concern. "You okay? What's gotten into you?"

I immediately pulled our faces together into a kiss. It caught her off guard. I poured my heart and soul in through the clumsy gesture. Everything I was and everything I wasn't was all stripped bare in that kiss alone. I felt my chapped lips against her soft, pillow-like mouth and our tongues danced with each other with a fiery emotion, uncontrolled, unbridled. Our hearts pounded in synchronization with music only we could hear, lovers if only for a brief moment. Everything about the kiss was pure electricity, pure music, raw energy. When I pulled away, she looked at me, somewhat confused. Then she smiled. "Where'd that come from?"

I shook my head. "Sorry, I just . . . I thought you were . . ."

Penny pulled me in and kissed me back, her soft lips sweet and her perfume giving me comfort, even in the rain. "I've felt it too."

I pulled away, surprised.

"It's okay, I've felt it too." We put our foreheads together and breathed hard as the rain poured and poured. Penelope giggled and looked up. "God, this rain! I fucking love it!" I smiled uneasily as she pulled away, her head tilting up at the sky again. "The rain is perfect."

I looked up myself and breathed out as Penny danced around in it. She was on molly, wasn't she? I felt out of breath, but I had no reason to be. I leaned on the railing beside me, feeling out of it. Soon, Penny leaned on the railing too, looking out toward the freeway down below. The cars rushed by. I didn't realize it before, but on the horizon, you could see downtown Honolulu from here, the skyscrapers lit up against the night sky.

"I was worried you died," I finally managed to say, chuckling for no fucking reason.

Penny gave me a look. "Why would you think that?"

I laughed. "Just—just something stupid."

Penny and I stood side by side, leaning on the railing, taking in the rain. I looked upward and let the rain soak my face. Lightning crashed in the sky as I closed my eyes.

"It's good, isn't it?" Penny asked.

I smiled uneasily. "Yeah, I guess."

She rubbed my arm. I looked at her, feeling too exhausted to feel much of anything. She simply smiled at me for a moment.

"Rach, can I ask you something?"

I shook my head and scoffed. "Uh, I guess. Sure." I studied Penelope, who looked at me like she had an exciting secret. "What is it?"

Penelope grinned at me with a calm but excited grin.

"Have you ever wanted to fuck God?"

CHAPTER 12

It was all in a moment, when everything came crashing down around me. One moment, where it all clicked that maybe everything wasn't fine after all.

One moment.

I was in a daze. I don't know how, but I was in a daze, and in mere seconds I was snapped out of it.

I looked hard at Penelope. Very hard. My face lost any pleasantry at all as she smiled at me.

"What?"

"Have . . . you ever . . . wanted to fuck . . . God?" she said, looking me dead in the eyes. I blinked. This couldn't be happening. I had run as fast as I could. How did it catch up? I mean, it was a fucking ghost-demon-thing but . . . how . . .

I stared at Penelope, the rain still pouring. "I'd imagine it's beautiful," she said. "I mean, that's what I always picture when people say they feel God inside them. I imagine he's fucking them. What divinity it must be, to be fucked by the purity of creation." She smiled.

"No, Penny . . ." I said with a frown. "Can't say I've ever wanted to fuck God. I think of him more as a friend."

She turned toward the freeway, looking out. "*I* want to fuck God. I want the best orgasm I've ever had. So good that no other orgasm could possibly beat it. I wanna be fucked so good it splits the heavens, man. I want to be part of something *more*."

What was I going to do? I was positive that Penny had been possessed or something by the Red. This was not the first time someone spouted weird existential stuff to me at this point. It had something to do with the Red. I didn't know what yet, though. Penny almost looked at the point of tears with how watery her eyes were. "Haven't you ever wanted something more? Haven't you ever wanted . . . an extraordinary existence?"

I swallowed, looking into her eyes. I shook my head. "I just want a normal life."

Penelope's face saddened, staring into my eyes. "You don't mean that . . ."

I searched Penny's eyes and swallowed. "I do. I've never wanted anything more than a normal life." I sighed out. "I . . . I never wanted to be special."

Penelope frowned, looking away, her cheek twitching. "I guess . . . I really am alone, then."

I shook my head, caressing her face. "No. No, you're not."

She then grabbed my hand and took it off her face. She looked back at me, disappointed. Then she started climbing the railing.

I panicked. "Wh-what the fuck are you doing?"

"Fucking God."

"Penny, stop fucking with me!"

Penny looped her leg over the railing. I tried to pull her off but she fought off my hands.

"Penny!"

Suddenly, I felt a hard smack across my mouth and couldn't help but stumble back. Penelope had slapped me. She glared at me for a moment before climbing to the other side of the railing and standing on the ledge, holding on to the railing and facing me. I became acutely aware of the cars speeding by down below. They were loud, zooming by without abandon, even in the rain. Penny clutched the railing, laughing. "Feel that, Rach? It's a great honor to live a life with meaning! To be blessed among the crowd! To be the chosen fuck buddy of God!"

"*Penny, stop!*" I yelled, clutching her and trying to pull her back my way.

Penny kept laughing. "Rachel! *You aren't meant to be just another drop in the ocean of mediocrity! You could be God's fuck buddy too!*"

No matter how hard I pulled, Penelope wouldn't budge.

"Rachel." She giggled, caressing my face with a hand. "It's so easy. You just have to let go."

My face crumpled. Tears poured from my eyes. "P-Penny, please."

Penelope's face softened with a warm smile. A sort of dreaminess filled her eyes. "You called me Penny . . ."

"Penny, please. You don't have to do this. P-please . . ."

"Shhh . . ." Penelope softly hushed before pulling me into a kiss. It was intense and despite the softness of her lips, she pressed in hard. My heart trembled as the rain kept pouring. Then she broke the kiss and leaned in toward my ear. "You like Van Halen . . ." She pulled away and smiled. "Might as well jump."

She pushed me and fell backward. Backward, to her imminent death toward the cars below, all the while watching me, a calm smile on her face.

"*Penny!*" I screamed.

As I looked over the railing, toward where her body should've been . . .

Nothing.

. . . There was nothing.

My eyes relentlessly searched, trying to find some sort of semblance of where her body could be.

There was no body to be found.

The Red had fucked with me again.

I watched down below, the passing cars speeding by, still in disbelief of what just happened. She was here . . . then wasn't. She was here, I kissed her, felt her, tasted her, and then she was gone. I was still processing this when I heard a familiar ringtone. Snapped out of my daze, I began searching for the sound and found a purse near the railing. It was fancy but I couldn't quite tell the color in the current lighting. The ringtone was coming from it, though. I dug my hand into the bag. That ringtone . . . It sounded like . . .

Mine.

I pulled my very familiar iPhone out of the unfamiliar purse and threw the purse aside.

Incoming Call: Penelope

I closed my eyes hard. Fuck. What was this? I ran under a bus stop cover and answered the phone.

"H-hello?"

"Rachel?"

"Y-yeah . . ."

"Where you been, girlie? Been trying to reach you all day!"

"Sorry . . ."

"You leave your phone off all day?"

"No . . . Just . . ." I had nothing. No excuses or anything for her.

"Look, we can talk about it later. Where are you? I'll get an Uber right now, we'll pick you up."

"What? Wh-why?"

"You haven't seen my messages? Trevon wants to meet with us."

"R-right now?"

"Yeah. It's about Dana . . . Didn't say much else."

"O-okay . . ."

"Give me your address and I'll pick you up?"

I did just that. Like a good little doggy.

"You're outside? In this weather? I'll come get you right now, 'kay, hun?"

"Yeah."

"Be there in a few . . ."

With that she hung up. I merely stared forward. This was another trap. It had to be. Nothing was real anymore. The Red was playing with me again. I couldn't—I can't tell what's real anymore. Rain was on my skin, oddly feeling warm, not particularly cold. Who knew, maybe not even the rain was real.

Who said the reality you think you inhabited was reality? Maybe it was like every fucking movie around Y2K. It was all a fucking illusion. Did I ever know Matty, Penelope, and Dana? Were they even real people?

For a moment, part of me longed to go to the spot I thought Penelope fell off . . . Maybe do the same thing. Anything to end this fucking feeling. The world was thick sheets of plastic wrapped around my head, slowly suffocating me until I begged for death.

None of anything was real.

As I stared blankly toward the passing cars, I heard one pull up behind me.

"Rachel? Hey! Rachel?" Penelope's familiar voice sounded out. I slowly turned toward her, mouth agape. She was yelling at me from the back of a silver Subaru.

What if I jumped off this bridge right now?

Penelope opened the door. She was wearing a hoodie and short shorts. "Come on! Get inside! You'll catch a cold out there!"

I contemplated jumping for a second longer before finding I didn't have the strength or willpower to even do that. So like a blind dog, I obeyed. Probably falling into yet another fucking trap.

Was this my existence now?

I got into the car and suddenly felt dry. If I was even wet to begin with. I closed the door and just looked down at my lap. Penelope gave the Uber driver the go-ahead and we started our journey back to Tropical Springs.

"This rain is crazy! How long were you out there, homegirl? You look *drenched*."

". . . I don't know."

Penny took a moment. I could feel her eyes go over me. "You okay? You look out of it."

"Yeah . . ."

"And what happened to your shoes?"

I didn't answer. The silence was uncomfortable as I felt Penny stiffen next to me.

"Rachel . . . wh-what were you doing on that overpass?"

Again, I didn't answer, only looking forward. Then a pair of hands turned my head toward where Penelope was sitting. "Rach, look at me."

Soon, I was staring into her eyes, glittering onyxes in the dim light.

"Rachel. What's going on? Why were you on that overpass, hun?"

Her flesh felt real enough. Her skin, her breath. She was a convincing imitation if I ever saw one. She stared into my eyes.

"Rachel . . . *let me in.* Talk to me. Tell me what's going on."

I stared back, wanting to cry. "Are you real?"

She searched my eyes with a little disbelief. "Of course I'm for real." She hugged me tight. I did not hug her back. "Rach, I told you, you can trust me." She pulled away and looked deep into my eyes. "I'm here for you. Whatever you need, I'm here." She kissed my forehead and pressed my head to her chest. "It's okay. I'm here."

A bit of me relented and clutched her back. Every bit of my existence and mortal coil hated myself for falling for another trap from the enemy. But I couldn't help it.

Eventually, though, I had to pull away, not wanting to be held too long for fear of being fooled yet again. I cleared my throat as she briefly caressed my face. I jerked my head away and sat up. "Um . . . What does Trevon want, exactly?"

Penelope seemed to be processing something, before nodding and sniffing in. "Uh . . . not sure." She seemed a little uncertain. "Think it does have something to do with Dana, though."

I nodded and turned away. I guessed I should have dreaded a confrontation with Trevon, but at that point, like I gave a fuck. Even if he wanted to strangle the life out of me, it'd have been a welcome reprieve from what the Red was doing.

I watched the plastic Honolulu mock me from outside with its cheap glory. The artificial, Mattel-made, Barbie-land, candy fuck of an environment that was outside. The bourgeoisie pleasure house that was so separated from everything real, dirty, and grimy. True beauty dies. It withers away and becomes ugly. It's the natural cycle, but the picturesque Honolulu remained consistent. As corporate and clean-cut as fucking Disneyland. The buildings might as well have had giant gumdrops, candy canes, and frosting. Clowns on cupcakes saying, "Eat me."

Truth was a fucking eyesore. It was a bitter medicine but one I longed for the taste of. One I desperately needed or I would dry up and my bones would become a spooky set piece in the dollhouse that was this place. Truth was an ugliness that just wasn't there.

I hated everything. I hated everything from the pit of my soul.

When we finally arrived at our destination, we crossed through the courtyard next to the pool. The blue light reflected over us and colored everything that way. I stopped for a moment and looked up, toward the building that I had called home base since this vacation began.

Staring down from a balcony was a familiar-looking old woman. One I knew was dead and shouldn't be there. She was clutching the railing and smoking, and even though she was so very high up, I knew she was looking at me. I blinked and smiled a little seeing her, as she stared down at me with a scowl.

"What're you looking at, Rach?" Penelope asked. She grabbed my hand, and began tugging at me. "Come on, we gotta go." I smiled at Jennings as she left my field of vision.

We got inside and to the elevator, Penny pulling my hand the whole way, my brains like marshmallow. I watched us rise higher and higher through the window.

"Hopefully it's good news about Dana . . ." Penelope chimed in, clearly trying to make some sort of conversation.

I just looked at her. I don't even know what my face was doing. Was I smiling? Was I crying? Was I completely straight-faced? Whatever look I gave her seemed to unnerve her. She simply looked back, a worried look on her face. Before long, she diverted her attention away and I did the same. The elevator continued to climb until we got near the top, at the floor with Trevon and Dana's penthouse suite. When we got to the door of their suite, Penelope knocked.

"Tre? You there?"

I focused my attention on the nearby ti plant. I studied it, not particularly interested in if Trevon answered the door.

"Tre—oop."

Penelope had pushed slightly on the door to find it open. Immediately, my danger senses went off. It *was* a trap. It was a fucking trap. Penny chuckled nervously. "I guess he didn't shut the door fully . . ."

Unlikely fucking coincidence. I swallowed hard. The Red was about to pull another fast one, huh? I tightened my fists. Penny pushed on the door, beginning to step in.

"Trevon?"

I stood my ground outside in the lavish hall.

"Tre? We're here . . ." Penelope noticed I was staying outside the suite. She motioned to me to move forward, but I stayed put. Not gonna fall for this again. No way.

Penelope, obviously getting a little frustrated, shook her head, but then proceeded to walk forward.

'Kay, but what if the Red hurt Penny?

The thought urged me forward even though my feet remained planted. Dana was *still* in the hospital . . . and Matty had ceased to exist. What would the Red do to Penny? Part of me wanted to run away. Not learn whatever horrible fate the Red had in store for her.

I couldn't run, though.

I didn't know what I was going to do, but I couldn't let it get Penelope like that. With a swallow, I stepped through the open suite door.

Aside from the odd, orangey lamp, the large, luxury suite was dark and seemingly empty. Fur rugs, expensive-looking vases and pillows, art deco furniture, and a staircase that spiraled to a second floor. The walls were gigantic windows, there was a large balcony outside, and if it weren't for context, this place would seem like heaven on Earth. Lightning cracked outside, briefly lighting up the hotel suite.

"Tre? Rachel and I are inside . . ."

"Over here . . ."

Penelope and I turned the corner of a wall and found Tre's silhouette. He was outside on a covered part of the balcony, leaning against the railing. I eyed a heavy-looking piece of art nearby. It was like a smaller version of the statue on the nearby cabinet. It was black, shiny, and had a shape that looked like a female body without a head or arms or legs, but bent in an abstract way. The base of the statue looked heavy, like something I could smash onto someone's skull, so I decided to keep it in mind. Just in case I needed a weapon.

Trevon was staring out into the bright lights of Honolulu as rain beat down onto the uncovered part of the balcony. It was a consistent pitter-patter as his silhouette stood against the lights of the city below. He stood with his back to us.

"What took y'all so long to get here?"

"Traffic. It's raining, Tre," Penny answered.

Trevon turned and looked toward me. His eyes were glazed over. In the dim light, they sparkled quite a bit, like they were very watery. He sniffled, entering the room. "Aight."

Penny nodded. "Well, uh, I guess we should get to it, then. Huh?"

I shot her a look. She seemed to be communicating something to Trevon with her eyes. I squinted.

"Yeah . . ."

They both looked at me.

My mouth eased into an almost sarcastic grin. "The fuck is going on?"

Penelope breathed in. "Rach . . . it's time for you to be honest . . ."

I blinked. "What?"

"You were the *only one* with Dana when she got attacked."

Tre scoffed. "You think we're stupid?" he said, almost seething at the mouth.

Penny looked Tre's way and held up her hand to him. "Tre, we don't know anything yet." Penelope swallowed and looked down before looking at me. "Look, you have to tell us the truth about what happened, Rach. We aren't letting you leave this room until you do." I felt like I was slapped across the face. What the hell? "The police still haven't found who did it, but all the signs are pointing to . . ." Penelope bowed her head, seeming unable to look me in the eye or finish her sentence.

I scoffed. "T-to what? What're they pointing to, Penny?" Trevon glared daggers at me; Penny shyly looked back at me. I knew what she was indicating. "To me? You gotta be shittin' me."

Penelope looked at a loss for words. "Y-you gotta admit, Rach. It doesn't look good. Police have been mostly asking us questions about you."

I felt hurt; my eyes stung. "You brought me here . . . to *accuse me*, Penny?"

Penelope shook her head. "No, not—not to accuse you! W-we just want *the truth*."

I scoffed. "*Bullshit*, you brought me here to stand trial!" I shook my head. "God . . . I should've known you're full of shit. All that postering in the car, and all that *pretending* to care about me—"

"I *do* care about you, Rach!"

"Yeah, okay—"

"I'm sorry but *our friend is in the fucking hospital right now*! And *you* haven't exactly been straightforward with your answers! Just tell us what happened, and—"

"I have! I've been very straightforward! I *don't know* what happened, Penny! I don't know how much more clear I can be about tha—"

"Why the *fuck* are you lyin' like this?" Trevon yelled at me.

"I'm not lying, Tre!"

"You a lyin'-ass piece of shit!"

"Tre, this isn't helpful—"

"Nah, nah, nah. Only fucking person there and she didn't see? What *fucking* bullshit!"

I shook my head "I swear—"

Trevon charged me like a raging bull on steroids, pointing a finger at me. "Don't you fuck with me, asshole! *Don't you fuck with me! I know it was you! I know! There was no one else in or out that bathroom! That's what the police said!*" Trevon yelled. I shut my mouth. Shit. "What was it? Always the bridesmaid, never the bride? What, someone beat your ass so you gotta take it out on Dana, huh? *Wish you were getting married to that bitch Greg, huh?*"

"Oh, you motherfucker," I spewed through my teeth. Anger burned through my veins now. "Really? You *know* it was me?" I began toward him too, and Penelope got in between us. Keeping us at her arms' length.

"Rach, come on, it's not . . ."

I shook my head, squinting, trying to get Penny's arms off me. "What do you know, huh? *What do you fucking know? You're just a goddamn stupid junkie on the fucking pills aga—*"

"Guys, stop!"

"Ooooh What you gotta say, huh? The fuck you gotta say? Let's hear it—"

"I'll kick your fucking ass, you stupid piece of—"

"Bring it! Any time, any day! I'll do you like you did Dana—"

"You fucki—"

"*Stoooop!*" Penelope screamed the loudest, angriest I ever heard anyone scream. "Let's just calm the fuck down!" There was a brief silence as Trevon and I glared at each other. The only sounds that could be heard were the pitter-patter of rain and everyone catching their breath. Penny swallowed before speaking. "Let's just take a few moments . . . and *cool down*. Okay, guys? This isn't helping anybody."

Trevon scoffed and backed away, a wry smile on his face. He sniffled. "Aight. Alright. Is cool. Ya'll wanna play like that. I get it."

"Tre, I said cool it."

Tre backed off and rubbed his head, looking into a dark corner. Penelope turned toward me. "This is not how I wanted this to go."

"What, you the judge in this kangaroo court?"

"I *just* want to know what happened to my frien—"

"Don't you think *I* wanna know too?" I breathed hard, tears streaming from my eyes. "Dana is one of my best friends in the entire world. I—I would never do that to her—"

"Rach, I'm not accusing you—"

"Then how come you don't believe me?"

"I just don't think you're telling the whole story!" Penelope said with conviction. "Can't you just tell us what actually happened? We—we *need* to know. The fact you can't just say what happened is super fucking sus, 'kay?"

My face crumpled; I shook my head. My body shook and I began sobbing despite my efforts not to. Penelope was clutching my arms. Tears streamed down my cheeks as I continued shaking my head. "Y-you wouldn't believe me . . ."

"I would! I promise I would. You just gotta trust—"

"It'd get you like Matty. It'd get you like Matty, I—"

Penelope squinted her eyes. "Rach, what're you—"

"I can't t-tell you. I can't. I—I—"

"You have to—"

"Please . . ." I begged.

"Fuck this." Tre said. I think Penelope and I both heard the click before we turned toward him because for a moment we both froze, my heart skipping a beat. Glimmering in the dark light, in Trevon's left hand was a revolver. It looked like one of those ones from an '80s detective movie. I had no idea what model it was . . . just that if he shot that, somebody was going to die. He pointed the hand cannon right at us.

Penelope stepped slightly in front of me. "Tre? Wh-what're you doing with that? We *agreed* we'd let the police handle her—"

"Move."

"Where'd you even get that? I—I don't think she did it, Tre. I—I *believe* her. And even if she did . . ."

"I told you to move."

Penelope shook her head. "It's not her, Tre. Come on, man. Put down the piece." Trevon didn't respond, still pointing the gun at me. Penny had moved so her full body was in front of me. "I won't let you hurt he—"

Bam.

Penny went down right in front of me, clutching her gut. "Penny!" I screamed, heading for her.

Trevon cocked the gun again. I stopped, looking the gun barrel dead in the eye. "Ah, ah, ah, ah," Trevon said, shaking his head.

Penelope was screaming, clutching her stomach, hands coated in blood. *"You shot me! Y-you actually fucking shot me! Y-you crazy fuc—"*

Trevon didn't break eye contact with me, holding his gun shakily. *"Shut up, Penny! Just . . . just shut the fuck up!"*

I held up my shaking hands, trying my best to not look directly in the barrel. "E-easy Tre . . . Easy . . ." I began to move little by little toward the statue, shuffling in a way I thought was inconspicuous. "Put it down, Tre . . . You're a lot of things, but not a murderer."

"Stop moving."

I obeyed. "O-okay . . . Okay . . . You're the boss. *You're the boss.*"

Trevon sniffled. "You gonna tell me what happened to Dana. You're gonna tell me why you did what you did."

I shook my head. "I—I didn't hurt Dana."

"You lie."

"I'm not! I swear—*I swear* I'm not! I'd *never* hurt her!"

"Then who did it?"

I paused, breathing hard, keeping my hands up. "Please . . . Y-you're not gonna believe me. I—I can't t-tell you, cus you're not gonna believe me."

"You gonna tell me . . ." Trevon then pointed the gun at Penelope. "Or Penny gets another piercing."

"Tre, *what the fuck are you doing*?" Penny said, her face twisted in agony.

"I see the way she looks at you. I ain't gon' leave this room till I know who's responsible for Dana's coma." Tre licked his lips "You *both* were with her that night. One of you's gonna talk."

I gulped. "Tre, point the gun back at me."

"I-I'm really bleeding . . . I—I don't wanna die," Penelope cried. "Please, Tre, I don't wanna—"

"*I said shut up!*" Tre yelled, briefly turning his attention to Penny.

I shuffled a bit more toward the statue. "Okay, okay! I'll tell you! Just point the gun back at me!"

"Nah, I said you better start talking!"

I breathed hard, closing my eyes. "Alright, alright . . ." I opened my eyes. I swallowed, feeling like I had a lump in my throat. How the fuck was I going to say this? "L-look . . . I was in the bathroom throwing up cus of the molly. D-Dana came in to check in on me." My breaths came faster and harder. "She—she just started losing teeth all of a sudden. Then something I couldn't see s-*slammed her* into the mirror. Her body—it began dragging across the floor by itself. L-like something invisible was doing it. Her . . . her arms and legs broke like f-f-fucking twigs by themselves. I *wasn't lying* . . ." Tre simply stared at me, a blank, unreadable expression on his face. "I know it sounds crazy but it's the truth! I swear, Tre! I fucking—I fucking swear that's the truth!" I shook. "I didn't do shit 'bout it, though, *so point that gun at me*!" I screamed. I shivered so violently my jaw couldn't help but jitter up and down. "Please . . . D-don't hurt her. It's me you want. If you want to kill me, kill me. But don't hurt Penny. Please . . ."

Trevon seemed to lose all malice in his face and dropped his revolver away from Penny. Penny was looking at me, completely lost.

"A ghost," Tre said flatly. "You're saying a fucking ghost . . . hurt my Dana."

I nodded. "Yeah . . . Th-that's . . . That's what I'm saying."

Trevon shook his head, scoffing. He turned around and began chuckling, shaking his head. I eyed the statue, which was now just a little out of arm's reach.

Then Trevon looked at Penny, who locked eyes with him while on the ground. He shook his head.

"I warned her."

Trevon lifted the gun and shot Penny in the head.

My ears rang and everything moved in slow motion.

I grabbed the statue, yelled something I couldn't even make sense of, and hit Trevon in the back of the head as hard as I could. His legs buckled with the first hit and he went down with the second. Soon he was down on the ground, bleeding from his head. I turned him to face me.

Where Trevon should have been, the white-skinned, yellow-eyed version of me was there instead. She just smiled at me, the grinding noise sounding off like cannons in my ears. It sounded like a fucking fighter jet. She laughed at me.

I screamed out, anger and fear fueling me as I brought the statue down onto her face. I brought it down over and over and over again. Warm blood covered my hands, warm blood covered my face. Her skull caved in, distorting her grin like an old rotted pumpkin that once had been carved for Halloween. Bits and pieces of her skull and brains flew with each strike I brought down upon her. For Dana, for Matty, for Penny. Hell, for me. I didn't stop pummeling until I was absolutely exhausted .

I breathed hard, closing my eyes. When I opened them, it was Trevon's corpse under me. I fell over, looking at my handiwork. Bits of brain matter were all over the floor, but everything above the lower jaw looked like bloody moosh as lightning struck again to reveal the scene to me.

My hands hurt and shook, my knees ached, my throat felt completely torn up from screaming. I felt like vomiting as the weight of what I did hit me all at once.

I just killed someone. I *just killed someone*!

"Ra . . . chel" Penelope's voice croaked almost at a whisper. I looked to where Penelope lay on her side. Blood streamed from a hole in her forehead and from her mouth. Her eyes were half open, though not necessarily looking at anything. Her breaths were sudden and sharp and her fingers twitched.

"Penny . . ." I said out loud.

I carefully turned her over and lifted her into my arms. Her eyes swam without any particular direction. "Ra . . . chel . . ."

"I'm here . . . I'm here," I said, leaning over her, more blood covering me.

Penelope breathed raspy breaths. "Don't . . . don't lea . . ." she croaked.

My face twisted, more tears falling out of me. "I'm not going anywhere, Penny . . ."

"Please . . . P-please . . ."

I think I've only heard a death rattle once before in my life, when my cat had to be put down when I was a little girl. Who knew humans dying would sound even worse? It was a wheezing sound as all of the sudden, Penny's body slumped. Her eyes were open, but there was nothing behind them. I broke down, crying into her chest as her head lolled back limply.

"No, Penny, no. Please no . . ."

For what seemed like hours, I sat there, holding Penny's limp body. My face hurt from crying and the blood on me became dry and sticky.

What was even left at this point?

I sat and wondered that, clutching Penelope's dead body like a sleeping baby. The rainstorm outside began to die down a little, leaving more quiet than I cared for. I couldn't think straight. Everything just felt so loud, even in silence. Penny was dead. Matty was dead. Trevon, I killed. What more could the Red do to me?

Thump.

My ears perked. I lifted my head after hearing something within the penthouse.

Thump.

On red alert, I carefully put Penny down and looked around. I grabbed the nearby gun and clutched it tight, beginning to get up.

Did I really think a gun was going to help me? No . . .

But what the hell else was I going to do? I listened intently and walked a few steps through the darkened penthouse, just a little past the two dead bodies. The hiss of the kitchen sink on full blast reached me, not too far away.

I raised the pistol, unsure of what was coming.

Suddenly the lights turned on. Nothing came forward. Shaking, I walked deeper into the penthouse, gun at the ready. I heard the sound of the TV turning on, and voices, but I wasn't sure what they were saying. Then I walked into the living room.

I . . . was not prepared . . . for this.

Dana sat in a wheelchair, arms and legs in casts. She was watching TV when she noticed me, pointing a gun at her.

Dana looked at me, wide-eyed and breathing hard.

"Dana?" I croaked out.

"T-Tre? Tre!" Dana then called out.

Suddenly, Trevon came from around the corner where the kitchen was, looking cleaner and more alive than I last saw him. "Dana? You oka—" Then he saw me holding up the gun. "Whoa!" He immediately put his hands up.

I shook. "Y-you're dead. Th-th-that's impossible. *You're dead!*"

"Rachel, just . . . put down the gun . . ." Trevon said, swallowing hard.

"I—I—I killed you! Y-you're not supposed to be . . ."

I backed up, to look down the hallway I just came from.

There was Penelope's body. Her head was completely smashed in, brain matter all over the floor. The only thing left of her face was her lower jaw.

I crumpled, clutching my head. "No, no, no, no . . ." I closed my eyes hard. A pit formed in my stomach as I dropped the gun and dropped to my knees. "No . . ."

"Call 9-1-1," Dana said, her voice shaking. Trevon quickly left.

I screamed, tugging at my hair. *"I didn't do this!"*

"*P-Penny? Oh God*—" The sound of Trevon dry heaving echoed through the penthouse. I folded over, clutching my stomach and sobbing.

Trevon peeked his head around the corner. He looked green. "P-Penelope . . . Sh-she killed Penelope. Dana, she—"

"I said call 9-1-1!" Dana yelled at him.

I crawled toward Dana, who stared at me with almost a sense of pity. Her lips trembled as I got closer. "Please . . ." I said. "I didn't do it. I didn't kill her. Y-you have to believe me . . ." I got to her knees and put my head in her lap. "Please, Dana, please . . ."

"F-first you attack me . . . now Penny?" Dana said, her voice straining. I looked up to find her teary eyed and fidgeting. "H-honey, y-you're sick. You need help. Help I can't give you . . ."

As she said this I saw a familiar white-skinned figure behind her, gleaming down at me from over her shoulder. The familiar grinding sound began as Dana continued talking. The other me smiled at me from behind Dana, who didn't seem to notice her presence. Not moving, not blinking, just staring at me with those wild yellow eyes.

I screamed and fell back.

The other me simply stared, smiling, grinding her teeth, the sound getting louder and louder.

I screamed and screamed and screamed. I screamed until I couldn't anymore.

CHAPTER 13

A void.

It was all a void.

A stinking, shitting, sewer pit of nothingness where existence was useless. There was no light in the pit, no sound. No anything. Empty darkness. Eyes weren't useful, neither were touch or smell. If even one could talk, who would you talk to? If even you could hear, what would there be to listen to?

It was all meaningless. It was all nothing.

I didn't know how long I floated through darkness, sinking deeper into the abyss. Briefly there were colors of blue and red as I fell, a storm brewing through nothing. Lightning hidden by clouds.

I saw faces. Rows and rows of porcelain-white faces with their eyes closed. A sheen of water slightly covering them. The faces were uncountable and numerous, different shapes, different sizes. All on top of one another, evenly and perfectly like a pattern on carpet.

I moved over them silently as they passed.

Where was I?

What even was this?

Back to falling through darkness. Bubbles came out of my mouth as I breathed out.

Was I dead?

"What even is death?"

What? Who said that?

"Is death really the end? If it's not . . . why fear it? When there's so much worse . . ."

Who the fuck was that?

I opened my eyes and I was leaning against a wall in a pitch-black room. My breath shuddered. The walls felt like cloth, but there was a sensation around my whole body. It was almost like a blanket wrapped a little too tight. A light across from me flared on, hurting my eyes. I couldn't move my arms, otherwise I would've shielded my eyes. They burned, they hurt.

"The coyote will always get eaten by the wolf," a gravel-like voice from the light said. My eyes still had to adjust. "The coyote is smart, a trickster born . . . But he will never match the wolf in ferocity."

Slowly but surely, a figure came into focus sitting in the corner. They were overweight and sitting on the floor. Long gray hair from what I could see.

"The wolf is something the coyote can never be. No matter how hard the coyote fights, or how clever his tricks, the wolf will have its way. It's fated."

The figure slowly but surely became clearer with each passing moment. I breathed hard, my eyes adjusting. "Wh-where am I?"

"Right where it wants you. We're almost at the point of no return." When the figure said this, it became very clear to me who it was.

It was . . . Jennings?

She was naked and the shadows hid her face, but it definitely looked like her. Her body sagged, wrinkled and grotesquely misshapen, not entirely human. Her frame was bulbous with thin stick-like limbs that drooped like elephant skin. She was sitting on the ground like some sort of lazy troll, propped up against a wall that was deep black, like obsidian. The ground was slick, covered with water, and there was a bluish tint to the light. A small bit of fog surrounded everything.

My throat felt dry as I swallowed, looking at her. "You . . ." I looked around and noticed for the first time that I too was naked. The wall I leaned against was glimmering and black. From what I could make out of the room, it was both an infinite void and an enclosed chamber. It was hard to tell in the dark, which was altogether both asphyxiating and spacious.

"We don't have long. Only this brief chance. This final warning." Jennings looked up at me, one of her eyes missing. "This is not the first time we've had this conversation. Perhaps it will be the last. Unlikely, though . . ."

"The fuck are you talking about?"

Jennings didn't look at me. She didn't even respond to the question, merely continued to look at the floor with her only eye.

"Hey. Answer me! Warning till what?"

"It's all happened before." Jennings smiled. "You think you're the first?" Her only eye drifted to me. "It doesn't play by our rules. Time, reality, it doesn't even live where we do. You and I are cursed to relive this conversation over and over again. Can never seem to escape the inevitable."

I blinked. "Who are you really?"

Jennings didn't respond.

I blinked, my face crumpling. Okay . . . Maybe wrong question. I thought about it for a moment.

"I-is the Red a god?"

To this, Jennings grinned a sneering grin. A mean, hearty chuckle came out of her. "God?" She shook her head. "You think *God* wants anything to do with us? He just stays up there, where it's cozy and safe." She laughed. "No . . . this?"

Her eye drifted up. It looked above me, almost to the heavens. "This is what God fears." A glazed-over look came over her eye. This was the best look I got at her empty socket. The hole looked like her eye had been burned out. "We've run out of time. It knows we're awake."

"Jennings, tell me what the hell we're dealing with."

Her eye drifted back down to me, wide and crazed. "Don't look at the red. Don't look at the red."

"What does that mean?"

Jennings smiled and laughed, louder. "Don't look at the red. Don't look at the red."

"Jennings!"

Jennings stood up, laughing and screaming at the same time. Black goo emanated from the wall and clung to her back as she walked toward me, like some sort of old chewing gum that was stuck to her. She lifted her goo-covered arms. "Don't look at the red, don't look at the red, *don't look at the red*!" her toothless mouth screamed.

Suddenly, as if there was a grenade inside her, she flew apart. Brain matter, tissue, organs, torrents of blood, it all burst from her like a water balloon.

I jolted awake to the sound of a latch clicking open. Back in the dark, unable to move. Lying down, though. My wrists and ankles felt like they were tied down, inhibiting any movement. I tried to sit up, but felt like I had something firm strapping me down, right over my chest. I couldn't do much other than lift my head. Soon, a bit of light leaked in. A broad, muscular man with a mustache and a Hawaiian shirt entered the room, eventually turning on vulgar yellow lights to reveal the room I was in had all the charm of a hospital room. IE: None. Behind the man was a shorter, thicker woman with a mean face and a white polo shirt holding open the door. She had some sort of equipment belt on akin to the belt a cop would wear. In the hallway, there looked to possibly be a third, much taller, balding man wearing a similar belt.

"How's our *Red Queen* after her nap?" the muscular man said with a strange sort of familiarity.

Red Queen?

The fuck?

"Where am I?" I asked, feeling like the world was spinning just a little too fast.

The man with the mustache smiled as he went to my bedside. "Your favorite hospital, same as yesterday and many days before," he said. He put his gloved hands to the nylon and Velcro restraints tied around my wrist, and his smile fell, his face more somber and serious. He stared at me hard in the eyes. "If I undo these restraints, we gonna behave today, Rachel?"

My right eye twitched, not liking the implications. "S-sure."

With that he began undoing the restraints on me. I read his name tag. *Michael.*

I leaned back and sighed, rubbing my wrists and looking around. I was wearing a white shirt, pajama bottoms, and a blue hoodie missing its pull string and zipper. On the wall next to me, I saw pictures of Dana and Trevon, older and holding two infant children in what looked like Christmas cards. There were crude drawings that looked like kids drew them. Next to them was a large piece of paper with marker and pen marks that said *My treatment plan*. Finally, there was a picture of my mom in her gray-haired glory; underneath were the words: *In loving memory, Samantha Hannigan.*

This last one caught my eye and maintained my interest as I stared at it. Mom? Mom was . . . dead? A sense of dread seeped over me as I stared at my mom, whose picture was staring back at me, bewildered. I was a little too overwhelmed to feel much of anything at the moment.

"Come on, time to get up. Doc wants to see you after breakfast," Michael said as he undid the last restraint. With some difficulty prying my eyes away from the little celebration of life pamphlet that had my mom's face on it, I finally willed myself to get off the bed, my bare feet landing on an icy tile underneath. I quickly found some shoes that didn't have shoe laces and put them on.

The walk into the main hospital very quickly made it clear what kind of hospital I found myself in. The mixture of a certain off-ness of the fellow patients dressed in normal clothes, the three people following me with large black belts among nurses in actual hospital scrubs, and the heavy-duty gates outside the windows of the halls told me exactly where I was. Some woman down the hall screamed at the top of her lungs incoherently. A psych ward. A psych ward for the criminally insane, if I had to guess. The halls were cramped and cold as the three guards, orderlies or whatever the hell they were, trailed me.

How long had I been here?

When did Dana and Trevon have those kids?

When did Mom . . . A pit sank in my stomach as I looked out the windows toward the prison-like chain-link fences outside. Had I been here for long? What happened after Dana and Trevon found me?

Was I actually crazy? How long had it been since I first arrived in Waikiki?

It wasn't long until I was led into a cafeteria that didn't look terribly dissimilar to a grade school cafeteria, with multicolored plastic chairs in different shades of the rainbow. Michael stayed with me as I got my food, some very basic eggs and bacon with a plastic spork instead of silverware and milk in a little carton. Honestly, the food brought to mind the little lunches they had for us back in grade school too.

I couldn't help but notice different, seemingly more coherent patients staring at me, but looking away as I turned my attention to them. You know the feeling where everyone but you was in on a joke? That's what it was beginning to feel like. It was like people were avoiding making eye contact with me by any means possible. The orderlies, or whatever they were, seemed to be playing this little game too. Everyone except Michael, who was eyeing me like a hawk with a fake smile.

"So what, you my babysitter?"

Michael chuckled. "Come on, don't say it like that. We're old buddies, aren't we?"

I stuffed eggs in my mouth. "I don't know, are we?" I chewed a little, looking toward a woman in thick horn-rimmed glasses who looked at me like I was Satan. "Kinda feels like you're either my prison guard or bodyguard."

Michael nervously chuckled. "Look, Rach . . ." he said under his breath with a hushed tone. "Doctor Higler just wants to make sure you get to your appointment on time. You know as well as I do that you tend to take little *adventures.*"

I lifted my eyebrows. "I do, do I?" I asked before taking another bite. News to me. Was that where I've been all this time? On a little adventure? "Well . . . guess I've just been a busy little bee."

After I finished up breakfast, Michael gently led me down a long hall with his gloved hand on my back. To Mike's credit, I never got creep vibes from him this whole time. His hand was appropriately placed, like a cop trying to lead a suspect away. Only difference was I did not have handcuffs. I once read somewhere that a psych ward was not a preferable alternative to a prison. That many prefer prison because it had more dignity. Considering how infantilized I was beginning to feel, I think that article I read may have had a point. Not to mention, at least with prison you're given a sentence, an expiration date for when you would get released. For a ward, it was indefinite. *Until you get better.*

How long had I been *sick*?

I walked and walked, eyeing metal doors and barred windows. For a moment, I thought a nurse in scrubs I passed was Penelope. But . . . that was impossible. I killed . . . I mean, Penelope was—she was dead. I blinked a few times and sure enough, it was a different woman altogether.

Maybe everything *was* just a fucked-up hallucination.

Before I knew it, Mike walked me to a room with large windows for walls, where a woman with a white coat stood in front of a desk. She was older, with a wrinkled but kind face. There was also a younger, twenty-something nurse with a clipboard sitting in a seat near the desk. The doctor smiled at me. "Rachel! Good to see you! Take a seat."

I looked over to where she pointed. It was a plastic chair very clearly attached to the ground. I glared at it, then her. Then I looked back at Mike, who folded his arms like some sort of bouncer. I sighed and then sat in the chair awkwardly.

Dr. Higler . . . That was the name on the woman's name tag. She sat at her desk, keeping a pleasant face. "It's been a while since we last saw each other, Rachel. Given the latest little incident, though, I thought this was appropriate."

I blinked. What the hell was going on?

The doctor started a timer, then she breathed in through her nose and smiled at me. "First off, how are you today? How are you feeling?"

I licked my lips. "Fine. You?"

There was an awkward silence as Dr. Higler looked away from me and wrote something on a sheet of paper. "That's good! Very good. I'm good, thank you." She sighed. "Let's, uh, let's begin by addressing the elephant in the room, shall we? You know why you were confined to your bed the last few days, right?"

I shrugged. "I called Mike fat?"

Mike, behind me, chuckled lightly.

Higler's face sharpened, glaring at the man behind me before looking back at me. Apparently, she didn't find the remark as funny. "Funny, but . . . This is not a joking matter, Rachel. I am being very serious."

I sighed. "Why was I strapped to my bed, Doctor?"

The doctor nodded. "I think you know very well what you did, Rachel. You are smart." There was a pause as Dr. Higler looked me up and down. "A technician is in the hospital." I blinked, merely staring at her. "Rachel . . . you attacked her with a sharp object. Stabbed her multiple times. You're lucky she survived. Consequences for murder could've been dire."

I shook my head, sighing before a laugh rose from deep in my gut. "I *literally* have no idea what you're talking about, dude."

Higler's kind face looked not so kind as she looked me up and down. "Are you messing with me?"

I shook my head. "Nope. I'm telling ya . . ." I glared at the woman in front of me. "I don't remember doing that. Doesn't even sound like me."

Higler lifted her chin. "Really? Is that so?"

"Yeah. Pretty sure you have the wrong gal. I've never stabbed anyone in my life."

Higler blinked a few times before squinting. "If I recall correctly, you're in here for an assault and a murder. So stabbing someone . . . that *doesn't* sound like something you'd do? I'm just trying to see the logic in what you're saying here."

I lifted my eyebrows, my mouth pointing into a slight grin. "See but . . . I—*I* didn't kill anybody. Penelope's death, that—that wasn't on me. *I* didn't do that."

Higler blinked, unimpressed. "Ten years, Rachel. You've been here ten years. We've had this discussion many times. You know *that you did what you did* . . ."

Wait . . .

What?

I stopped for a moment, blinking. "I-I've been here ten years?" I said.

Higler's face was stiff as a board "Ten and a half, technically. And still! It still seems like you fail to cooperate with us." Higler leaned in. "I don't know how many times I have to tell you, Rachel: We are here to *rehabilitate* you. We're *not* enemies. We're not *the Red*. You need help. You're a person who's unwell, and we're here to help you."

I went slack-jawed, unable to completely process the information. Ten years? Ten years since Waikiki? How the fuck had it been ten years? In the blink of an eye. I'd been here that long? I was in my forties now?

"Don't you want to mix in with other patients? Go to the common room? Get some new friends? You can't be part of group activities until we get this behavior problem under control. The medication can only help so much. To a degree, you are responsible for handling your symptoms."

I scoffed, looking down at the ground. "Ten years. Wow." Was I really that far gone? Ten years of my life I just . . . don't even remember? One moment I was thirty, the next I was . . . forty?

"Rachel . . . Rachel, can you please make eye contact with me when I'm talking to you?"

I looked up, furrowing my brow. "Have I . . . have I really been here for ten years?"

Higler looked at me with something resembling sympathy. Then she sighed. "I'm upping your prescription. Clearly, we aren't doing enough to combat your symptoms." She tapped her pen and shook her head. "I really thought we were getting close to a breakthrough with you. I'm . . . Well . . ." She looked deep in thought. "Frankly, I'm a little disappointed."

She stopped the timer.

"Behave for the next two weeks and we will see about reinstating some of your privileges."

I stared at her desk, not at her. Dazed. "How did my mom die?"

Higler seemed caught off guard by my question. "I'm sorry?"

"How . . . did my mom . . . die?"

Dr. Higler sighed and nodded. "Um, I *believe* it was a heart attack, if I'm not mistaken. I am deeply sorry for your loss. Loss of a parent is rough."

I sat still, still completely in disbelief. Ten years gone. I was off the rails of the crazy train, and ten years were gone. Where was I through all of it? I lost my family, I lost my friends, I lost everything.

I had nothing left.

I sat there for a moment, stunned.

As much as I felt heartbroken, though, something inside me refused to believe everything. Maybe it was what Jennings said, that the Red had me exactly where it wanted me. My little supposed delusion. Ten years? Really?

There was just . . . something a bit off. One thing that didn't quite add up. I glared at the doctor. The way Higler talked . . . Call me crazy, but doctors tend to use more medical lingo in their speech when addressing a patient. I mean, it was a longshot, and a very subtle thing. But she didn't . . . quite speak like a doctor should. I mean, nowhere in her speech did she actually address whatever I supposedly was in treatment for. Couldn't hurt to ask. I had nothing left to lose, right?

I swallowed. "Remind me . . . What is my official diagnosis again?"

Higler took a moment to process, then grinned wryly. "Session's over, Rachel. Time to go back to your room."

I squinted. That wasn't an answer. "I'm serious. You never once stated what exactly I'm diagnosed with. And—and what exact drugs are you prescribing me? What's the name of my medication?"

Higler's face was stiff. "Rachel, I'm not in the mood for games. This is aggressive behavior."

I couldn't believe it. I figured it out. She wasn't who she said she was. She wasn't a doctor.

"You don't know what I'd be diagnosed with, do you?" I asked. There was a twitch in Dr. Higler's face. A small one, but it was there in her right cheek. "And you don't know the *exact* meds I'd be prescribed."

Higler merely glared at me, stone-faced.

I blinked, realizing some more things. "Dana always said she never wanted kids, now she suddenly has two? And—and my mom *never* went by Samantha. She hated being called that. Her friends always called her Sammy."

"Rachel, come on, it's time to go," Mike said, creeping up behind me.

I grinned as a realization came upon me, my heart beginning to pound hard in my chest. "None of this is real, is it? You don't even have a name for the hospital, do you?"

"Rachel, I'm not gonna ask again." Mike started to grab me but I shot to my feet, away from him, and unfortunately into a corner.

"No, no, no. This isn't right. This isn't right. It's the Red again."

The quiet nurse in the corner immediately stood up. "Calm down, Rachel."

"The Red isn't real, remember what we talked about?" Doctor Higler insisted. "*The Red isn't real.*"

"J-just drop the fucking act already! I'm onto you!" The nurse crept in and Mike kept his gloved hands up as he moved in. I laughed in disbelief. "Ohhh, you motherfucker. You're good. I almost fell for it. I almost fell for—" Mike grabbed me and I scratched his face as hard as I could. "Get the *fuck* off me!" Mike yelped in pain but continued to muscle me. "Let me go!"

Soon, other big, burly people with big black belts began to enter the small room and restrain me.

"We're not trying to hurt you!"

"Nooo! Get off! I'll fucking kill you! Get off!"

"Nurse! Sedative!"

"Get off me! Get off me!!" I screamed at the top of my lungs as I thrashed about, the big, burly people putting me into some sort of hold and slamming my face against the desk so hard I could taste the metal. My legs kicked and kicked as someone pulled the back of my pants down. Soon after, I felt something long and metallic stab into my butt cheek that hurt like hell.

"It's okay, Rachel. It's okay . . . You're safe."

My body went limp. Someone pulled back up my pants. I let out a small involuntary whine before the big, burly people pulled me off the desk, holding me up somewhat.

Higler stared at me analytically, moving her jaw side to side. My vision swam as I stared at her.

"What are you thinking? Back to her room?" Mike asked.

"No . . . I believe Ms. Hannigan has earned herself some ECT time."

Mike seemed hesitant. "You sure that's a good idea? I mean, she's—"

"Of course I'm sure. This has gone on long enough. Take her to the room. No arguing, Mike."

Mike sighed. "Whatever ya say, boss." His voice began to distort. "*Whatever you say . . .*"

I was dragged unceremoniously across tile floors, my feet trailing behind as the orderlies held me by the arms. It seemed like the hallways never ended. The ground was wet, like there was a leaky pipe somewhere.

The hallways got dark, then light, then dark again. The ground was completely covered in water. The world spun as I heard Dr. Higler's heels clack on the tile behind us. The group of large people that surrounded me seemed to grow taller the more I looked at them; I almost couldn't even make out their faces because they were mostly covered in shadows. My vision swam. In the distance, there were flashes of red and the blurry figure of the man with the hat. My vision twisted and turned and twisted again. The scared patients in the halls as we passed—their faces distorted, elongated until they were unrealistic. Soon, I wasn't even sure if what I was looking at were human faces anymore. Drool dripped from my lips as I turned my head. I felt the world going upside down and inside out as the lights of the hall continued to flash.

"Rachel! Rachel!" a voice said to me from the side. I sleepily looked over as Dana, in full nightclub attire, yelled at me, her mouth becoming bigger than the rest of her body and her eyes drifting completely separate ways. "You'll never be as good as Penny, you hear me? You fu—" Her voice became muffled and muted as the world turned this way and that.

Suddenly, for a brief second, everything went dark.

Everything came back and I was being placed on a table. The features of the various doctors and nurses around me in hospital scrubs were completely twisted and distorted. One nurse's eyes were a little too wide to be human, and her grin looked blank and menacing. A doctor on the other side of me looked like his nose was too big and his eyes were too little.

"ThE PaTienT isalmostready Forrr heR TreatmeNT," one of the nurses said, her voice slowing and speeding up.

Higler appeared near the nurses, normal looking and undistorted. She looked me in the eyes as the nurses strapped me in with leather straps.

"Ten years! Ten fucking years I've had to put up with your *bullshit*! All you do is bitch and moan and bitch and moan and bitch! Never even asked *me* about *my* problems!" Higler said with a ravenous tone, nearly foaming at the mouth. A nurse shoved something rubber into my mouth. "Do you ever think of anybody other than yourself? You ever ask *me* how *my* fucking day was? *It's all about you!*"

A nurse slipped a jagged metallic headpiece attached to wires onto my head. I tried to struggle against it, but even with the straps around my arms and legs, the nurses held me down. Despite my struggling, the metal headpiece was perched atop my head, its sharp edges digging into my forehead and drawing blood. I moved my head this way and that, trying to get it off desperately, but I couldn't. It felt like a vice grip digging into my brain. A new wave of panic set over me, even though my body couldn't do much to resist or to fight. I tried begging but the words couldn't find their way out past the muffle. *Not like this! Please not like this. Punish me some other way. Please don't do this to me! Please!* Higler was pulling out her own hair in chunks, frothing at the mouth. Her eyes bulged out of their sockets, her flesh turning oily and pinkish and bubbling, her head jittering toward the side, front teeth growing more prominent.

"It's like that time you were little with that *stupid fucking bunny rabbit*! Nobody cares! Nobody gives a *fuck*! *You don't matter, Rachel! You don't fucking matter! Do you hear me?*"

A surge of electricity shot through my body and searing pain followed. My body arched as every vein I had burned. I shook spastically and uncontrollably as an electric current surged through every fiber of my being. The light above me flashed on and off above me. My mind rushed. Panicked. I couldn't focus. *How was I going to get out of this? How was I going to get—* Higler looked more twisted, hairless except for a few strands, large front teeth and purplish pinkish veins that looked glossy in the lighting.

"Get her again! Again! *Again!*"

Another surge of electricity seared through my body, causing it to shake uncontrollably. I shut my eyes hard as the white-hot pain flooded through me. When I opened them, one of the ceiling panels was moving directly above me. A corner's worth of a hole stared back at me, yellow eyes looking down at me, unblinking, a wide shit-eating smile peering at me from the darkness. Oh God. Not again. Please God, not again. I couldn't take that *goddamn* familiar smile anymore. Not that stupid *fucking* smile. It was *horrid and it wouldn't leave me alone, why the fuck wouldn't it leave me alone?* I began to cry, and heard the grinding sound. I blinked, and when I opened my eyes, the other me was lying on the ceiling above me, looking down at me, giggling uncontrollably. But she wasn't alone. Trevon, Penelope, Matty, Dana, and Kai were all lying on the ceiling too, face down, arms and legs completely straight. They didn't even look real with their faces remaining hidden, turned toward the ceiling. I screamed at them as the other me lay perfectly still, other than her belly moving with her laughter. The light flickered. I looked down, back at the nurses.

All of them had ripped off their skin, revealing red skull faces. All the red skull faces stared at me with blank black holes. Blood had been smeared haphazardly all over the walls. Electricity surged through my body. I blinked again, and all the nurses were completely skinless corpses, bleeding everywhere, pulling out my innards and greedily stuffing them into their mouths. Disemboweling me, eviscerating me. Their exposed muscles and veins glistened as their hands ripped through my belly, teeth tearing at my bloody intestines and stomach with excruciating, sharp, and agonizing bites. I looked back up at the other me and screamed at the top of my lungs from behind the mouthpiece.

I screamed and screamed and screamed.

But there was no escape.

There was never going to be an escape.

The Red would never let me go. Even if I outsmarted it or beat it at its own game . . . it would never let me go.

CHAPTER 14

The black-haired woman on the TV screamed and screamed as skinless people feasted on her bloody entrails.

Rachel couldn't help but laugh at the fucking dumb movie. People actually filmed this? What kind of Hollywood exec. actually gave the okay for people to film this shit movie? The effects looked cheap and the damn thing was getting old. Dumb protagonist kept falling for the tricks of the evil entity or whatever.

"What a stupid bitch." Rachel laughed again, finding amusement from what she saw on the screen. With a bored and tired motion, she yawned and grabbed the remote, immediately pointing it at the screen. Did they not have good TV in Waikiki? She turned off the dumb movie, watching the screen fade to black.

Rachel blinked and folded her mouth in disappointment before stuffing another strawberry in it. When was Dana going to contact her? They had been at the hotel for a few hours since getting off the plane, and Rachel was getting restless. When were they going to go out for drinks? She wanted to actually see Waikiki! Not be locked in some damn hotel room.

Rachel sighed and looked out at the balcony outside. Rain hit the glass with a vengeance as the palm trees hung on for dear life. Lovely weather outside, really.

Rachel, this isn't making any sense . . .

Rachel got up off the couch in her hotel living room and walked to the bedroom.

"Baby?" she asked aloud, opening the door. Penelope was sitting on the bed. Mint-green dress, her back facing Rachel as she entered. "Babe, you get any word from Dana? 'Bout when we meet with Matty and her?"

"Not yet, love. Still waiting," Penny said brightly, completely transfixed by the lovely weather outside. Thunder cracked outside as the dim light of late day poured in. Wind howled ferociously and the trees bent like they were going to be pulled from their roots.

Rachel thought for a moment about just how lucky she was. To be finally on vacation to Waikiki with her girlfriend after all these years. She sighed. She couldn't help but think, as she stared longingly at the woman she loved: *This is the woman I'm one day going to marry.*

"That—that's not what I'm thinking."

Rachel imagined all the dates they had been on together. About the time they went kayaking on rapids, and the other adventures she would've never agreed to otherwise.

"Babe, do you hear that?" Rachel asked, looking around the room.

"Hear what, my love? All I can hear is the storm. It really is such lovely weather we're having," Penelope said, keeping her back to Rachel.

"It's like . . . someone is narrating."

. . . .

. . . .

. . . .

I blinked in a stupor, processing the almost-silence. Rain beat hard, really hard, against the glass door that led to the balcony.

I was . . . back in Tropical Springs?

I took a moment, breathing hard, leaning on the edge of the foot of the bed, before sliding down to the floor. I put my hand to my head and shut my eyes tight.

What was wrong with me?

I looked out the glass door and at the raging storm outside. It was unreal. Completely unlike any storm I'd ever seen. The wind howled ferociously. Was that a hurricane?

Was I in hell?

I thought back to the psych ward I was just in. Thought about everything that had happened. My breathing became erratic, and I clutched my head.

I—I was fucking losing it.

I didn't know what's going on anymore.

My body trembled and I felt like puking. What was real anymore? I sat on the floor of my hotel room, tears pouring out of my eyes. I leaned my back against the foot of the bed before letting out sobs.

Was it ever going to end?

I fell over to my side and curled up in a ball on the carpet. I just wanted it to end. I was tired; tired, and didn't want this to continue. Was I cursed to live like this forever?

I don't know how long I cried on the floor. Could've been at least an hour. Was time even relevant anymore? I felt . . . broken. Broken beyond repair. My thoughts began wandering as my tears came to a crawl. I stared at nothing for the longest while.

Finally, words came out. Words I didn't expect. I smiled.

"P-Penny . . . d-do you wanna know how I met Greg?"

No response. I didn't need there to be. I swallowed back the bile and snot at the back of my throat. "It was . . . it was a cloudy day. A—a pool party. I didn't even see him coming." I breathed in a harsh breath and shuddered. "I had just wrapped up a fling with this one girl . . . and, uh, I don't know, wasn't in the market for girls at the time. He w-was a friend of a friend that was moving. It was a going away party for that friend. Greg was . . . charming. So goddamn charming." I breathed in and out. "We wound up in the pool together at some point. Horseplay . . . cus Greg was all about horsing around. Somehow, we wind up under water, my legs wrapped around his waist. W-we had our first kiss underwater. It was like a fucking movie scene. Time stood still . . . my hair flowed like ribbons." My eyes stung. "I—I didn't know he had a girlfriend at the time. I—I didn't care. I was . . . so entranced. He was like a magnet to me. I didn't know . . ." I shook my head. "S-sometimes I wonder if . . . if what happened to me was karma. If everything after is what I deserved for being the other woman. I wonder . . . if I deserve to be happy."

Penelope kept quiet. I lifted my head, feeling tired. I dug into my pocket and pulled out my phone. I went to Instagram, to my blocked list, and found his name. I stared at his profile picture. I swallowed, then pressed unblock. A calm serenity came over me as I looked over his account. Pictures of him on the beach with some new, much prettier, younger girl. A girl who looked like a model. Who looked like she filled every desire he ever had. I stared as he seemed so unbothered without me. So unaffected. His life went on . . . Mine didn't. He and his girl looked . . . happy.

You were easy to get over.

I stared at the pictures of Greg and his new woman—a happy couple. Then I closed my phone and placed it with the screen down in front of me.

It didn't matter anymore.

Maybe it never did.

I sat up and hugged my legs, sniffling. I looked outside. To be honest, it didn't look like there was much outside the balcony. Just gray nothingness and rain. I stood up, tears falling, and walked to the glass door. Wind blew, definitely sounding like a hurricane; the rain beat against the glass like tiny bullets about to shatter the damn thing. I closed my eyes hard, listening to the rain.

What beautiful music.

"Hey, Penny . . ." I said before opening my eyes. "Do you wanna walk in the rain again?"

I turned.

Penny's skin was bleach-white, a vacant smile on her face. Her eyes were yellow and staring at me.

A loud, thunderous grinding sounded off in my ears. I clutched them in agony and grit my teeth.

I backed away, my head feeling like it was gonna explode.

The grinding sound shifted, sounding like men chanting in an unfamiliar language. Chanting the same thing over and over again. On instinct, I looked toward the glass door and could very clearly see the man with the hat standing on the balcony. His red skull face dripped as his vacant eyes pierced into my soul. My eyes widened as I realized I could now see him clearly, with his suit and black trench coat. I felt sick. My body was numb and on fire all at the same time. A sharp glass-like pain filled the veins in my arms and hands swelled, growing more pronounced, and I shook like a leaf. I was burning, freezing, in seering agony as the worst pain I'd ever felt lurched through me. Only burn victims would know the blistering feeling I felt. The man with the hat opened the glass door very calmly and casually, letting some of the weather in. Thunder cracked and my hair blew frantically in the wind and rain.

The other me emerged out of the shadows of the nearest corner of the door, moving like a stop-motion figure. I dropped to my knees from the pain, needing to vomit. When I looked up, the other me was pushing the other Penny to the bed and crawling on top of her. Her hands dug into Penny's stomach and moved under Penny's skin as both stared at me, grinning. I lurched forward, still in immense pain and trying to hold back vomit. The man with the hat walked in and turned his head stiffly, coldly, toward the other me and Penny. The two were vibrating, uncontrollably, as the other me lowered her face into Penny's.

Finally, I threw up. Plain water gushed out of my mouth. I looked down for a second to see a faint white substance in the water before looking up. The chins of the other me and Penny had combined, fused together like two bits of gum stuck together and pulled apart. An animalistic shriek echoed as their mouths melted into one. Both pairs of eyes rolled back into their skulls as they mercilessly shook. Arms sprouted out, multiple long, white, spindly arms from their combined torsos. The creature rose off the bed like some sort of spider, still shrieking, loud, louder than the chanting. My hand began to shake violently. I looked down and couldn't help but notice the veins in my hand squirming like snakes beneath my skin. I looked back up as the spider-like abomination ripped both the other me's and Penelope's faces off like a Band-Aid, revealing two red skulls combined together without a lower jaw. The man with the hat then turned his face slowly toward me, and the large *thing* began to move.

I didn't wait around to find out what it was gonna do.

Fighting through the pain, through pure primal instinct I immediately booked it.

I stumbled through the doorway of my bedroom, the burning pain lessening as I got away from the creatures. The window in the living room area of my hotel room was beginning to crack, the storm getting even more out of control, entire trees and umbrellas flying by. I almost slipped on tile as I passed the kitchen and made my way to the front door. My hands fumbled clumsily with the lock, hands still shaking and feeling like they were asleep. That agonizing, acidic feeling lurched throughout my body again and I looked behind me to see the double-faced skull of the abomination beginning to peek out from my bedroom, jittering all the while. My hands finally got the door open and I rushed out. A torrent of water was pouring out into the dark hallway from Jennings's room as I passed it.

I was in a full-on sprint toward the elevator. The hallway twisted and turned. I looked behind me. The creature made its way methodically, and it had definitely picked up a rhythm and speed, filling up the cramped hallway, having gained more arms and skulls. The other hotel room doors were bursting open, pouring out waves of water as my feet splashed through. I got to the elevator and immediately tried prying it open.

Voosh.

A tidal wave of water rushed out of the elevator, pushing me back and completely soaking me in salty seawater. My back hit a wall as I lifted my head and gasped for air. A surge of white-hot pain shot throughout my body, and I looked down to see my fingers bending backward, quickly and frantically at random, switching between being hyperextended and normal. The bones felt like they were breaking all the while.

The creature had gotten closer, almost in reaching distance. My head started to tilt to one side, jittering farther and farther and farther. My arms began to snap and bend the wrong way as the creature loomed. Sharp cracks sounded in my neck as the thing approached, and a lily-white hand started to creep out of its mouth. The creature rumbled and screeched as I got up as quick as I could and began running, my neck, arms, and head resetting themselves to the right position, pain lessening again. I ran and ran before slipping, my back hitting stairs that weren't there before as I headed downward. My body rolled to the bottom with a solid thud. The hotel hallway looked like it went down farther.

The chants got louder again, and up ahead in the hall, the man with the hat was calmly walking toward me, one slow, methodical step at a time. I was trapped between them—but the creature behind me shrieked loudly, prompting me to get up and run—right toward the man with the hat. My head began feeling like it was squeezing into itself and my skin felt like it was being peeled by a blowtorch. Even if I wanted to give in, to let the Red have whatever it wanted, this *pain,* it—it was unbearable! Completely and utterly! I'd never known a worse— A hallway opened between the two monsters and I headed that way, turning the corner and completely losing sight of both. There was a sudden shift in gravity as I landed on my side. I looked up and the hallway was completely on its side, water splashing down from the doors above. I got up and ran, water pouring atop my head as I passed underneath. The man with the hat was right behind me, still calmly walking forward. No rush or pep in his step.

Suddenly, the floor from under me caved. I looked up as the open door I fell through got farther and farther away before I landed in a pool of water.

I lifted myself out to find that it was filled with naked, floating people that were completely still. I swam through them, looking behind me in the labyrinth. A bunch of white arms were emerging from the door in the ceiling I had fallen through, like the legs of a spider. I darted my gaze away and found a staircase that led upward.

I was back in a dark, dry hotel hallway. I breathed hard, catching my breath a moment.

My back suddenly twisted unnaturally, and my mouth stretched out, unnaturally hinging, before returning to normal. I looked back, and the spider abomination was peeking around the corner.

Gotta keep running. Couldn't stop. I ran ahead and found a slightly open door. When I opened it all the way, there was a large, lit-up screen with two naked figures.

"Ohhh yes." It was my own voice. "Fuck yeah, Greg. Fuck . . ."

The room was set up not dissimilarly to a movie theater. I looked at the people watching. They all had long black hair, tied up the exact same way. All were dressed in the same red dress. In perfect synchronization, they all turned their heads toward me, like stop-motion figures. They were all other mes . . . all smiling the same way with those hideous yellow eyes.

I backed away, looking behind. The abomination was on the ceiling, crawling toward me much faster than before. I ran even faster, but this time the agonizing burning sensation didn't go away. My hands and fingers still uncontrollably bent and twisted the wrong way in front of me, bones beaking and resetting themselves all the while. The world almost seemed like TV static; everything was blinking. Different sights passed by in the hallway: A skinned man eating the flesh off a gutted Penelope's face. Dana and Trevon sharing the same naked body, a corpse, with legs where their arms should be. Matty laughed at me with burned-out eyes.

Finally, I arrived in the main lobby, but it wasn't the hotel lobby anymore. Water fell from the ceiling as I found myself on a balcony in a large cathedral-like room with towering, jagged walls that seemed to be ever moving, ever changing. There was a lake-sized pool of water below, filled with dead, naked bodies. I looked to my side to see the man with the hat walking up the stairs directly toward me, radiating a certain sense of purpose as he headed up, the light from the water reflecting off him. On the staircase on my opposite side was something that looked kinda like a pale, wet, and naked Penelope with barnacles on her face and a bullet hole in her head, her lower half completely twisted backward. Her limbs moved like they were broken as she climbed up the stairs, her eyes rolled back into her skull.

"Raaaacheeeel . . . Raaacheel . . ."

Behind me was the abomination, looking more like a strange bloody mass of white arms and red skulls. It opened its mouth and a pair of white hands covered in goo and viscera began crawling out. Soon, the other me in the white sundress appeared, her belly bloated like a balloon. She stood up normally, not in fast motion, covered in what almost looked like afterbirth, clearly pregnant and staring at me with those lifeless yellow eyes. All three figures approached me. I backed away, finding my back at the railing of the balcony. Cornered. I looked over the railing. The water looked about fifteen or twenty, maybe thirty feet down.

Everything in my body began screaming in agony. Veins pronounced themselves in my arms, swelling, and I howled in agony as the three figures crept toward me. Quickly, I climbed over the railing of the balcony and without much thought for the fall, I let go and jumped, diving down.

The fall felt short as I dropped into the people-infested water. Sea saltwater snuck into my nostrils and burned, and it was only once I was in the water that

I saw that the floating naked people were just a bunch of other mes, floating lifeless and still. My hair flowed as I swam farther and farther down, past more and more floating, dead mes with lily-white skin.

I kept going down until I breached the surface of the dark water. I gasped for air as my eyes stung from the vibrant white of my surroundings. There was a light fog as I looked around, the water suddenly only waist-high. Nothing but water, for miles and miles around, and a blank, overcast sky. I shivered, the air on my seawater-wet skin making me cold. Behind me, the man with the hat floated above the water. I froze. He was standing perfectly still, looking directly at me. I breathed hard, staring at his meaty skull face, blood dripping. His hollow eyes seemed to look through me as I stared back. Aside from my heavy breath, there was nothing but silence.

In a slow, methodical movement, the man with the hat looked up, away from me. Cautiously, I turned. In the middle of this ocean-like place, there were white stairs and a white door. What the hell?

I didn't have time at all to process what happened at the hotel. But now? Now I was looking at my surroundings and beginning to wonder . . . where the hell was I? I looked back at the man with the hat. His blank, skull face simply remained pointed in the direction of the door.

Okay . . .

I looked back toward the door. It stood tall and erect, but normal looking. Like a door that one would see in a modern suburban home. Slowly, I walked forward, still trying to get away from the man with the hat. The water slushed below me as I stumbled. Hesitantly I began climbing the short staircase that was maybe only four or five steps in total. It didn't take much to get to the top, though they were tiled like bathroom tiles and slippery. I got to the door and hesitated.

Was it a bad idea to open this door? Probably.

I looked around, though. There was literally just this door and miles and miles of what looked like ocean. That and the man with the hat standing atop the water. There was nowhere else to go that I could see. I took a deep breath and grabbed the doorknob, finding it relatively easy to turn. I turned it and looked back at the man with the hat.

It was like a doll coming apart piece by piece as he fell to the drink below, his arms, limbs, and head just dropping off at the same time into the water. Soon there was only a black trench coat and hat floating in the sea. I stared at the hat floating for a moment. What was *that* about?

Swallowing, I turned back to the door. My hand trembled as I clutched the doorknob. What the hell was beyond this door? A small part of me was telling me to not open it. To just try to find a way, any way but the door, to escape this endless sea. Maybe swim for all eternity if that's what it took. Drowning in whatever plane or dimension this was didn't seem so bad in comparison to whatever the Red had in store . . . But a more overwhelming part of me wanted to see the other side. A deeper, more primal instinct. I *needed* to see the other side. I *needed* to know what was behind the door.

I could feel my heart in my chest as I pushed open the door. The white light was blinding as I stepped through, and I had to close my eyes hard as I moved forward. I stood for a moment, shivering. My eyes had to adjust as I reopened them, with the white being so blinding.

The severity of my situation quickly became clear to me. Everything was plaster white. The sky, the ground . . . and then the other things. I wasn't sure what the hell they were at first. At first glance they all looked like oddly shaped trees. Rows of oddly shaped white trees among a glistening white field. There was something large ahead of me. One tree was bigger than the others by miles, so big that it disappeared among the skies. It moved and creaked slightly back and forth like there was wind. As far as I could tell, though, no such wind blew. I looked behind me. The door had completely disappeared. Behind me were more of the strange white trees standing erect atop the glistening white ground. I was standing in the middle of this strange field. All alone.

I walked forward, and a small bit of water rippled under my feet. I looked down at the floor. Immediately, there was a familiar sight.

Faces.

Faces stacked upon each other. Faces upon faces for miles. They were endless, like some sort of strange tile that took up the world. They were white, like they were made of plaster or something, but there was still a skin-like texture to their surface. The thin layer of water covered their faces, rippling as I walked, trembling all the while. When I looked up at the strange trees, I realized they weren't trees at all. They were . . . sculptures. Sculptures made out of the same white plaster-like material, with strange shapes. It was like someone had made interpretive art with human anatomy. On one, a head had a torso placed on top of it. Underneath the head were five buttocks attached to backward legs. Arms stuck out of the torso at the top like antennae. Another statue was like a torso with a bunch of legs emerging from it. Another torso was beneath it and they were held up by an arm with its palm planted on the ground. I couldn't count how many of these strange sculptures there were. It almost felt like I was walking among a large cornfield or apple tree orchard. These seemed deliberately and meticulously planted.

As I got closer and closer to the large tree, I began to see it was more of the same . . . just done on a much more intricate scale. It was like a coral reef made up of strictly arms and legs. It was maybe eight or ten feet wide, but extended like some sort of weird ladder up toward the heavens. It creaked softly back and forth, emitting a sound identical to a tree blowing in the wind. My body shook in its presence. I was seeing something few humans had ever seen before. I couldn't help but be bewildered by its sheer size. It looked . . . infinite.

Obeying the primal curiosity yet again, I reached out and touched it. The skin on the arms and legs felt dry, like wood or bone. They had a sandpaper-like texture to them. I wrapped my hand around one and looked up. These arms and legs seemed to go up for miles, disappearing among low-hanging clouds.

I put another hand a little higher, and my foot onto an arm near the bottom. I didn't know why, but . . . I wanted to climb.

I had only just begun climbing when the sky and everything around me began to turn a shade of pink. Soon, the color darkened, and a bright light emanated from above. Without thinking, I looked up.

It was . . .

The most beautiful thing I had ever seen.

A bright red light emanated from the heavens, basking me and everything around me in the color, and I could do nothing but stare at its glory. Soon, the red light became all I could see. I felt . . . amazing. Like something warm and sweet washed over me. Like a heavenly warm shower of ambrosia. I had no pain anymore. No sorrow. Greg no longer mattered. Neither did Dana, Trevon, Matty. Not even Penelope. I was . . . cured. Cured of everything that ever haunted me. I smiled as I stared into the bright, red light. I finally saw the truth. The truth of the world, of suffering, of divinity.

I was cured of my suffering.

Cured of sensation and feeling.

I was cured of being Rachel.

I stared at the light, my eyes aching gloriously as they began to burn away, the warmth I felt becoming a blistering, searing heat. My skin bubbled and burst. I chuckled. It all . . . made sense now. Everything. I couldn't help but laugh because the answers had been there the whole time. I laughed because it was the funniest and most delightful truth I had ever known.

Jennings was wrong.

The red is pure and it is glorious.

The red is pure and it is glorious.

The red is pure.

And it is glorious.

EPILOGUE

Honolulu Police Department Audio Recording #367482

"Check. Testing 1 2 3 . . ."

. . .

"This is Detective Jordan. The date is April 24, 2024. This is in regards to the investigation of the deaths of Rachel Hannigan, Penelope Albright, and Matthew Vasquez. Please state your name, ma'am."

"Um, Dana Jackson. Well . . . it would've been if the wedding happened. Dana Harding. That's my current legal name."

"Why don't you explain what happened the night of the eighteenth of April, 2024. The night before the incident."

"Um . . . well . . . It was my bachelorette party. Rachel was . . . *jumpy* after being attacked by that old woman. The night of the party, we were going to a club and Penny offered her . . ."

"Offered her what?"

". . . Fuck it. Offered her molly. At some point in the night, we were at the club and completely lost track of her. Found her unconscious in a bathroom stall, covered in puke. Immediately we freak out. She wakes up and is kind of awake but not awake."

"And you didn't take her to the hospital?"

"Figured we could handle whatever was going on. More accurately, I guess, Penny didn't want the law involved. Took an Uber back to the hotel and got Rachel to her hotel room. Woke Matty up, who was . . . understandably pissed. Penny and Matty got into an argument when Rachel began uncontrollably convulsing. Her eyes rolled into the back of her head. It was scary . . ."

"What happened next?"

pause

"Um, she . . . she snapped out of it. She was weak and woozy, but you would've never known she just had a seizure, or whatever it was. Matty had her in his arms and she began acting like it never happened. It was . . . weird."

"Weird how so?"

"Like . . . I don't know how to describe it. It was like Rachel was doing a—a bad Rachel impression, you know? The way she talked, it was—it was really weird. I've never seen her like that. She kept grinding her teeth . . . I don't know, the person I knew . . . She just wasn't acting like herself."

"Let's skip ahead to the voicemail and texts on your phone. What was the context of those messages?"

"Well, I set out to find supplies, you know, to take care of her. Not easy at three or four a.m. here in Waikiki. Penelope told me what to get. We assumed it was some sort of overdose, so she gives me a list of supplies. I found a Walmart across town that's still open so I took an Uber over there. While on my way, get a text from Penny. She tells me something's really wrong with Rachel. Fever, throwing up, we may have to take her to a hospital. I call her, still in the car. We talk, and all of a sudden I just hear this . . . screaming in the background. Like a—like an animal. I'm pretty sure it was Rachel. Penelope told me to hold on a second and hung up the phone. At this point I say fuck the supplies. We need to get Rachel to a doctor or something. Tell the Uber driver to make a U-turn.

Head on back. I guess I didn't hear my phone on the ride back or there was some sort of connection issue cus I didn't see the voicemail till after everything went down."

"Have you listened to the voicemail?"

"Yeah . . ."

"Mind if we play it?"

"Go head."

voicemail is played

"Hey Dana, Penny here. Don't know why you didn't answer, but here's the scoop. We got Rachel to calm down, but listen . . . there's something *wrong* with her eyes. The whites of them, they're, like, the most red I've ever seen. She keeps complaining about 'em. I've tried calling 9-1-1, Matty has too, but the call keeps dropping for some reason. Matty and her are in the bathroom right now but it's not looking good. We might just take her to the emergency ro— Matty? Matty, how are things in there? Matty?"

end of voicemail

"Let the record show that the body of Matthew Vasquez was discovered in the bathroom by the officers responding on the scene at six fifteen a.m. So, Dana, at approximately five a.m. a guest at Tropical Springs in the room sixteen sixteen, room directly below the crime scene, reported hearing a woman screaming outside. You said you were walking through the courtyard around that time?"

"If I had to guess, think it was that time, yeah. I thought I might've heard something, but I wasn't sure. Was walking through the courtyard, by the pool cus it was the quickest way to get to Rachel's side of the hotel. While walking I noticed the voicemail and listened to it. That's when I heard what sounded like it might be screams and . . . I'm sorry. I'm sorry."

"Take your time. Box of Kleenex right there."

"Thank you . . . Fuck . . . Um. I don't even know how to describe wh- what I saw. It's like a bad dream. One moment I'm walking. Next . . . my friends are fucking dead in front of me. It was like . . . two big fuckin' water balloons dropped and they were filled with blood. Through it all, I could kind of make out Penelope's face. But Rachel . . . s-somehow her face was completely scraped off."

suspect cries for a moment

"There was—there was this bloodstain on one of the balconies . . . I know it was from her. I know that's where Rachel lost her—"

incoherent sobbing

"Rosa Hernandez, the maid who reported the incident, said she found you taking pictures of the deceased. You have to admit, doesn't exactly make you look innocent in all this. In particular, you took pictures of your friend Rachel's body. Now, why would you do that?"

pause

". . . I don't know to tell you the truth. Something about how Rachel didn't have eyes anymore. Like—like they were burned out or . . . I don't understand it myself. I will tell you that my fiancé can't even look at me, though. Wedding's postponed . . . probably off for good. I don't blame Tre. I'm disgusted I did it."

pause

"I keep . . . getting this feeling. This nagging feeling that makes me sick to my stomach . . . Ever since taking those pictures, it keeps me up at night."

"What's the feeling?"

". . . Like whatever happened to my friends . . . it's only just begun . . ."

End.

ABOUT THE AUTHOR

Nicholas J. Ripley is the frontman of the punk rock band Futilitarian Librarians as well as the author and primary visual artist of everything related to Project Suncloud. Born in Las Vegas to a pair of dancers, "Uncle Nick" has been professionally involved in the arts since the young age of nine years old, when he got his first professional acting and modeling gig. Besides playing with his band and working on Project Suncloud, Nick also writes as a film critic for FilmSnob Reviews. When he is not doing anything artistic, he enjoys watching horror movies, playing old video games, and spending time with his cat/co-author Arya Stark.

To discuss booking Nicholas J. Ripley for media or speaking events, email: projectsuncloud@gmail.com

If you've enjoyed this book, please consider leaving a review on Goodreads. I appreciate every bit of support, and it would mean a lot. Thank you!

-NJR

Website:

patreon.com/ripleyjnick

Instagram:

@nickjripleyofficial

ALSO BY NICHOLAS J RIPLEY

A Winter for Doves Parts 1&2

Upcoming Standalones:
Mino
Stray

Project Suncloud:
A Hunt for Wolves
The Vindictive Queen
A Mourning for Vultures
A Grave for Sparrows

Comics:
Dog Mom of the Dead

AUTHOR'S PLAYLIST

"Pull Me Under" by Dream Theater

"Washing Machine Heart" by Mitski

"Freaks" by Surf Curse

"Nikes" by Frank Ocean

"True Faith" by New Order

"The Adults are Talking" by The Strokes

"Alison" by Slowdive

"Self Control" by Laura Brannigan

"Cigarette Duet" by Princess Chelsea

"Good Luck, Babe!" by Chappell Roan

"Hazel" by Far Apart

"Be Quiet and Drive (Far Away)" by Deftones

"The Bitter End" by Placebo*

* NJR recommends listening to this at the end of the book

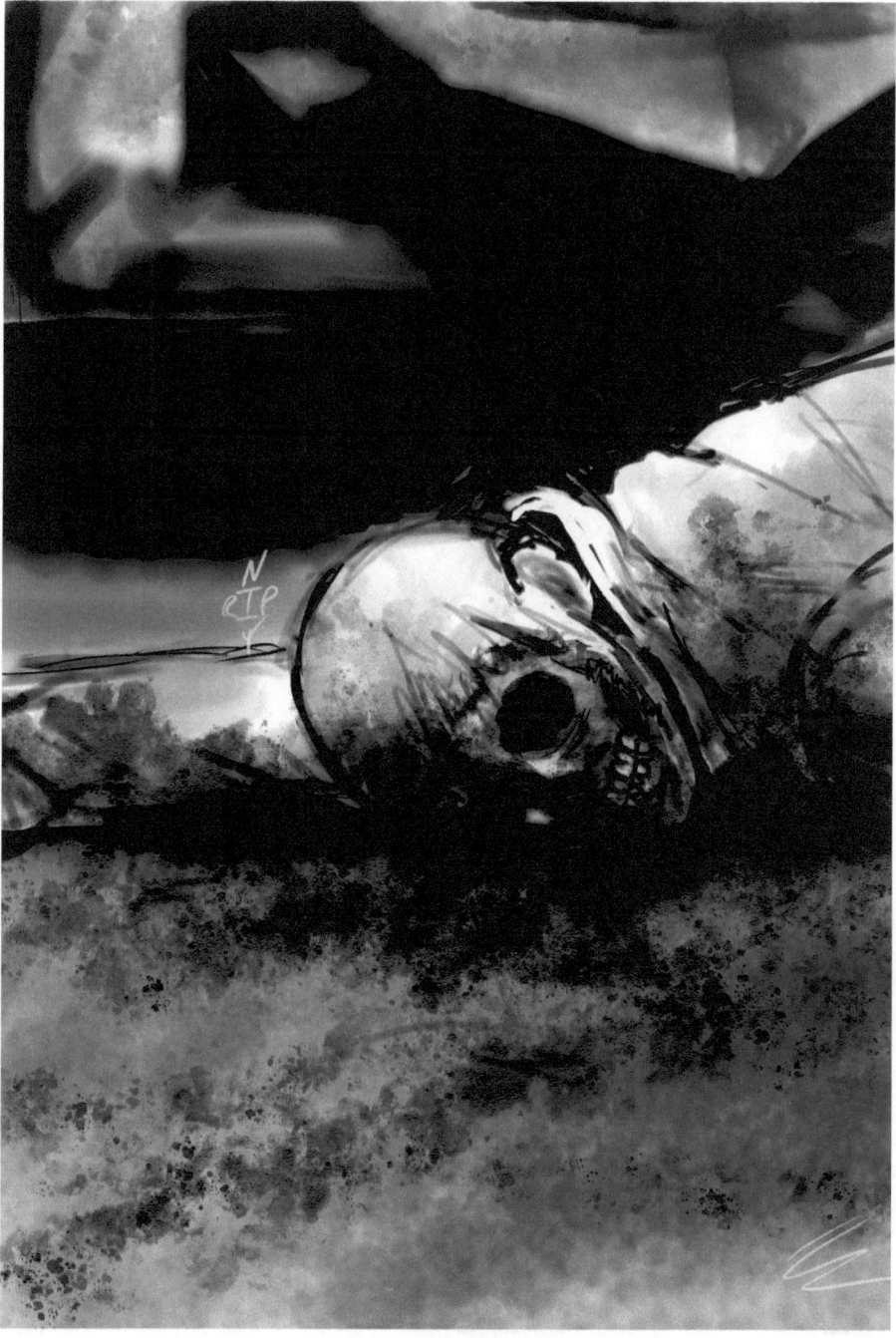

www.ingramcontent.com/pod-product-compliance
Lightning Source LLC
LaVergne TN
LVHW041909070526
838199LV00051BA/2547